Labrador

LABRADOR
KATHRYN
DAVIS

ANCHOR BOOKS
DOUBLEDAY
NEW YORK LONDON TORONTO SYDNEY AUCKLAND

AN ANCHOR BOOK

PUBLISHED BY DOUBLEDAY

a division of Bantam Doubleday Dell Publishing Group, Inc.
666 Fifth Avenue, New York, New York 10103

ANCHOR BOOKS, DOUBLEDAY, and the portrayal of an anchor
are trademarks of Doubleday, a division of Bantam Doubleday
Dell Publishing Group, Inc.

Labrador was originally published in hardcover by
Farrar, Straus and Giroux in 1988. The Anchor Books edition is
published by arrangement with Farrar, Straus and Giroux.

Library of Congress Cataloging-in-Publication Data
Davis, Kathryn, 1946–
    Labrador / Kathryn Davis.
        p.   cm.
    Originally published: New York: Farrar
    Straus Giroux, 1988.
    I. Title.
[PS3554.A934924L3   1990]   89-17995
813'.54—dc20   CIP
ISBN 0-385-26515-8   AC

DC

For Eric

What is this face, less clear and clearer
The pulse in the arm, less strong and stronger—
Given or lent? more distant than stars and nearer
   than the eye

T. S. ELIOT

And what about the children who do not want to be loved?

ISAK DINESEN

Labrador

"Once long ago," Rogni said, "an old woman in a flowered housedress sat on a kitchen chair steeping tea in a cracked brown teapot. She was the Nurse-of-Becoming; she was getting ready to imagine two sisters. Only she made three mistakes. First she imagined Willie, the elder, without a sister. Then she imagined Kathleen, sister if ever there was one, mooning after the impossible. And third, she imagined them without a history, like the earth without form and void—which is how that other storyteller started things off. This old woman was greedy and filled with rapture at the prospect of seeing them rise from the steam of her teapot, and she thought about how she would take them, like damp and rumpled handkerchiefs, and shake them out into the little lace-edged things that they were— Willie a rectangle, Kathleen a circle—and hang them over the cookstove to dry.

"Listen, she is gulping down her tea even now, in her small square house in the middle of the tundra, where the bake-apples speckle the muskeg in late summer. But how will the sisters eat this fruit? She gave them no mouths. She is a terrible thing, the Nurse-of-Becoming, watching the two sisters stiffen and then catch fire at the edges because she has placed them too close to the stove. She has a tiny pig-like nose and huge flat eyes like the animals that live in caves. She lets the sisters burn and the black pieces of them drift through the air of her kitchen; she puffs up her cheeks and blows, and they fly, in bits, everywhere.

"In the beginning, this is how it was."

THE ANGEL

Into my eye, Willie. A fleck of you flew in there, making a tear well up—that little shining star you saw and swept onto the tip of your finger to suck. It fell and fell down the dark shaft of your throat, trickling into your heart, where it glowed. The room filled in with light. I must have been about two years old and you—you were six, all dressed up in a red-and-green plaid dress, the bodice smocked with X's and O's of white thread, the sleeves puffed. You leaned over the edge of my crib and brought your face down, closer and closer, so that it was enormous, like the moon when it rolls across the horizon, when it has stopped being the moon and is imperious, rolling up and unrolling whole oceans. The black centers of your eyes got bigger, your nostrils got bigger, too, and then your mouth opened. "Kitty," it said.

What did you want? You were just a six-year-old girl on her way to school. You were just a six-year-old girl whose red plastic purse dangled from a gold chain worn across the wrist. Maybe you were finally going to give me one of the religious pictures that you accepted from the boy whose mat was adjacent to yours at nap time—shiny pictures of the Lamb of God that, ordinarily, you would never let me touch but would show to me mysteriously behind Mama's and Daddy's backs, as if we were doing something wrong.

"Kitty," you said to me, and the black oval of your mouth was so close to my face that I thought my name gave off a smell like milk. "Say, Goodbye. Say, Goodbye, Willie."

But my love for you tied my tongue, and then you whirled around and all I could see was the sparkling absence of you, which turned, little by little, into rosebuds: the flat, high walls on every side of me where scolding, bunched-up cat faces peeked out of the petals. Shadows of birds flew there, Willie, and I began to cry. "Hush," said Mama, "hush." Her hands were firm and wet and the shadows of birds flew across her face—so many faces, Willie! —and the flying had to it a whiff of flowers. She lifted me up. There was an egg to eat far away. *Snip snip* the top lifted off and out came the steam. This was in the kitchen.

For a long time this was the only day there was. There was the quiet morning out of which so many things flew— the dark fleck and the star and Mama's wet hands; the birds and the yolk of the egg—before afternoon came and you took me with you to the lake. On the dirt road I looked down and saw your long thin feet in ballet slippers the same whitish pink as your skin—in fifth position, you told me, the most difficult position of all—the T of your feet marking that exact place on the dirt road forever. You pointed to the west, where the mountains of the Presidential Range stuck up, still covered with snow on their peaks, and you told me that if we were standing there we could see all the way to the seashore where, long ago, our mama and daddy had participated in an event called a honeymoon. There the world fell apart into black rocks, against which the sea crashed over and over, like the boy in the story who hit himself on the head with the hammer. "Kiss me, my darling," our daddy whispered. You described it all to me: the bright red lips of our mama puckering up, the way her eyelids fluttered and then flapped closed. "You're not supposed to look," you told me. "That's how you fall in love."

It was early in the spring and under our feet the road was dry, but the ditches were filled with mud and running water; off in the woods we could see humps of snow, those sleeping beasts whose only desire it was to cart us off on their backs to the blue-black countries marked by the stars. "They're sleeping now," you said. "We've got to be very quiet."

Mountains stood all around us but the road was flat, cutting through the places scooped away by the glacier. White pines and red pines grew on either side of the road, and the only way a person could tell the difference between the two was to pick one of the little bundles of needles. If it was a white pine the needles were five to a bundle and you could bend them without breaking them; the red pine needles were two to a bundle and brittle. "Pick a tree," you said, "and if you can guess what it is before you pick the needles then you'll get your wish."

But all I could see was two green waves, chinked and ripped with sunlight. My eyesight was terrible, although we didn't know that yet. "Green," I said, pointing. "Green, green, green, green."

"Oh, Kitty," you said, and you were laughing. "Well, okay, make a wish anyway. Go ahead."

I screwed my eyes shut as I'd seen you do over your birthday cake, and there we were, the two of us, standing together on the dirt road, with the lake winking through the trees in the distance. Then I felt your arm brush against mine so that, just for a second, the little hairs caught onto each other. "I can't," I said.

Of course I could, now. And I wonder, would it have made a difference if I'd been able to tell you what I saw? Because, instead, you made a wish for both of us, and I don't think it's any secret that it was your wish that floated upwards in its silvery pod, calling attention to itself. "I wish," you said, "that we could live forever." And then you grabbed my hand and we walked together to the lake, where the pollywogs swam in jerks through the green ooze near the shore; where you reached way down into the back pocket of your shorts and handed me a piece of butterscotch wrapped in foil, and as I sucked on it I could see the moon printed on the sky, exactly like the vaccination mark on your arm, and I was perfectly happy.

I know we were happy then, both of us. You would pirouette through the house, dazzling me so that I could scarcely observe Mama and Daddy's dreary spawn: the knitted wool streaming from between Mama's fingers; the blue words which filled up the yellow pages of notepads rising in towers around Daddy's sorrowful face. What did they think they were doing? Were they trying to turn the downstairs of the house—*their* kingdom of chairs and tables and brownish lampshades—into wool and paper? It was a shifty thing they were making, and they worked at it purposefully and independently of each other, so that the parts didn't fit together. I thought there were walls everywhere, but it was through these that you apparently danced, showing me the gaps.

In those days there was no top or bottom to you—you were a beautiful, whirling X—the tips of your fingers and toes sending out a shower of sparks whenever they came into contact with some part of the world's surface. The star from my eye that you'd swallowed had swelled to become all of you. My dancing sister! You were the North Star— the one Mama and Daddy planned to wish on, but they had to catch you first. Believe me, *I* never wanted to catch you. I only wanted to keep you, forever and ever, in view. "Wait for me," I'd call, as you disappeared around a corner, and it was your glittering wake I'd follow, up and up, all the way to the third floor, where, in more opulent times, servants had lived their complicated and exhausting lives. The air in those third-floor rooms was hard to breathe; it was thick with an adult residue—whether from Mama and Daddy or from the souls of dead servants, we couldn't figure out—but we chose to put up with it. At least there was almost no furniture: each room had a single metal bedstead, painted white, like the one I woke up in after the masked doctor plucked my tonsils out of my throat; each room had an empty dresser where the heartless nanny would set our pink bowls of gruel before heading back to the dining room, where choice cuts of meat and handsome suitors awaited her. "Listen to her laughing," you'd tell me, but I was less interested in your story than in the spectacle of you telling it—in the possibility of seeing a piece of fluff riding your head like a lucky passenger.

We were orphans. Our parents had both been killed in a freak accident involving a threshing machine, leaving us at the mercy of our nanny's whims. While she frittered away our rightful inheritance, we sat cross-legged on the attic floor, dipping into our pink bowls with our spoons, gobbling up mouthfuls of stale air. But this was better than the life we'd lived before—oh, far better!—because we could sit with the skirts of our dresses rucked up high on our thighs, revealing our white cotton underpants, and no one cared. Nor did they care that we'd made a pact to love only each other, and when we curled up on the mattress ticking to sleep—my small fat body nestled within the curve of your bones—we dreamed the same dreams. I was never frightened *then*. I trusted the weight of your pale forearm across my chest and I trusted you, Willie. It was a long time before I figured out the perfection of your plan: how you always made me tell you my dream first and then, your face taut with astonishment, you would whisper, "That's just like my dream! That's my dream exactly!" I saw magic unstiffening, rising to parade on its thin legs around the room; I didn't recognize it as the sly animal of your invention.

Labrador

There were six rooms on the third floor of the house and we moved from one to another, trying them on like dresses. Two of the rooms were too small—more like closets, really; one had a stain on the ceiling shaped like a witch-face; one had a hole in the wall that showered plaster when your back was turned; one was the favorite home of spiders. The room we chose was at the corner of the house and had two dormer windows: one facing north towards the mountains, the other west towards a stand of pines—high bare poles at the tips of which we could make out a smear of vegetation. You explained to me that it would be through the northward-facing dormer that we would first catch sight of the silver wings of the planes, flying across the top of the world from Russia, carrying in their bellies the bombs they would release to drift down slowly—which, you insisted, we would have to catch in our arms like footballs and then set carefully on the lawn, blowing on them to cool them off.

We were only permitted to come into this room together. This was your rule and you enforced it scrupulously the first time you found the pink bowls slightly—oh, so slightly—shifted from their places on the dresser.

"I'm sorry," you said, shaking your head from side to side, to let me understand that the whole matter was out of your hands. This was the autumn when I was five and you were nine; the autumn when tent caterpillars took up residence in our family tree. Your head had gotten smaller as I'd gotten larger, as I began to see all of you. There it sat, a small white triangle above your long white neck; your long red braids whipped against your shoulders as you confronted me with the evidence. Was it your boredom that made you look for such mistakes? Was it your sadness at growing bored that made you so angry with me, as if I'd remained small and dull on purpose, in order to mock your brilliance? "You'll have to be punished," you said.

We were afflicted for the first time, that autumn, with the

inevitable presence on Saturday nights of Mrs. McGuire, whose recollections of her Irish heritage extended back to the Tuatha De Danann, those earliest persecuted settlers of the Emerald Isle. Mrs. McGuire was at least one million years old, of this we were certain, and the years had caused to spring from the pores of her wedge-shaped face thickets of whiskers, as if the entire inside of her head was filled with nothing but hair. Her greatest pleasure was to take one or the other of us on her lap, where we would sink, ball-like, into the frightening socket of her pelvic basin. Hapless orphans!—once lodged in place we would have to submit to the nuzzlings and nibblings of Mrs. McGuire's wild, Celtic mouth, the cabbagy odor of her body, her insistence on engaging us in a pointless game called Chin-Chopper. Meanwhile, Mama and Daddy, dressed up and erotic as loons, drove into Conway to the Palm Tree Lounge where, according to Mrs. McGuire, they flagrantly courted the Devil's attention.

Following my infraction of the rules, you left me all alone with Mrs. McGuire for an entire Saturday evening. You packed up your blue baby-doll pajamas in your pink quilted suitcase and left me all alone while you went off to spend the night at Cissy Fenster's. You didn't even like her, Willie! A chilly wind blew; all the fissures in our house were widening, letting in bugs and mice and, as the sun went down, an insinuation of bilge. I sat at the kitchen table in *my* pajamas—big things made for a boy and printed with friendly cowpokes—eating the sick-child's supper of poached eggs on toast and cambric tea in a Limoges cup that Mrs. McGuire prepared for me. She didn't know how, as Mama did, to hide the string in the egg that was the chick's ghost and, as usual, the toast was burned.

She was nothing more than a lonely old woman— certainly no more irritating or desperate than Daddy—but her loneliness had so skewed her features, like the cauls worn by the afflicted infants in her tales of childbirth, that she seemed like a thing on loan from another universe. She *watched* me eat. I felt like a creature of her devising, chewing minutely. There was an electric clock shaped like a teakettle on the wall above the sink—I knew how to tell time and I knew, as well, that if we were silent on the quarter hour Mrs. McGuire would tilt the trowel of her face ceilingwards and intone, "There is an angel passing overhead."

"We have to wear socks for dancing," I offered, out of the blue, at quarter to seven. "At kindergarten." Mrs. McGuire sat dabbing at the corners of her eyes as if she'd just finished having herself a good cry. I thought of you, Willie, safe in the Fensters' low-slung house, eating something like chicken à la king on toast points, fastidiously removing pimientos.

Mrs. McGuire patted her lap, signaling the end of dinner; all the water that ever was, in which swam the souls of hapless children like myself, funneled down the drain of that lap. "Come here, my precious darling," crooned Mrs. McGuire, "and I will tell you the story of my second cousin Patrick McCoo and the bloody milk cows." There stood Patrick McCoo, his blighted herd lowing outside the window, as he watched the steam rise from the enamel pan in which he boiled the bloody milk. In this way he could discover the identity of the witch—on this occasion it was a Mrs. Fiona Houlihan, whose body grew so hot it burst open at the fingertips, from which spurted fountains of blood, boiling fountains of blood, which sizzled when it hit the cobbled streets of Dublin.

"But that is not the worst of it," said Mrs. McGuire, "that is not the worst of it by far. Can you believe that faithless woman refused to admit that she'd bewitched those cows?" Mrs. McGuire opened her mouth, approximating awe at such perfidy, and as I peered down her gullet, it looked to me like a tube where a snake might hide, preparing to spring out at me. I admit, I preferred this tale to the ones in which coffins made their slow, air-borne way through people's parlors.

Eventually, Mrs. McGuire let me slide down from her lap, so that she could make a cup of tea for herself, and so that I could go to the bathroom to wash my face and brush my teeth. It was a very cold night, unusually cold for that time of year. During the night, in addition to all the other things that happened, Mama's tomato plants withered, because she wasn't there to cover them with bran sacks, and Mrs. McGuire scalded her wrist while pouring water from the kettle. You, of course, don't know any of this, but I know you'll believe every word of my story, because you always said I was lacking in imagination. Resourceful Willie, with your fabrications! I combed my hair and ran a washcloth over my face before presenting myself to Mrs. McGuire, who sat earnestly rubbing butter into her wrist; I wondered, at the time, whether it was a kind of penance Catholics did when they thought no one was watching.

The burn was my good luck—it precluded the possibility of the usual good-night kiss and hug, the possibility of Mrs. McGuire's features imprinting themselves in my face like a design in a cookie. I promised to say my prayers and then made my way through the pantry, where the glazed eyes of rabbits and waterfowl stared at me from the lids of tureens and pâté molds; the chill in this part of the house was constant and dull, like gunmetal, and it extended all the way up the stairs, down the hall, and into my big and watchful bedroom. Mama had left the night-light burning; its clown-face glowed from the wall socket. And, of course, your letter was lying there on my pillow when I pulled back the chenille bedspread. "Dear Kitty," it said. "The old hag has got you now." I could only read my name, but the printing was large and furious; it wasn't until the next day that Mama told me what it said, and then you got punished

—but I suppose you remember that. I put the letter on my dresser and climbed into bed.

The noise was coming from the third floor, almost directly overhead. It was coming from *our* room: a noise like something thick being slid through a slot—like something thick sliding *itself* through a slot. I wasn't frightened. I got out of bed and ran up the stairs, and I felt the way I did on Christmas mornings, nudging with my toe the full weight of the stocking at the bottom of my bed.

The room was empty. It was empty, but the noise issued from its center, from the place where bands of moonlight coming in through the two windows appeared to intersect. But that's not right—there was no sense of intersection, only of thickening, of tremendous thickening. Meanwhile, the noise reduced to a thinness that I no longer heard but felt, like a hair caught in my mouth, impossible either to remove or swallow.

I stood there shivering in my pajamas, waiting. I stood there, small and bold, until, eventually, all I could hear was the ticking sound of old wood; a mouse moved around inside the walls, rolling ahead of it a nut or some other round thing—inside the walls of our house, Willie. The little round nut that was me rolled around and around inside the walls of our house, away from the currents of watery moonlight; around among the pieces of wood nailed together a long time ago by our great-grandfather, when he was alive and trying to impress the young lady whose eyes you are supposed to have inherited: bluish-green and—this is what Daddy said, not me—unforgiving. *House*, I thought, trying to bring myself back out of the walls of it and into my self. Eight gables—because our great-grandfather was a lover of literature and a show-off; a mansard roof with slate tiles; stone columns holding up the porch roof; a cellar a man could stand up in. People oohed and ahhed, but only from a distance. A summer house! Once upon a time the shake shingles were honey-colored, before the long winters turned them gray; once a young man sat with his new bride on the porch and it was the truth, then, that she owned all the land as far as her unforgiving eyes could see.

My hands and feet were cold. Mrs. McGuire was at the foot of the stairs, yelling my name. "Kathleen! Kathleen!" she yelled, and the wind was blowing, making the pine trees bend all together from side to side.

"You've been walking in your sleep," Mrs. McGuire pronounced, as she led me back to my room. "I'll have to tell your poor mother to put a pan of water under your bed."

Several days later I was walking up the driveway on my way home from morning kindergarten, when I saw bright orange flames billowing out of the northward-facing dormer: a great and dramatic gesture, like a woman welcoming her lover home after a long absence. Mama was standing in front of the house, idly nipping the air with a pair of pruning shears, while she surveyed the tangle of shrubbery that rose up all along the front porch. "Look!" I shouted. She turned, first to face me, smiling; then she tilted back her neck so that Grandfather's old fishing cap—a green thing with a large visor like a duck's beak—fell into the grass, as she followed the line indicated by my finger. She looked intently upwards for several seconds and then walked up to me, puzzled. "What is it, sweetie?" she asked.

The flames were lively and I could see that they consumed nothing, only played against the flaking green paint of the window casing. "I thought I saw something," I said. "A plane or something." I never thought I was crazy; I was too literal a child to entertain such an idea. Instead, I ran into the house and up the stairs to the third floor, where I found the door flung open and the room filled with flames, in the way a box might be filled with moths: all that separate and distinct movement, that articulation of wings beating everywhere at once within a container. The flames gave off no heat; there was no smell of wood burning; no roaring or crackling. In fact, the room was dead quiet.

You see, when I was a dull child of five, decked out in pale blue glasses, the luck that cannot be contained in the great inertia of heaven, but which is generated there and then dispelled, entered our house.

I stood in the doorway watching the flames, and one by one they winked out, beginning at the edges of the room, until all that was left was a single tongue of fire suspended at the room's exact center; it seemed to address itself to my presence in the doorway with the same frank and unwavering interest I'd noticed in babies, as they rode the aisles of supermarkets in their mothers' shopping carts. And then, just as the burden of such scrutiny was beginning to make me blush, the flame vanished, and all around where it had been the room sprang into focus. I walked carefully. Through the west window I could see each needle on each of the branches of each of the pines; through the north window I could see Mt. Chocorua's conical peak of granite, as pristine as a milk tooth against the blue sky. I picked up the two bowls and then put them back down again on the dresser, knowing that I was replacing them in their *exact* positions—exact even as to front, back, and sides, although they were a uniform pink and perfectly round. Then I went downstairs.

You might say that everything had gone back to normal, except that normal, at least for the moment, no longer seemed to include the possibility of disaster. I followed Mama around outside, helping her pull up weeds, gathering them together into a small pile and then carrying them off to a larger pile behind the woodshed.

"You're such a good helper," Mama said, and then the little breeze that was always waiting for its chance flew out of her mouth in a sigh—that sound which, if things were their old selves, would indicate that being a good helper wasn't enough. But I knew differently.

"Shouldn't we burn them?" I asked, wanting to see ordinary fire for the purpose of comparison.

Mama shook her head. "They won't burn," she said, and even though, I guess, what she meant was that the weeds were too green and damp, it was an ominous statement. I walked a little ways off, to put distance between myself and that place where weeds were immortal, and when I looked back Mama was stamping down the pile with her foot. She was so small and thin—it was easy for me, at a distance, to mix her up with you, Willie, especially when she'd tucked her prematurely gray hair up under that silly hat. Her expression was serious and seemed to have risen to the surface of her face from someplace deep inside her, where there was a leak.

What else was there for me to do but wait for you? I stood watching for the flash of yellow at the end of the driveway that would signal the arrival of the school bus and, with it, your queenly descent, your desirable nonchalance as your schoolmates' arms and faces rose to fill all the windows of the bus in homage. "So long," I heard you call out, and then you were walking towards me, cradling your books against your chest.

"What's the scene, jellybean?" You spoke out of the corner of your mouth, like a thug, as you'd been instructed by Jojo Melnicoff. Remember him? The one who threw his milk at you because he loved you so much?

You continued walking right past me and I saw how you'd unbraided your hair, how it fell, kinked and sparkling, all the way to your waist, out from under the little blue beret you wore that fall. Your hair was the color of fire and it flickered in my face as I tagged along behind you, so that I made the usual mistake, assigning to you the role of source, as if all my experiences had their first expression in your body—your eyes, your mouth, your immaculate shrug.

"Willie!" I called out, and you looked back over your shoulder at me. "I saw something in the room."

You stopped walking and turned to face me. "What were you doing in the room?"

"I didn't go in," I lied. "I just stood in the doorway."

"You'd better be telling the truth," you said. You bent down to fiddle with your shoelaces, waiting, I now realize, for inspiration to hit. Then you straightened up. "I saw it, too," you said, reaching out one arm in my direction, to let me know that we should confront this thing hand in hand, like the orphans we were. "I think it's a rat," you said. "And I think it's got bubonic plague."

You began to drag me towards the porch, but already I was on my way to the third floor: I could see myself floating upwards like a feather in a draft, in the draft made by your excitement. How I loved you, Willie—still love you—more than Jojo Melnicoff ever did! I loved you so much that I could even bear the possibility of seeing the room's secret pass into your hands, where you might wrench it into a different shape. I don't think you ever believed in mutability, you were too much an agent of its process, just as a saint can no longer operate on faith, once she has looked into the face of God.

We entered the room together; it was empty and cold, and through its windows I could see clouds unwinding with great rapidity—ragged, thin clouds—from an invisible spool. "Look!" you shouted, and I jumped. But there was nothing there, nothing at all.

"What're we going to do?" you asked. "The rat," you pointed, "it's bigger than I thought."

I pushed my glasses up high on my nose. "I can't see it," I said. I wasn't trying to ruin your game, you understand; I only thought that perhaps the room's mysteries were various and randomly visible.

"That's a shame," you yelled, "because it's coming right at you!" With your eyes you followed the rat's movement from the corner of the room, across the floor, and then up my legs, at which point you made with your white spiky fingers for my throat. "It's got you!" you screamed. "You're going to shrivel up like a leaf, and then you're going to die! You're going to be covered with pustules from head to toe!"

"With what?" I asked.

"Oh, no," you moaned, "this is terrible." Your hands moved from my throat and then you were holding on to me, rocking me back and forth. "There isn't any cure," you whispered. "Don't die, Kitty. Please don't die."

We were orphans and we only had each other. We looked at each other and I saw your face very clearly, the way I'd see everything at the end of a long car ride, after Daddy pulled the car into the driveway and turned off the ignition. I saw tears forming in the corners of your eyes, the corners nearest the bridge of your nose which, in their slight downward curving, have always made me think of the scrollwork on a violin.

You threw yourself on the mattress, out of which silverfish traveled, in their great alarm, in many directions. You sobbed and sobbed, and you were speaking as well, but I couldn't hear a word you said, because your face was pressed into the blue-and-white mattress ticking. Do you remember? I sat beside you on the bed and stroked your hair the length of your back. It felt wonderful. And I said your name over and over: Will-lie, Will-lie, Will-lie—each syllable equal, like breathing.

Finally you rolled over and looked at me. I don't think, in all the ordeals we went through together, that I ever saw you look ugly. But such translucent skin as yours tended to reveal the places where blood and sorrow pooled just under its surface. Your eyes were pink, and the miracle is that when you cried you didn't end up looking like a rabbit.

"It's happening again," you said. "Stop it!" you yelled.

And then you touched my arm. "Don't look so worried, Kitty. I'm not mad at you."

"You're not?" I caught a glimpse of the little feather that was myself peering in the window.

You pressed your fingers to your eyes. "Everything gets so *tiny*," you said. "And thin. Like the outside of a balloon when it's about to burst." You opened your eyes and then shut them again. "Stop doing that!" you said. "Please."

"I'm not doing anything," I told you.

"Don't you know what I'm talking about?" you asked. "The faraway-and-wrong look? You know, don't you, Kitty?" You were pleading.

"Maybe," I said. I was thinking of room 12—of the kids in room 12. That was, in our small rural school, the receptacle for the halt and the lame, the retarded and the hostile, the children in whom God's sense of proportion had faltered: huge children towered over tiny children; children spoke all at once, in a rush of melodious labials, or they spoke more slowly than the land's rebound from the weight of the glacier, and their words meant nothing at all.

"It's everywhere," you said. "Isn't it?"

We held on to each other, and over your shoulder I looked around, cautiously, for the bright and mismatched plaids and stripes; for the pale faces snagged on a single thought; for the alien shoes. I was frightened, Willie. I could feel the room rise so high in the house that it passed through the roof and then flew away, beyond Mama or Daddy's reckoning, beyond the reach of the pines or the mountains, beyond the gravitational pull of the small round world. We might have vanished altogether, except that something more powerful than gravity landed on the roof. It made the extinguished sound of a fist hitting a dummy, by which I understood that we had fallen under its jurisdiction. You never heard a thing. Nor did our parents as they stood, arm in arm, in the doorway, both of them a little breathless from the long climb.

"What is it you kids *do* in here?" Daddy asked.

"We play," you said. You pinched my wrist, warning me.

"I wondered what became of these bowls," Mama said. She scowled at the floor. "One of these days . . ." she said, bending down to draw a line in the dust.

They both stood, uneasily waiting, like visitors. I felt my heart sailing around in my chest.

"Lemma," a voice said, the lips opening to speak within my ear. The voice was clear and rigid, as if it had never been softened through use, like a shirt pinned to a piece of cardboard. *"Lemma."*

That was the first time I heard Rogni's voice.

It was all that I had of him at first, just that word, *lemma*, like a slice of a larger word dissolving slowly on my tongue. *Lemma* defined the shape of those late-fall afternoons, when darkness came earlier and earlier, when my heart was filled with that excessive joy that is transformed, by every child who has ever felt it, into dread. It is not as if there was original sin, you see, but instead colossal apprehension, which called forth darkness out of light.

One morning in November, cold wet air blew in off the Atlantic and, with it, rain that froze as it fell, sheeting the world in ice. Cars couldn't hold to the roads but spun wildly around and around, plastering their drivers like campaign posters to telephone poles. When the storm hit I was already at kindergarten, sitting on the floor among my classmates, all of us on our little mats, watching Miss Kern count the milk money. "I'm missing fifty cents," she said. "Who forgot?" Suddenly the lights went out and the room grew tricky and strange, as if all the wooden blocks and games were jumping from shelf to shelf and there wasn't a single thing Miss Kern could do to stop them. She continued to count the money; so intent was she upon that hoard of quarters that she didn't even look up when the tall bearded man with eyes as black and moist as a seal's appeared in the doorway.

This was Peter, the janitor. His blue work shirt had long wrinkles pressed into it, contributing to our belief that he lived in the school basement, sleeping on the cement floor next to the furnace. One tongue of fabric stuck out over the front of his dungarees—you told me that you thought he was handsome. "You folks doing all right?" he asked Miss Kern, who looked up guiltily, as if, under cover of darkness, she'd been hiding our coins in her pockets.

"We're fine," she said, dismissive. "Thank you."

Peter walked over to where Miss Kern sat tucking an upward-curving strand of hair into the downward curve of her pageboy; he stood extremely close to her—unnecessarily close, it seemed, so that I could feel Raymond Naples on my left and Becky Fine on my right moving forward on their mats and then stiffening, waiting to catch a glimpse of adult interaction. We *all* waited; this was the secret place into which we knew, someday, we would tumble, whether we wanted to or not.

"Candles," Peter said, handing Miss Kern a box. "The power's out everywhere. Ice on the lines."

Did her fingers touch his as she took the box? Of course not! Miss Kern had a fiancé to whom she was devoted; his picture was on her desk, positioned so that she could see it whenever she looked up: a man with a horse-like face wearing a soldier's hat. He was stationed in Germany and sent Miss Kern letters, which she would read to us—she would pause, deciding which parts to keep to herself, and during those pauses we would see her face light up in a way that made us feel embarrassed.

"Here," Peter said. He reached into the back pocket of his dungarees and took out a pack of matches. We'd all seen this gesture before, through the towering windows of our classroom: Peter lighting a cigarette as he slouched against the jungle gym, and then that first plume of smoke floating across the playground.

"I don't know," Miss Kern said. She set her red lips primly. "We have rules about playing with matches."

"Jesus Christ," Peter said, "I'm not suggesting that you *play* with them." And then he turned, quickly, on his long stork-like legs; for a fraction of an instant I felt his eyes on my face, fixing me with a look of pity and amusement.

"Please go," Miss Kern said, but he was already out the door, walking casually, as if he didn't know that the Devil's long red tail twitched with glee to have won another soul. Would we get to see it? The Devil's scaly arms breaking through the concrete playground, dragging Peter down to hell? "Children," Miss Kern said, laying a polished red fingertip against her lips. But the name of the Lord, spoken in vain, was like the sparrow that had gotten into the room one day, flying from wall to wall and hitting against the windows—we could feel the wind of its passage across our faces, dangerous and thrilling.

In darkness we drank our milk and ate saltines. Miss Kern told us a story, but I wasn't listening—I was thinking about the long brown corridor at the other end of which, in room 8, you were sitting at your desk—the front desk near the window which Raymond Naples had told me was the pet's desk—and I wondered whether room 8 was filled with candlelight and whether you were worried about me, your little sister, so far away in such a quiet and unfriendly building. The milk tasted sour. I looked over to see if Becky Fine was drinking it and, as I did, Raymond Naples's legs knocked against mine, enhancing my sense of loneliness.

Lemma, that the man puts his penis in the woman, I heard. *Lemma, that the man puts*—and then an exhalation of breath, a falling away of sound, leaving a silence that was filled, in the next instant, with the distant wailing of sirens.

I waited, then, for Miss Kern to say the word at which

we would all spring into action; I strained my ears to hear the sound of the approaching planes with their deadly cargo. I knew from your description, Willie, that we'd be alerted by sirens. But Miss Kern remained transfixed by her story, the round blossom of her face yearning towards us, as if the story alone might forestall disaster.

"Shouldn't we go outside?" I asked.

"Whatever for?" Miss Kern lifted her eyebrows, warning me to hold my tongue.

I understood the predicament of Chicken Little, as the blue sky fell in shards into the barnyard. I looked at the huge jars of poster paint arranged on the shelves in the back of the room and, as I looked, I saw them shattering, the reds and blues and yellows mixing together across the walls and floor into the mud of aftermath.

"Kitty Mowbrey!" Miss Kern yelled. "Where do you think you're going?"

"Outside," I said. I was halfway across the room, making my way to the door.

"You come right back here, young lady," Miss Kern instructed.

And so, for the rest of that dark morning, I sat on a chair in the principal's office, in the company of the large snapping turtle, a masterpiece of taxidermy, which we all knew was not really dead but had been frozen stiff by Miss Mullen, as punishment for having bitten off her ears. This was why she coiled her gray hair on each side of her head, like earmuffs—she had to hide the scars. From time to time Miss Mullen would look up from her desk and smile at me the smile of a bad fairy devising a new spell. You'll be sorry, I would think, until the terror rose like mercury along my spine, filling my brain. Outside, the sleet began to let up, and through the small window in the far wall I could see a sky as weary and crumpled as an old piece of folding money. A truck passed by, salting the road that wound down the hill and into the woods that surrounded our house. The planes never came. Still, I could not believe that the world's fate had been consigned into such unreliable hands as those of the Misses Kern and Mullen. This was the spell cast down upon me in that office, Willie: how watchful I became, checking for the consequences of adult stupidity; I could not stop looking through that small window, hoping to catch out of the corner of my eye the edge of a hem or a shoelace, as the dead drifted past its panes on their way to heaven.

I rode the bus home with my schoolmates; I rode next to Bobby Hallenbach, who confided in me that his sister bled regularly and mysteriously from between her legs—that there was nothing she could do to stop it. "It'll happen to you, too," he said. "It happens to girls." I saw myself as flat as a glove from which the hand had been suddenly removed; I saw myself in a box among other gloves, and this was called a cemetery.

"The world might end first," I told him.

"No, it won't," he said seriously. "Because of God."

When I got home Daddy was sitting at the kitchen table eating a bowl of tomato soup, talking to his boss on the phone. This was during one of his periods of employment, working as a stringer for the local paper. "Where?" he said into the phone. "Are you sure?" The soup steamed up his glasses so that I couldn't see his eyes; I could hear, far off in the house, the sound of the vacuum cleaner. "I'll be right there." He hung up the phone and then looked at me, spooning soup into his mouth. "Kitty?" he said, and removed his glasses, wiping the lenses on the sleeve of the heavy sweater he wore all the time once the weather got cold—the sweater Mama had knitted for him in the first year of their marriage, while you were growing inside her. "Thank heavens you're home," he said.

He opened his arms and I ran to him, feeling his long arms close around me like tongs, burying my nose in the chickeny smell of his armpit. "Kathleen, stringbean," he said.

"Daddy," I whispered into his armpit.

Then he let go of me and I stood back, smiling stupidly into his face. "I had to go to Miss Mullen's office today," I announced.

"Miss Mullen? The nurse? The short one with the red nose?"

"No," I said, "she's the principal. Miss Kern sent me there after the janitor came."

"Why?" he asked.

I wasn't sure how to answer this. "Well," I said, "I think I was bad."

"Does your mother know about this?"

I paused. "Daddy," I asked, "is it true that the sirens mean the bombs are coming? And then we have to catch them?"

"Who told you that?"

"Willie," I said.

He frowned. "A siren means lots of things, Kathleen. An ambulance has a siren, so does a fire engine. There's a siren that goes off every day at noon in Conway. And as for catching bombs—if we're ever big enough fools to start a war, that'll be it. Not even Willie Mays could catch one of those things."

"Oh," I said.

He peered at me over his glasses. "The janitor," he said. "Isn't Peter Mygatz the janitor at your school?"

"His name's Peter," I said.

"Right." Daddy stood up and pulled on an enormous canvas coat, of the sort I'd seen in pictures of ladies and gentlemen riding old-fashioned automobiles. "The letter writer," he said, stroking my hair back from my forehead and kissing my nose. "A wasted life, Kathleen."

"What do you mean?" And I held my breath, Willie,

waiting for that evidence of parental omniscience we'd always wished for and dreaded—waiting to hear that Daddy already knew about the janitor's perdition.

"Peter Mygatz," Daddy said, "has a Ph.D. from Harvard. He has a Ph.D. from Harvard and now, when he isn't mopping the floors at your school, he's sitting in that bread truck he calls a home—you know, that eyesore near the cranberry bog—writing letters to the paper." He walked over to the door and stood looking at me sadly. "You've got a good head on your shoulders, Kathleen. Remember that."

I didn't want him to leave. "Willie," I said, "is in love with him."

"What?"

"Well," I amended, "the kids say she's got a crush on him."

"Great." His gaze floated up to the corner of the room above the plate rail, and then his gray eyes narrowed, as if in consultation with an invisible deity. "Your sister, I'm sorry to say, is a lousy judge of character."

"Bobby Hallenbach says Willie's a heartbreaker," I said.

He was almost out the door now, his feet straddling the threshold. "Listen to me, Kathleen," he said. "When I get home I'll personally show you a picture of the human heart. It's a muscle, nothing more. Okay?"

And then he was gone, although he left behind emotional yardage I couldn't understand—great sheets of it that settled slowly over everything in the room, as if we were in transit, preparing to lock up, wary of dust. I guess he knew how it would happen: the little crack running up the heart's center and the two halves falling apart like an eggshell, out of which nothing would hatch. You fell in love with the janitor so effortlessly while, for the rest of us, you made it so difficult: we piled our offerings around your feet and learned to settle for acknowledgment. That's why Daddy got you the pony for your birthday, only to hear you christen it "Peter." Admit it, Peter was a ridiculous name for that moody creature whose greatest pleasure was gnawing on the barn. Do you remember? That was the November of the pony, of the janitor, of Mrs. Naples's death on the county road, of Rogni. Of course you didn't know about Rogni. Not then. I kept Rogni to myself.

In the room, in the small gray room, I sat in the corner on the floor eating a peanut-butter-and-jelly sandwich, while Mama continued pushing her vacuum cleaner around and around downstairs. Then I heard the car start up in the driveway and I went over to the window and watched it disappear. I'd wrapped myself in a blanket because I felt as isolate and sad as a child lost in the woods.

Lemma, I heard. *Lemma, that the man puts his penis in the woman. That it spreads out everywhere inside of her, that it makes her rattle and rattle until the pieces begin to fall off, the long pieces and the short pieces and the pieces shaped like cups and bowls and the pieces that have no shape but are like moisture.*

I turned and saw a figure printed on the air, its delineation recognizable yet wrong, like a photographic negative held up to a window. The figure occupied the whole center of the room, extending from floor to ceiling and, while it didn't move from that place, within its contours it shifted and seethed, as if bringing itself into focus; no matter how intently I tried to stare at what seemed to be a face, all I could see was a teeming pool through which eyes swam like dark fish, within which the oval light of a mouth opened and closed.

I pulled the blanket up over my head and the voice began again, louder this time: *Lemma, that all matter is blasphemy.* There was a pause and then the voice exploded into a single ball of noise. The noise was everywhere and it went on and on, suggesting that there had never been anything else—that the great noise of our world's ending was our daily bread, our home and family, our green pastures.

"Kathleen," a voice whispered. "Kathleen." The explosion poured out of the room, swallowed back down into that whispering throat. I felt a hand draw away the blanket, gently, cautiously, as if *I* were the most fearful thing in the universe. I still held on to the remainder of my sandwich, which I'd squashed into a lump; it was like a souvenir from a foreign country. There was a person crouched down in front of me, looking at me warily—a man with eyes as startling as the eyes of a friend who has always worn glasses and suddenly removes them for the first time in your presence. "Kathleen," he said, enunciating carefully. He looked so sorrowful that I reached out to touch his arm, but he drew back. "Not yet," he said. "I'm too new and dangerous, and so are you. We have to be very careful, do you understand?"

I nodded my head, even though I understood nothing. The man stood up and I saw that he wasn't very tall, but that the upper part of his body was full and muscular, like that of Vern Hawkings, the farrier, whose proportions only seemed correct when he was riding a horse. "Where did you come from?" I asked.

He looked all around the room, swiveling his head on the strong column of his neck, and when he saw the two pink bowls he smiled. "There's another of you, isn't there? Willie?" The lids of his eyes fell a notch, so that I became aware of his lashes—each lash as thick and black as if I was looking at it through a magnifying glass, set against the deep blue field of his gaze.

"Willie's my sister," I said. "She's in school now. She's older than me."

"I know," he said. "But she's going to be back here soon, and then you'll have to go downstairs. You must keep her away from me, Kathleen."

"Why?"

"I don't have any explanations," he said, walking over to look through the west window. "Those are the rules,

Kathleen. As this world is made, I might weaken." He extended one arm and motioned for me to join him at the window, which I did, reluctantly. "Don't be afraid," he said. "You are, aren't you?"

I nodded my head. The skin of his hands, where they rested on the pitted wood of the windowsill, was white and perfectly smooth, like polished stone, and I thought that if I could see his palms they would be unmarked by those lines with which the superstitious content themselves about their destinies. I *was* afraid, Willie. I was afraid of my own body, with its cuts and scabs, like a thing coming apart at its seams. Through the window I watched the bright yellow capsule of the school bus, bringing you home.

"I'd never hurt you, Kathleen," he said. "You have to believe me. See, the sun's coming out now. And then it will go down, over there behind those hills, and this day will be finished. That's how it works here. You measure time's passage, don't you? You count days and you consult clocks— and so you live with desire. I'm just beginning to under-stand that."

The school bus pulled up at the end of our driveway, and I saw, for a moment, a blue spark—your jacket—before you vanished into the pines. "Desire?" I asked.

He touched his chest. "Here," he said. "I think you feel it *here*. Something like a ball of glass filled with air? Like the instant before creation. Is that what desire is like?" He ran one finger down the pane of the window. "It isn't fair," he said. "It isn't fair that it should be the ending as well." And then he looked down at me.

He looked down at me, Willie, and as he did I saw his whole body speeding upwards, growing to a great height. His fingers laced through mine—the skin cool and supple, gloving fire—to yank me loose from the pocket of our house. Briefly, I felt myself snag on the intricate webbing of laundry hung out to dry, sheets and pillowcases, shirts and trousers—the temporal extrusions—then I was free. The house no longer contained me; I passed through layer after layer of color: the green of a world filled with leaves and scarves of lively air, jittering against my legs as my face and shoulders pressed upwards like a prow through the paling blues of sky, where the wetness of clouds coated me over, making my body slippery and fluent. I couldn't see a thing, as if my eyes were closed; but they weren't, I know: I reached my hand up to make sure, and I could feel the open place behind the lashes.

So I entered the language of the angels, the dangerous territory through which quills shot—where the heart of a human child is most vulnerable. A wing folded around me; I was bound in by pinions, the hooks and barbs of enormous feathers; the other wing rose and fell, beating a dark chord, and we flew, higher, through the thick yellow rapture of souls stewing in heaven's pot. And then there was the silver and judgmental silence.

"Look, Kathleen," said Rogni, pointing to where I could see myself standing on a silver and empty plateau under a silver sky. "An event is taking shape here," he said, "if only you knew how to recognize it." Wind blew at me from all directions, and in the distance I could see great white bears, reared up on their hind legs, dancing across the horizon. But this wasn't a real horizon—it was the edge of all created things—it was the place where God's desire faltered. The music to which the bears danced was inaudible and ran through my bones like a *chinging*, as if I was a hoop being tapped across a schoolyard by a metal wand. I was alone.

Willie, I heard. It ought to have been *my* voice. I was, after all, a five-year-old girl, carried suddenly away from her home—from the scratchy chair where Daddy would hold me on his lap each night and read me stories about friendly and loquacious animals—it ought to have been *me* who called out to you. And I could see, through all those plates of color, piled one on top of another to make a crystal, like the lens of a miraculous telescope, you. I could see you stooping down beside the place where the stream that ran along the edge of our property pooled; you were stooping down to pick up a pebble and I could see the white shapes of your fingers closing around that greenish-brown egg; you put it in your mouth and sucked on it. I could taste it: like sucking the flavor from a coin, elemental and sharp.

Then the angels—among them the one called Rogni, who thought you were his—gathered in a nest of hot spokes and anguish, wondering. Who were you? You tilted your head forward; you listened. This was the place where the orphans came to wash each other's face. The water was the color of Coca-Cola, but perfectly clean. The grit in it was bits of dissolved rock, bits of shining mica. You made your eyes into slits, because you were always suspicious. Could you hear them? I could see the blue of your jacket moving up and down, slightly, with your breathing. Your lips were parted and I felt each breath: soft, soft, softer—a breathing out, a breathing in, a gathering of breath, a gathering of the smallest silver particles into walls, ceiling, floor.

I stood then at the window, its panes congealing into a solid barrier of glass, beyond which the world filled in with darkening vegetation. And then I heard a door slam far off in the house, signaling your arrival.

"Kathleen, you'd better go now," Rogni said. He sat down heavily on the mattress, like a person. I noticed that he was wearing work boots and that they were scuffed and nicked, as if with use. I hesitated, watching as he bent down and began to undo the laces—his fingers were shaking.

"Are you going to bed?" I asked.

"I'm going to lie here," he said. "That's all." He removed a boot and a sock, and I saw his foot—long and white and more beautiful than any foot I'd ever seen—more beautiful, even, than yours. "Kathleen," he said, *"please."*

Still I didn't move. "You scared me," I said.

"I'm sorry." He tugged off his other boot, peeled off his

sock, and stretched out across the mattress. "I thought it would be all right. This body—" He shook his head from side to side. "It's cold. It's a cold house to live in."

"We can't afford to heat all of it," I said. "It's warmer downstairs."

"What?" His head was turned on the mattress, looking at me, a dark blade of hair falling across his cheek. And then he smiled. "Oh," he said, "I see. But I meant *this*." He reached out and ran his fingers down my forearm, so that all the hairs jumped up, expectant.

"Are you going to live here?" I asked.

"I'm going to stay here. Just for a while."

"Are you hungry?"

"Kathleen," he said, "she's looking for you."

There was something in the way he said "she" that broke my heart—if only for a second—in a fierce and adult way, because I knew that I was hopelessly inadequate and that the only thing in the world that he wanted was you. Since then I've come to see that I was wrong: that the transaction to be made was more complicated, involving all of us. But at the time I was afflicted with a simplicity of vision that didn't account for complication. I could close my eyes and see those bears—their rapturous dancing—projected on the undersides of my eyelids. I could open my eyes and see *you*.

You were sitting at the kitchen table—its surface a changeable still life of keys, toast crusts, unopened mail, the star-shaped piece from a jigsaw puzzle, which meant that the swain with the mandolin would go through life without a nose—you were drinking a glass of milk, your upper lip white, your body sleek and elusive, turning in the chair to watch me as I came into the room.

"Did you hear the news?" you asked. "Raymond Naples's mom is dead. She hit a tree near Tyler Bog this morning."

I began crying and then continued crying softly as you sat on the green chair staring at me. The kitchen was hard to see, as if we'd fallen under the surface of the lake, into the domain of the pike with teeth like knives. A pot rattled on the stove and I could hear you swallowing milk.

"The whole school's going to be invited to the funeral," you said. "That's what Jojo Melnicoff says, anyway."

"I'm not going," I said.

"Do you think Mrs. Naples is in heaven?" you asked.

"I don't know," I said. "I guess so."

Gusts and breezes of excitement made you toss around in the chair. "Her body isn't," you said. "Jojo says we'll get to see her body at the funeral." You tied your braids under your pointy chin and made a face at me, rolling your eyes upwards and lowering your lids, so that all I could see were crescents of white.

"Cut it out, Willie."

On all sides of me the mustard-colored walls inched closer; the refrigerator motor began its low humming and I felt as if some process had commenced by which my soul would be pressed out of me—a little gelatinous blob that you would catch in a blue bowl.

"When I die," you said seriously, "I'm going to take my body with me."

"I don't think you can," I said.

"How do you know?" You were sitting very close to me, so that I could see, dancing on each of your irises, pricks of light shaped like butterflies. "It's my body," you said. You stretched out one leg and pointed the toes—a white, sparkling line which you raised slowly, indicating the path of your ascension. "It's *my* leg," you said.

In fact, I didn't go to the funeral. I stayed home instead, with Daddy, decorating the dining room with crepe-paper streamers and balloons for your birthday party. We rarely used the dining room, except for special occasions, and the smell in it was ceremonial and inhuman, compounded of old varnish, mildewed fabric, and a mysterious sweetness, like almond extract. A long, dark room, papered in green, down the length of which ran an immense mahogany table

—do you remember the chairs, how they were carved to look like bamboo, and painted gold? Where do you suppose they are now?

That table and those chairs, the bust of Kermit Roosevelt on the sideboard—was it true that once upon a time our family had been wealthy, but the wealth had been squandered by our peripatetic grandfather Jasper Mowbrey, whose face looked out from behind the yellow and blue balloons affixed to the gilt frame in which he now resided? He was a fine-looking man, Jasper was, whom Daddy resembled exactly, feature for feature, except that Jasper's expression was filled with a numinous and unthinking glow, common to all self-styled nineteenth-century explorers, while our father's expression changed from minute to minute, depending upon his proximity to any member of the human race.

"Will they be here soon?" I asked.

"The Napleses are Catholic," Daddy answered. "They may never get home."

During the four days intervening between the accident and the funeral I'd helped keep the pony a secret, standing beside Daddy in the half-light of the barn, touching the little creature's soft brown nose as it bent down to gobble up oats. And I'd kept Rogni's presence a secret as well—a simpler task, because he hadn't reappeared. The room remained empty of all traces of his existence. At least I couldn't see any: the mattress wasn't dented from the weight of his body, nor was the dust on the floor marked with the shapes of his feet. Metaphysicians tell us that there's no such thing as a trace of the future—that's why time is asymmetrical. I looked, Willie, believe me, I looked. But I was only five years old—how could I recognize the imprint of desire when I didn't even know the meaning of the word?

Meanwhile, desire triumphed. Our family argued about the appropriateness of a birthday party on the evening of a funeral. We could celebrate it the following day, according to Mama's suggestion. But you were adamant. "Saturday is my birthday, not Sunday," you said. You provided a guest list, which included the names of people who were specifically *not* to be invited. At the head of this list was Jojo Melnicoff, whose attentions you felt, no doubt, would distract you from the romantic offerings of Peter Mygatz, whom you had invited secretly one morning during recess. Should it have been a surprise to me to find him—an early arrival—filling our doorway with his large and diffident frame? Probably not, since in the afternoons while you were still at school I'd been in the habit of rummaging through your closet, where I'd found his navy-and-maroon scarf folded up under a pile of stuffed animals; where I'd found, in the bottom drawer of your musical jewelry box, a drawing of a red-haired girl dressed like a bride, holding hands with a tall, bearded groom. When I pulled the drawer out, the lid of the box flew open and the miniature ballet dancer twirled around and around, her lips painted on askew, sneering at me.

"Hello," Peter Mygatz said, when I opened the door to let him in. He was wearing one of those tweed jackets with leather elbow patches, like Mr. Simms, the sixth-grade teacher, and he'd recently showered, making the hairs of his beard lively and electrical. "Miss Kern's room," he said. "Am I right? What're *you* doing here?"

"I live here," I said.

He made no attempt to hide his surprise. "You mean to say you're Willie's little sister?"

"Who is it, Kathleen?" Daddy called from the dining room.

I couldn't bring myself to answer. Instead, I led him—feeling the heat and heft of him behind me, as if he were the celestial body to which I'd recently become satellite—through the kitchen, depositing him near the sideboard on which Daddy knelt, wrestling to tape a long banner that said HAPPY BIRTHDAY WILLIE across the wall. I knew I had an ally in our father, you see, even though I didn't understand that it was an unreliable alliance, based upon his bitterness, the sources of which were beyond me.

"Hello, Nick," Peter said.

Daddy whirled around, his arm brushing against the cool marble cheek of Kermit Roosevelt. Under different circumstances, I suppose, it would have looked normal—those two intellectual and relatively unkempt men having a conversation in a dark green room—but there were balloons, Willie! There was the faintest aroma of cake!

There were the blue pores of their faces in which masculinity welled up, and I'd seen the alternative.

"What do you want?" Daddy asked.

"Your daughter invited me," Peter said.

"My daughter!" Daddy looked at me, but I shook my head. "Look," he said. "Willie's ten years old. And you, you're what? Thirty?"

"I'm twenty-nine," Peter said. He fiddled with the white tissue-paper wrapping of a small package he held in his hands. "She was very insistent," he said.

Daddy put down the masking tape and climbed off the sideboard. "I don't think you understand," he said. "Let me spell it out for you. Musical Chairs, you know the game? Ice cream and cake."

The dining-room windows faced out onto the porch, beyond which stretched an expanse of meadow filled with grayish and dead grasses, surrounded on all sides by the tall poles of the pines. In the center of this clearing I could see Rogni standing absolutely motionless, staring up towards the house. My heart began to whir in my chest and I imagined, crazily, the possibility of confrontation: Peter Mygatz lying on his back amid dead grass, the plate of his face broken into pieces by a single blow of Rogni's fist.

"Insistent," Daddy said. "The government's insistent,

but I don't see you falling all over yourself to make *them* happy."

"Come on," Peter said. "You know it's not the same thing. I like Willie. She's a nice kid."

"Sure."

"I didn't want to disappoint her."

Daddy came over and set his big hand on my back. "Kathleen's *nice*," he said. His hand rested there, like the humps on the backs of old women, and I thought how if I were to sit, humped and nice, tossing out bread crumbs to pigeons, you wouldn't notice me; you would stand lounged up against a lamppost, a sailor's knee wedged between your thighs.

"Do you want me to leave?" Peter asked.

But as he did so, several cars made their way in procession up the driveway, the faces of mothers peering out anxiously, sizing up the house in which their children would be spending the afternoon. Could they see those spiders, the size of fists, clamped to the eaves of the porch? Could they see Rogni, as he walked from the center of the meadow to the house?

"It's too late now," Daddy said. But I knew that wasn't true, that all he had to do was say the word and the janitor would be gone, gone, gone. Rogni looked up as he approached the porch; he smiled at me, then turned to the right and disappeared behind the woodshed.

Now we could hear the back door opening, the sound of feet walking across the kitchen floor, the sound of high-pitched and sudden voices. "It's snowing!" you shouted, as you ran into the room, followed by your guests. "It always snows on my birthday," you told Peter. We were, the three of us—Peter, Daddy, and myself—the fixed and motionless figures consigned by medieval painters to positions as observers of the Mystery, our mouths slightly open, our limbs frozen in gestures of worship or solicitude. You brought the smell of snow with you into the house; small flakes of snow, widely spaced, drifted down outside the window. I watched as Daddy walked over to help you out of your coat. There you stood in your green velvet jumper with its pearly heart-shaped buttons; you stood regally patient as he bent to kiss the top of your head, where the snowflakes melted into diamonds, where the desires threatened to spring forth all at once from their sac, like a hatching of mantises.

Meanwhile, your guests shed themselves of the somber outerwear provided by their mothers in deference to the dead—the dark coats and jackets they'd been instructed to keep on throughout the funeral—and revealed themselves as children. There was a plastic record player in the corner of the room on which Cissy Fenster, awkward in tiers of yellow organdy, placed a record. "I've got the bell-bottom blues," sang Teresa Brewer, " 'cause my sweetie is a sailor and he's sailin' somewhere on the seas . . ." Two boys stood staring at the magic lantern on the sideboard, brought back from the mission house in Hebron by Jasper, before he chose to disappear off the face of the earth. "This is neat," one of the boys said. He was wearing a red bow tie and his hair was slicked back from his forehead; I didn't know his name. The other boy was Rodney Hallenbach, Bobby's older brother, captain of the Safety Patrol. "We've got one of those," Rodney lied, "it ain't so neat."

Presents filled the center of the table in a colorful pile, to which I saw Peter add his offering. He set it down furtively and then turned to me and winked, as if we shared a secret. I felt a tangle of hatred under my breastbone. There you stood among your schoolmates, smiling, while our father stood sadly watching you smile.

Lemma, I heard, *that in order for there to be rapture there has to be a trap.*

Someone extinguished the lights and Mama appeared

holding the cake, its ten small points of flame wavering as she walked to the table, singing as she walked, her thin voice basted like a metallic thread through that adolescent panel of sound. She put the cake at the head of the table and handed you the knife. "Make a wish!" someone yelled. A record was skipping on the player—*highest hill, highest hill, highest hill*, it insisted. You took a deep breath, as if you were about to dive into the lake—as if you were standing on the dock in your knit bathing suit, your expression proud, assuming an audience—and then you blew the candles out. "I wish you were dead," you said, to no one in particular. "I wish you were dead like Mrs. Naples and the maggots were eating you up." Benny Stroup began to cry, and you drew the knife from the cake, licking it clean of frosting, to extend in his direction. "Can't you take a joke, Benny?" you asked. You began cutting the cake with great precision, shrugging off Mama's hand impatiently, when she set it on your shoulder. "Yeah, Benny," said Rodney Hallenbach, "can't you take a joke?"

I heard the sound of the brass drawer pulls jingling against the mahogany surface of the Queen Anne highboy in the living room, as if someone were walking past it.

Lemma, that the number-two traps are baited with red meat, that the white fox is dizzy with lust, that she made a compromise in order to become matter, I heard—the striking of the anvil bone against the inside of my ear.

You began opening your presents and I stayed in the room long enough to see what was in Peter's package: a thin silver chain, which he got up to clasp behind your neck, drawing apart the shiny drapery of hair in order to expose the nape. I wondered if you could feel his breath on your skin and the thought made me sick. But the smile on your face was a limited and private one, telling me nothing, and I was sure you never noticed when I left the party, slipping through a narrow space between the two huge sliding doors, which, in the days of Grandfather, had remained open, connecting the dining room and the living room.

Rogni was standing in front of the fireplace on the caribou-skin rug, running his eyes back and forth across the mantel, assessing that museum of Mowbrey family history: the porcelain goose girl beloved by our poor abandoned nana; Grandfather's beaded slippers; a Mason jar in which the woolly-bear caterpillar I'd found in the woods was now a slick black worm throbbing in its cylinder of fuzz; a biography of Anna Pavlova, long overdue at the Conway library. Rogni lifted objects, blew the dust off them, and put them back, frowning. "Kathleen," he said, "I need your help." He was peering into a small stone bowl filled with a brick-red and powdery substance. "What's this?" he asked.

"I don't know," I said. Later, when I was fourteen, I'd learn its name—iron hematite—and that it had been bestowed upon our grandfather by Bella Tooktasheena, the Inuit woman who wrecked his marriage. "Where've you been?" I asked.

"Where?" The room was lit by the snow, falling faster now, clarifying and sharpening—as if, were I to reach out and touch the edge of the sofa, it would cut my hand. Rogni shook his head. "I keep forgetting," he said, "what it's like for you. All these compartments." He opened the drawer in one of the end tables and took out a red lacquer box. "In the universe there is a planet, and on the planet there are many countries, and in one of the countries there is a forest, and in the forest there is a house, and in that house there is a child with a little red heart in her body." He opened the box and took out a single metallic blue jack. "See, Kathleen, it doesn't stop." He held the jack on the palm of his hand. "Is this Willie's?"

"How would I know?" I asked.

"But she's your sister . . ." he said, and then suddenly

his mouth fell open, so that I could see a flickering of light where there should have been only a dark vault, a tongue. From the dining room came the sound of tearing paper and I heard you exclaim, "Oh, Nancy Drew!" The light inside his mouth flared up for a second and then winked out.

Willie, the danger was everywhere, as it always is, except I was, if only briefly, immune—I was beyond history, where an old woman in a floral housedress stood, her back to me, an emerald ring on the fourth finger of her right hand. *Old fat thing*, the ring asserted placidly, and she removed it from her finger and placed it in the very back of the top drawer of the Queen Anne highboy. She placed the ring in the drawer and then stood twisting the hem of her floral housedress between her thumb and ringless finger. This was *our* universe, Willie, and I was standing on its threshold—all there was was a thin rectangle of light inching across the hardwood floor, making its way up the old woman's body like a lover's hand—*our* universe, in which you were getting up to dance with a janitor named Peter, whose sole pleasure was the joining together and then slipping away of your fingers from his as you jitterbugged to Perry Como.

"This is impossible," Rogni said, and I blinked. The old woman was gone, although I couldn't get rid of the image of the loose skin of her ankles, hanging down over the tops of her red high-heeled shoes like dewlaps. He went over and stood near the door, listening. "In the hierarchy of angels, Kathleen," he said, "nine in number, I am the lowest. The lowest. What are they doing in there?"

"Dancing," I said.

"Is that all?"

I narrowed my eyes. "If you're an angel," I said, "why do you need me to tell you what they're doing?"

"Because I can't see through the door," he said. He sounded angry. "I need something of Willie's," he said. "Are you going to help me or not?" And then he sat down on the sofa, hunched up, his hands over his eyes, like the see-no-evil monkey that perched on the end table out of which the red box had come. "When they paint their holy icons," he said under his breath, "men rarely look between the legs."

"Why do you need something of Willie's?" I asked.

"It's all right, Kathleen," he said, "maybe you should just go back to the party."

"No," I said. And then I had an idea. "There's a ring," I said. I dragged a chair over to the highboy and climbed up onto it, but I couldn't reach the top drawer. "It's in here," I said.

I watched as Rogni stuck his arm way into the drawer; watched as he drew forth the ring, which emitted a green and aqueous twinkle. "This?" he asked, and when I nodded my head he looked at me sternly: this was the first time I recognized on his face a typical adult expression. "You're sure it's hers?" he asked.

I looked away. "Uh huh," I said.

Rogni slipped the ring into his shirt pocket, where it made a tiny bulge down near the seam. "It's very important, Kathleen. I have to get the story right. If I don't, something very bad might happen."

"Like what?"

"I don't know yet. And I could be wrong."

"Maybe you shouldn't take it," I said. "Maybe we should put it back." I thought about how, once upon a time, I fell in love with you, Willie, and I stole your blue mittens, which I hid under my pillow to fondle at night. You remember this, of course, because you were the one who found them there and took them to Mama, who made me give them back to you. In consequence of this I knew that it was bad to steal and that my greatest punishment had been your scorn.

"I could be wrong," Rogni repeated. "She's like a

funnel of wind and this stone is so hard." He touched it, tentatively, through his pocket.

"What if somebody looks for it? What if they see it's missing?" Fear was turning around and around in me, trying to find a comfortable place to lie down.

"That's a chance we'll just have to take," Rogni said.

Chairs scraped against the dining-room floor and I heard Mama say, "Where's Kitty? Has anyone seen Kitty?" I guessed that it was time for the party to move to the barn, to where the pony hung his doleful head, his forelock adorned with a large red bow. "She's probably upstairs eating gruel," I heard you say; it was the first time you betrayed our secret and I knew we'd never be orphans together again. From that day forward we always had our parents to care for us, and I realize now that in giving ourselves over to the care of others we invited in the whole world, that sphere of green and blue stuck through like a pomander ball with weapons.

A herd of feet moved across the pantry floor and out the back door; I could hear voices rising into the cold air, inflated and bright. "Kitty?" Mama called from the foot of the stairs. "Kitty, are you up there?" She began climbing, and Rogni looked at me beseechingly.

"I've got to go now," he said. "Before she comes back down."

"No no no no no no!" I wailed. "Don't go. Not today. Oh, please don't go." I was hysterical, and I could feel each sob as it formed inside me. "If you wait till tomorrow, I'll help you find something better. Maybe one of Willie's ballet shoes?"

"I'm not a thief, Kathleen," Rogni said. "I've got what I need. And I'll bring it back soon. I promise."

"Who cares?" My hysteria sputtered and died, leaving me sullen. "I don't want the dumb ring, anyway."

"I'm sorry, Kathleen." Rogni walked to the door, the

one we never used, with its fanlight of wavery old glass. "Goodbye," he said, pulling it open, letting in wind filled with big flakes of snow that settled like stars everywhere. For a moment I was all alone, and then I felt *her* brush against me—the seething bulk of her; the tumultuous cabbage roses—tearing the room apart. Or was it only the wind and snow? And had it been Nana who, one day before she got sent to the nursing home, pulled open the drawer and showed me the ring?

"I hate you!" I yelled. The door swung shut, and when I ran over to the window all I could see was the meadow, from which every color had been removed except white. The sky was hung with fibrous sheets of cloud. "I hate you," I said again, softly. This time I meant *you*, Willie. Then I put on my coat and boots and went out to the barn, where your guests were taking turns feeding hay to the pony.

You stood off to one side, talking to Peter, who stood with one arm stretched out, his fingers stroking and stroking the pony's withers. "Hey, Willie, look at me!" yelled one of the boys from where he perched high above our heads on a rafter. You didn't even bat an eye.

"Get down from there before you kill yourself," Daddy said, but he didn't sound like he cared. He was staring at you as if you were a member of Mrs. McGuire's ghostly tribe, come to rest in our midst, portentous and fleeting.

"Easy," Peter said. "Easy, boy." The pony was shaking its mane and stamping its hooves. "Keep it down in here."

I can't remember how long it was before you noticed me, but when you did you left Peter's side and walked up to the pony. "Want a ride, Kitty?" you asked.

I shook my head, and Daddy suggested that the pony had probably had enough excitement for one day.

"I want Kitty to have a ride," you insisted. "I'll just lead them around." You stared at Daddy coldly. "It's *my* birthday," you said.

And so I let myself be lifted up onto that warm and

breathing back; I let you lead me out of the barn to where I felt myself tangle in a cloak of weather, so that I couldn't see a thing. The pony's hooves made no noise in the snow, and the only way that I knew we were moving was through the bunching and unbunching of its muscles under me.

"Why'd you leave the party?" you asked.

"I don't know," I said. The pony snorted and began to trot, making me bounce around.

"That's a lie, Kitty," you said. "That's a big fat lie."

"No, it isn't," I said.

You laughed. "You know what happens to liars, Kitty? Liars get punished." You laughed again, and then I understood from the gathering of strength under me that I'd been released. "Hang on!" you shouted, and I heard the flat of your hand smack against the pony's flank; at the same time the full force of the wind smacked against my face and we sprang forward. I knew that we were moving very fast, even though I could see nothing. I felt as if I were clamped onto one of those mechanical horses stationed in supermarkets and shopping centers—those horses that rock and buck with the insertion of a coin. Only now the mechanism had gone crazy, overcharged with current, and your invisible hand fed in dime after dime, as if the resources of retribution were infinite. I buried my face in the pony's mane and hung on; in this way I knew that I was still alive—I could smell sweat.

The pony was galloping towards the pines at the foot of the meadow. I only realized this later: at the time I had no idea of direction, although I did know that the open space through which we bounded was hemmed in on all sides by trees. Of course, the trees were very old and were spaced far enough apart that even an out-of-control pony might slip through safely—slip through to find itself falling down the steep declivity on the other side and into the streambed below.

We would have died, Willie—your new pony and I

would have gotten up from that wreckage as two differently shaped and surprised ghosts—but we didn't, because suddenly a voice exploded through the swirling of wind and snow:

*This—is—*NOT—GOING—TO—HAPPEN!

I raised my head and saw the angel standing there: the dark pinions extended as if for flight, the rigid and prismatic robes, the heart's fury made visible, burning through the chest, its heat so intense that everywhere around it the snow disintegrated, leaving the air empty and black, the ground on fire. The pony stopped dead in its tracks and I could feel its rib cage opening and closing, opening and closing, under me.

"Kathleen," the angel said, "you have to breathe now."

And then I saw that we *were* in the rocky place at the bottom of the hill and that there spread out around our feet the shadow of an accident. I began to scream, because I could see the sharp edge of a bone poking through the pony's hide; the way my neck bent back, like an envelope opening to receive a message. I screamed and the shadow seeped into the earth, leaving a dampness on the small round stones so that they glistened brightly. Then the angel covered his face with his hands and wept. "Kathleen," he said, "the damage is done. How old you'll grow to be! And she—she will be my sweetmeat and my affliction." In the hollow where we stood, above which the pines rose up like accusing fingers, it grew cold and the snow fell, once again, everywhere, landing on the sleeves of my coat, on the pony's back, on Rogni's dark hair as he stood there shivering.

"What I did was wrong," he said. "I wasn't supposed to interfere like that."

"I'm sorry I said I hated you," I said. "I didn't mean it."

"But I'm hateful, Kathleen. When I entered this body I was your guest and I stole from you. When I entered your house I was your burden: I let you do my work so my hands would be free." He stared down at them—gloveless, the fingers extended like white snakes, lacking joints, too too long. "I've gotten involved," he said.

And I thought, *Now* I'm being punished. Although, if he couldn't see through a wooden door, how could he see into my heart? "It was a lie," I said.

"Kathleen, come here." I walked over to him and he reached out, the soft tips of his fingers brushing my hair back out of my eyes. I was crying. "What was?" he asked. "Shhh. Shhh."

That was when he told me his name. He told it to me twice and asked me to repeat it after him, and as I did I heard Daddy yelling, "Kitty! Kitty!" and I heard you say, "It wasn't my fault. She must've kicked him or something."

Rogni put his finger to his lips. "Listen," he said. "There isn't much time. Soon they'll be here and you'll have to tell them how the pony jumped down the bank and how you held on for dear life. By the time they get here, I'll be gone."

"Where'll you go?" I asked. "Will you ever come back?"

"You'll see me again," Rogni said. "I promise."

I could hear the dull sound of feet pressing through new snow, and then something the size of a mote, out of which light radiated in shafts, passed through me, leaving a thin tunnel. I was alone in the hollow, watching Daddy stumble down the embankment, his face white and frightened, his glasses askew. You followed, picking your way gracefully from hummock to hummock.

I might have lied to protect you, Willie, but I didn't. Now I think I know why; now I understand why I chose to avoid the power assumed by the protector. One lie had been enough.

It was like a shipwreck, the end of that day, with our family marooned in our own house, trying to find out which of the foods were edible, what liquid fit to drink. Meanwhile, you sat in your accustomed posture of bored royalty, eating a scrambled egg. "I don't know what she's talking about," you said, after I described for the hundredth time the way you hit the pony's rump. "She's making it up."

"But, Willie," Daddy said wearily, "why would Kitty make something like that up?"

"I don't know," you said. "Why don't you ask her?"

Mama held me on her lap and I was wrapped in a quilt, because I couldn't stop shaking, because the path of the angel's flight felt as if it had been threaded through with a noose of ice, by which I might be lifted up to dangle like an ornament, like the salvaged artifact I was, far far above our parents' outstretched arms. I didn't think I could stand so much attention; it was bad enough having to insist on my innocence.

"I'm awfully tired," you said. "I'd really like to go to bed now."

Our parents exchanged one of those looks by which children are made to understand their position as foreigners in the dark principality of a marriage. Our mama assumed her usual role of petitioner, widening her eyes: she wanted Daddy to believe, you see, that you were just a child; she wanted him to participate in her belief that children are not capable of malice. You were her own daughter, Willie —how could she have been so stupid?

"All right," Daddy said, swiping at his lips with a paper napkin, although he'd eaten nothing. "Maybe we should all go to bed. Maybe we all need to get some sleep."

You got up from your chair and hurled yourself into his lap. "Oh, Daddy, I love you so much!" you said. It was like a handkerchief waved from the deck of an ocean liner: a violent gesture filled with the foreknowledge of separation.

"I love you too, Willie," Daddy said.

Then you unwound yourself from his arms and came right over to receive Mama's good-night kiss, looking me straight in the eye as you did so. "Aren't you going to wish me a happy birthday?" you asked. I felt caught off guard, just as I would while walking in the woods, when a tree would let loose a branchload of snow to land, with a sudden chill, on my head. "This birthday of all birthdays?" you pleaded.

"Happy birthday, Willie," I whispered.

The snow fell faster and faster outside, encasing us all. In Labrador, Willie, the snow sometimes rises in drifts so high that a person can walk up to the bell in the church steeple and set it ringing with their hand. In Labrador there is always too much of something or none of it at all. Jacques Cartier called it "the land God gave to Cain." For my part, I think of it as your kingdom—the kingdom of the queenly Willie, whose neck I would have broken gladly, had it not been so fragile.

"There was," Rogni said, "at the turn of the last century, a young American woman who traveled alone to the island of Skiathos, off the Greek mainland. The passage was rough but she was content enough, taking pleasure in the way the whole world seemed to shift beneath her feet. 'It's like a dog turning over in its sleep,' she told the captain, when she ate with him at his table. He thought she was charming but proud, and so he made her a gift of a small bottle in which he'd erected the model of a ship. 'A trifle,' he said, 'something to occupy my lonely hours after people such as yourself are fast asleep.' Then he put his hand over her hand, but just for a moment, and the other passengers at the table were embarrassed, and looked down into their bowls of tripe.

"It was the young woman's good fortune, upon arriving at her destination, to locate a small villa on the island's southern coast. The villa was made of white stone and sat high on a hill crisscrossed by goat paths. In the mornings the young woman watched old women in black dresses climbing up and down these paths, picking up pieces of wood to start their fires.

"Her name was Clara Loomis and her father was the

Dwight Loomis who invented a small valve indispensable to the working of a machine used in smelting ore. So, you see, she was very rich. But she was also a mystic, having fallen, as a girl, under the spell of her pietistic great-aunt, who took her along on her pilgrimages to the cave of the visionary Johann Kelpius. This early fascination led her, one turbulent summer night, into the salon of Wilhelm Steumphig, a mesmerist of no small ability. A thunderstorm, as if on cue, provided the appropriate background noises for his pronouncement. 'You must go to Skiathos, my dear!' he said. 'The light there, alone, is of a purity unsurpassed anywhere in the world. And it is there that you will find your spiritual twin.' Clara wrote the island's name on a piece of paper ceremoniously handed to her by Steumphig's servant, a Leni-Lenape Indian. 'I'll go,' she said.

"By this time Steumphig was a little in love with her, and might have regretted her decision, had he not been aware, like the captain, of her pride. He thought he'd have an easier time of it wooing her upon her return. It was Steumphig's belief, you see, that mystical encounters had a humbling effect. This was because he'd never had one himself.

"Clara walked, every day, all over the island. The goat paths led everywhere: up the steep hills where the olive trees grew, down into the grassy bowls where peasants lived in small cottages called *kalyvas*. She ate oranges and figs and dates. Her legs became very strong. Up hill and down she walked, looking for her spiritual twin, but all she found were the hardworking and matter-of-fact peasants. At night Clara would sit looking out the window of her villa, which faced the sea. Then she would notice, as the sun went down, individual islands springing into focus, and each time this happened she would think, Perhaps I'm in the wrong place. Perhaps I should be over *there*.

"The captain's gift sat on the table, almost touching the

tip of her elbow where she rested it, as she looked out to sea. This was an unusual version of the customary ship-in-a-bottle, in that the bottle was filled with a blue liquid within which the ship floated, more like a shipwreck-in-a-bottle. It made Clara uneasy, yet she couldn't bring herself to throw the thing away. Sometimes she picked it up and shook it boldly, to watch the masts jiggling from side to side.

"There was, on the island's northern shore, a monastery presided over by a monk named Hieronymous. Clara heard about this from an old woman whom she met one day in the village, as she stood watching the fishing boats set out—blue and red and yellow—in the first light of dawn. The old woman approached Clara. '*Kali mera,*' she said, '*chari mou.*' Clara spoke enough Greek to understand the old woman, who explained that she'd noticed Clara wandering around the island and wondered if perhaps she was looking for the monastery. It was hard to find, located on the wind-ward coast, in a small cove. The old woman gave Clara directions. It was rumored, she said, that the monk Hieronymous had killed someone and that he'd now chosen to live out his life as a penitent. It was a crime of passion, the old woman said, committed in his youth.

"Did I say that Clara was beautiful? Because she was. And as she made her way north the following day, across the island's high central spine of rock and shrub, she imagined the effect of her beauty on a man whose life encompassed lust and murder and atonement.

"The monastery was built out of a darker rock than that found on the southern coast, and it was surrounded by the black fingers of cypress trees. Clara arrived there in late afternoon. She wasn't tired. Her skin was golden from so much walking in the sun, and her hair was the color of honey and hung in a thick braid to her waist.

"What did she expect? An old man whittled down to a holy thinness? Something like the ascetic Kelpius, whose portrait hung above her great-aunt's bed? As Clara approached the monastery, the wooden door swung open and out came a tall figure in black robes. He was, perhaps, forty-five or fifty, and even in his robes she could see that this was a man who spent his days in physical labor. His face was almost black—his eyes blacker still. 'God be with you,' he said in Greek. Then he led Clara into the monastery, which was cold and dark. The walls were empty; a single wooden bench faced an altar upon which many candles burned. 'Not a great artist, I'm afraid,' Hieronymous said, pointing upwards. Clara was startled. She thought he meant God. 'The mosaic,' Hieronymous said. 'You've come to see our mosaic?' On the domed ceiling Clara could see the face of Christ Pantocrator; he held a small globe in his hand. 'Oh!' she gasped, and the monk bowed slightly. 'The resemblance is accidental,' he said. 'I didn't notice it at first. Or, perhaps, we've come to resemble each other over time, like an old married couple.' 'Perhaps,' Clara said. She stood waiting. It had occurred to her, you see, that this man was the promised twin. And if the monk is twin to Christ, she mused, what does that make me?

"But whatever communion she expected was not forthcoming. 'I have to go attend to the hives,' Hieronymous said. 'You may stay here to pray'—and here he smiled slyly, so that Clara felt anger welling up in her heart—'if that is your inclination.' 'Thank you,' she said. 'I belong to no organized religion. Still, I would like to sit here a moment. It was a long walk.' 'As you wish,' the monk said. He strode to the door and then turned so that he was facing Clara. Behind him the sky was bright blue. 'This is a holy place,' he said, 'and, as such, open to all people. But there is an anteroom—the door is there, to the left of the altar—and, as you are a woman, it is forbidden that you enter that room. I trust you to honor its sanctity.'

"Clara sat down on the wooden bench and took a deep breath. Even though Hieronymous was gone she could feel his black eyes watching her from the ceiling. She tried to focus her attention on the candles, but her gaze kept shifting to the left—to the door. 'Why,' she said out loud, 'should a mystery be withheld from me, simply because of my sex?' Her anger at the monk's mocking voice transformed itself into righteousness. 'After all,' she said, 'I've traveled a very long way.' And so, after several minutes had elapsed in this fashion, she got up and opened the door.

"Now she found herself in a small room without windows. There was a chair in one corner and a box on the floor—a box about the same size and shape as a steamer trunk. Everything was covered with dust. Clara blew the dust off the lid of the box and saw that it was carved with a representation of the Anastasis: Christ was raising Adam and Eve from Limbo, lifting them up like dolls, while the Devil writhed, bound and gagged on the floor, surrounded by a flying mass of broken locks and oddly-shaped keys. She only hesitated for a moment, and then she opened the box. There was a soft moaning noise—it might have been the hinges.

"The box was filled with bones, a jumble of bones. The disorder was so complete that, at first, she noticed nothing unusual. But then, here and there, she began to see stirrings, small purposeful movements: the bones were arranging themselves into a recognizable form. At the very last, from somewhere at the bottom of the box, a skull flew up to settle on the tip of the spine, and then slowly rotated to face Clara.

" 'It's taken you long enough,' the thing in the box said. A string of armbones reached up and a fingerbone slid across her cheek. 'So pretty,' the thing said. 'For whatever good it'll do you. Where is he now?'

"Clara was terrified. 'What *are* you?' she asked. The thing in the box laughed. 'You'd do better to ask who I was. The beautiful Margarita, betrothed of Iannis, whom you now know as the monk Hieronymous—that's who I was. Who, because she dared to smile at other men, became the subject of his sainthood. Who, you might say, died to make him holy.'

"The thing raised its other arm from the box, and Clara saw that it was holding on to a small, ivory-handled dagger. 'What do you want from me?' Clara asked. 'Ah, my dear, you've got it backwards,' the thing answered. 'It's only a matter of time before he finds out that you disobeyed his orders. And then, as surely as the sun rises every morning, he'll try to kill you. I am merely providing you with a means of defense.'

"As Clara took the dagger from the thing's hand, she could hear the sound of the front door to the monastery opening, and the sound of the monk's feet crossing the stone floor. 'As beautiful as you are,' the thing said, 'I was more beautiful by far'—and then it collapsed back into a pile of bones.

"'Ah, there you are,' Hieronymous said. Clara stood, caught in the act of closing the lid of the box, preparing herself for the monk's fury. But he was smiling. He came over and put his arm around her waist. 'Let's go outside,' he said. 'The sun is shining and it's so gloomy in here.' Together they walked beneath Christ's stern face and through the front door. 'Sit down,' he said, pointing to a grassy rise. 'Here's some wine and some goat cheese I made myself.' 'But I don't understand,' Clara said. 'I thought you'd be angry.' The monk poured wine into her glass and handed it to her. 'Why should I be angry?' he asked. 'I knew from the moment you arrived that you'd go into that room. Besides, you're so beautiful. How could I be angry at so beautiful a woman?' The monk leaned over and kissed Clara. She had been kissed before, but always politely and tentatively, by young men of romantic, rather than passionate, disposition. Now she was frightened by the force of her response. And so they became lovers, and the night closed over them like a hand.

"The next morning Hieronymous was standing at the water's edge, looking out to sea. Clara came up and stood beside him, shyly. 'There's a storm coming up,' he told her. 'If you're going to get back before it hits, you must leave immediately.' 'But I want to stay with you,' Clara said. 'That's not possible,' he answered. His voice was cold. 'You disobeyed. How could you think that I'd want you to stay here with me?' Clara began to cry; she threw herself into his arms, and as he tried to push her away he suddenly froze. 'What's this?' he asked. It was the dagger, which she'd slipped into the pocket of her long green skirt. 'Where did you get this?' he asked. His arm swung in an arc and the dagger flew through the air, landing in the sea. 'You were going to kill me, weren't you?' Clara began to back away from him. 'Don't worry,' he said, 'I'm not going to hurt you.' He laughed. 'You pitiful thing,' he called after her, as she walked up the hill away from the water. 'You could never hold a candle to Margarita.'

"Clara returned to America. This time the passage was smooth, which was fortunate, because she was with child. Her father arranged for her to spend her confinement with an old couple in the country; the ignominiousness of her eventual reappearance in town, carrying an infant girl, was mitigated by her bravado. Clara became an outspoken champion of free love. She explained to anyone who would listen that this was the logical result of her earlier mysticism. Union was what was important; whether spiritual or physical, it didn't matter. When asked about the consequences, she grew fierce. Her love for her daughter was complete. They went everywhere together. The child, whom Clara had christened Margarita, was dark and wild, like a little gypsy.

"One night, shortly after Margarita's fifth birthday, Clara was returning from a gathering at a house in a bad part of town, near the waterfront. As usual, Margarita was with her, tagging along at her side. Suddenly, out from behind a corner of a building, there sprang a crazy man—he was dressed like a sailor and had a dagger between his teeth. Before she knew what was happening, the man thrust the dagger deep into Clara's heart. Margarita started screaming and the man ran away. 'Mama, Mama,' Margarita said, but nothing happened. Clara was dead.

"It was only later, while she was sitting upstairs in her mother's room, as the downstairs filled with sorrowful and whispering friends and relatives, that Margarita found the bottle. Clara had hidden it in the very back of her wardrobe, on the floor, behind her shoes. The child picked it up and looked into it. She could see a ship suspended in blue water. It was a pretty thing, the way it swayed back and forth, and it was perfect in all its details: the masts, the decks, the miniature crates and barrels. Margarita squinted her eyes and looked closer. Something was moving up one of the shrouds. So hard to see—she pressed her eye up against the glass! A man was climbing the shrouds. He was climbing and his back was to her, and then, all of a sudden, he turned around. She smiled, because, you see, she recognized him. It was Jesus Christ. Margarita knew. She'd seen the pictures."

Of course, he came back. From time to time, during the years following your birthday party, Rogni would reappear and tell me stories. The story of Clara, for instance, he told me on a dreamy afternoon during the summer of my tenth year. I'd been sitting on a hill in the sun, eating a piece of melon, when, from amid the teeming around me of insect life, his body gradually pulled together—a darker shape within that particulate cloud, giving off as refuse a scattering of grasshoppers.

"Kathleen," he said, "why are you smiling? That's supposed to be a sad story. Clara dies. Didn't that make you sad?"

"Well," I said, "sure. But the little girl has Jesus in a bottle." I sucked on the melon rind, extracting every last bit of juice. "Besides, I'm happy because you're here."

"I didn't get it right," he said, looking off across the valley, where the hot white bands of the roads held the green and lavish world together. Then he turned to face me. "I'm worried about you, Kathleen," he said. "I'm unreliable. I come and go. You ought to have some friends. You don't have any friends, do you?"

I was so embarrassed by his solicitude that I could barely

stand to tell him the truth: how I was the tallest girl in school; how I traveled its hallways like Gulliver among the Lilliputians; how my heart was broken daily by the sight of the graceful arms of my classmates, curving around their books as they climbed, without stooping, from the school bus. "Most of the kids I know are morons," I said.

"Clara was proud, too," Rogni reminded me. He leaned back on his hands in the grass and, for a moment, the outward contours of his body were like winds and dust in orbit around a small, dense star. Such metamorphosis, I'd learned, generally preceded flight.

"There's Amy Gertner," I said. "I guess you could say she's my friend."

Amy's father was the Episcopalian minister in Conway; she was as unpopular as myself, so that our friendship only served to intensify our positions as outcasts. Once I spent the night at her house and it was a horrible experience, confirming my belief in the ubiquity of adult irrationality. At the dinner table Reverend Gertner presided, waving the serving fork over a platter piled with chicken parts. "Well, Kathleen," he consulted me, smiling. "Which do you prefer, white meat or dark?" I warmed to his hospitable smile. "White," I answered, "please," at which he speared a thigh and dumped it on my plate. "Picky, aren't you?" he sneered.

"Amy's okay, I guess," I said. "And there's Mrs. Klink, the science teacher. She let me borrow her binoculars." I held them up, by way of demonstration. "I saw an indigo bunting this morning. That's a kind of finch." I didn't tell him that Finch was my secret name now, nor that the secret name I had for you was Grackle.

"And what about Willie?" Rogni asked, as if he could read my thoughts.

"I don't know," I said. "I hardly ever see her. I don't know what's happening to her."

Rogni got up and looked down the hill, to where a troop

of Cub Scouts was making its way, single file, in our direction. "She needs you," he said.

"Yeah," I said, "sure." I looked away, angry, to watch as the pack leader unfolded a large map, then gestured magnificently, extending his arms outward like the Reverend Gertner. When I looked back, Rogni was gone. Something like a small cloud passed across the face of the sun and I thought it was him. "Thanks a bunch," I said.

And then the Cub Scouts were all around me, tumbling and making merry noises. "Listen up, fellas," their leader said. "Leave the girl alone." He approached me and I knew, from my experience with Daddy, that he was nervous, because of the way that telltale section of his jawline jumped up and down. "Look," he said. "This is Roundtop, right?"

"No," I said. "Roundtop's over there."

"Damn!" He folded the map and put it back in his pocket. "Sorry," he said, running his hand over his crew-cut head. I watched as the individual hairs flattened out and then sprang up row by row. "There?" he asked, pointing, making sure.

I nodded; carefully I began gathering my things together into my pack.

"Well," he said, "they never have to know."

I shrugged and got up. "This is just a hill," I said. "It doesn't have a name." I spoke loudly, so that I could not be accused of complicity, but the little boys were busy playing keep-away with one of their regulation beanies. It wasn't until I started to walk away from them, down the hill through the dense, whiskery stems of the late-summer flowers, that I heard one of them say, "It is *too* her sister."

Willie, there was no getting away from you. Grackle. Of course, no one else saw you that way; Grackle Willie, the avid flitting eyes, the fanned-out and obtrusive tail, the *cheek cheek cheek* passing for song. What others saw was a thin, white-limbed fourteen-year-old. You commanded admiration and censure, both of which I'd seen in the faces of our schoolmates' parents, on the rare occasions when you would let me tag along with you into town. Certainly most of them had seen you—your body the curved bow, the taut string, the arrow itself, preparing to fly and then flying—in the production of *Nutcracker* last Christmas. A black-haired woman with iridescent eye shadow came up during intermission to introduce herself to Mama. "Such talent," the woman said sternly. "You must not let such talent go to waste *here*." She waved her arms around, taking in the whole brown auditorium, with its rows of folding shellacked chairs, its residual odor of disinfectant and bananas, through which wafted the alien notes of Emeraude, My Sin, Tigresse; on the walls were the murals in which dim, patriotic giants played flutes, or shook hands with Indians, or raised flags. The woman handed Mama a card. "Call me," she said, and then walked back to her seat with that same strangely kneeless swing of leg from hip socket by which you had taught me to recognize ballet dancers. "Well," Mama said, dropping the card into the vastness of her alligator bag. She appeared shy and embarrassed. "Let's not tell your father about this, all right, sweetie?" She smiled. "This can be our secret."

The thing is, Willie, I wasn't surprised by her desire for secrecy. I'd noticed the look in your eyes when the young man lifted you from the floor—your arms and legs extended in glowing points—I'd seen how his hand disappeared under all that sequined tulle and I had made a guess at where it was he held you steady.

Ever since your tenth birthday party, you'll remember, our family had preoccupied itself with trying to figure you out. By day you were Willie the ballerina, your hair pulled back tightly from your face, fastened into a small knot at the top of your head; you carried the blue bag with you everywhere, in which you kept your leotard and tights, your expensive new toe shoes. You hummed in the mornings, standing in front of the bathroom mirror, one leg raised straight out to the side so that your foot could rest, like a small bird, on the towel rack. By day you were the dancing Willie, recognizable and quick; it was at night that you became something else. I think it was because you could not stop spinning—you told me once how you would listen to the grandfather clock on the first floor, how its separate ticks would fly, one by one, up into your room, until there was no space left.

"It's not so bad," you told me once, "when *they*'re still up. You know? Then I can hear good old Dad's clinking ice cubes and good old Jack Paar. But then they go to bed. And then I'm the only person awake in the whole world. It's like I'm never going to fall asleep. Do you know what I mean, Kitty?"

Oh, Willie, I wanted to say "yes"—I wanted so much to be like you that I would have endured the curse of insomnia, if only we could be orphans together again. But I was a champion sleeper; I was the girl who'd remained asleep when an entire set of shelves mysteriously detached themselves from my wall one night, spewing books and dolls everywhere.

"I listen to that dumb clock," you told me, "playing its dumb tune. It doesn't always play the whole thing, it only does that when it's going to strike. You ever notice? Ding-a-ding-dong, ding-a-ding-dong. And then I think about heaven—how when you die you go to heaven and it never stops. There isn't any way out."

You were sitting on the end of my bed, staring down at one of the rag rugs our mama bought every fall from the blind woman with the gray felt slippers and drooling dog.

"Some people go to hell," I said.

"Thanks, Kitty. That's very consoling."

Then, because I started to whimper, you leaned over and took my face between your hands. You held on tight and whispered something, but your hands were pressing against my ears and I couldn't hear a word of what you said. And then you were gone.

For Daddy, I think, the solution to what we all came to refer to as your *problem* had its sources in the past—maybe in the precise moment when your palm slapped against the pony's flank. It was on his suggestion that you spent an hour, every Wednesday afternoon, in the company of young Dr. Varney, whose habit of moistening the thick pads of his lips with his tongue, prior to asking you a question, you duplicated over dinner with terrible accuracy. You were always such a talented mimic, Willie, and you possessed the mimic's gift for defining personality in terms of weakness. Dr. Varney's approach, evidently, was slangy and conspiratorial. "Hey, kiddo, how goes it?" you would drawl, stretching out your legs and crossing them at the ankles. And then you would sneer, your upper lip rising like a curtain to reveal that row of tiny, even teeth. "Jerk," you would say.

Daddy retained through all of this a scholarly determination. Whatever the nature was of his private "research," he seemed to draw solace from his endless note-taking, as if killing off the idea of entropy might help you sleep. His journal entries, during those five years, before he gave up—before you moved out, providing your own solution—testify to this determination. "December 10, 1959," he wrote. "Spent day shoring up back foundation wall. Guilty as all hell. House on verge of collapse. Great diligence called for. W. unchanged. Conscience as seat of counter-entropic energy? Political ramifications unlimited! Letter to Dulles. Reread Henry Adams." There followed a drawing of three doughnut-shaped objects: the first, whole; the second cut in half, rendered in cross-section; the third outlined in dots. "W. to Varney's, p.m." he continued. "In car W. describes childhood fear of light fixture over bed. Replace tomorrow."

He wrote pages of this stuff, interspersed with perfectly

rational plans for newspaper articles; plans for fixing up our house, accompanied by lists of supplies and schedules. On the first page of one of these ledgers he'd taped a photograph of our house when it was new. In the photograph three women posed in the front yard among plantings of ornamental shrubbery, long waving arms of delphinium, clumps of loosestrife. The women wore high-necked blouses and long dark skirts, and they held baskets filled with flowers, while behind them the house rose, every line true, every window sparkling, into a cloudless sky.

I think, Willie, that this was the way he understood your problem: in the beginning there was grace and brilliance with which, as time wore on, the world's multiple hands would begin tampering, like a mob of fans dismantling an idol. There was a caption printed under the photograph. *Time's arrow reversed*, it said. And so he continued to drive you to Dr. Varney's office; he remained hopeful.

Understand, he *had* to. He had to because his sorrow was not all for you, some of it was reserved for himself. That's why he began to spend more and more time at his desk, writing. He'd pretend he couldn't hear you tossing around upstairs in your bed and, if he couldn't block that out, then, I think, he'd pretend what he heard was the sound of generative activity: a spontaneous creation with a name more redemptive than "daughter."

Mama, on the other hand, was fatalistic. Her vision of the world included the possibility that, on a designated morning, the planet might leap from its orbit to freeze in the far reaches of space; on a designated morning you might come down to breakfast with the thin sheen over you of the sleeper. She wept, remember, one Easter morning, because no one was able to locate, where she'd concealed it among the windflowers, the porcelain egg from Italy, with its window through which you could see the Tuscan landscape: plane trees and a sugary road. "It's a sign," she said.

These were *our* parents, Willie.

And do you remember how Mama took you to see Rosina, that local woman who grew herbs all around and inside the turquoise-blue trailer in which she lived? On every surface—even on top of Rosina's television set, which you told me was always turned on—sat clay pots filled with tangles of vegetation, drooping their strange leaves over hundreds of salt and pepper shakers. Rosina had a mustache, and a voice so beautiful that new mothers would hire her to sing their colicky infants to sleep.

You never made fun of Rosina. In fact, you seemed to look forward to the time you spent with her, drinking tisanes or more potent concoctions from doll-sized teacups. But, despite the ease with which you were able to fall asleep across her huge lap, her cures were limited to the trailer.

Eventually, Mama resorted to psychics—to a Dartmouth professor who claimed to locate clear channels in the brain with a dowsing rod; to an ancient member of the DAR from Tamworth who threw the *I Ching*. Mrs. McGuire, unsolicited, suggested that Mama mix some of your menstrual blood into a glass of port wine and give it to you at bedtime. "Then the poor benighted child must say her prayers, kneeling, mind you, at the foot of the bed." She paused, letting this all sink in. "A prayer once in bed calls the Devil to your head," she explained.

One morning, on my way to breakfast, I found a drawing on the wallpaper at the foot of the stairs: a banana-shaped object filled with smaller, wobbly objects, many of them labeled: fenchlet, the doorway of Merbus, Kitty's bone-garb, hooma. You were lounging on the porch in nothing more than a large gray T-shirt, slyly watching Daddy through the window, as he sat drinking his coffee and reading the paper. "What?" you said, when I asked you about the drawing. "Oh, *that*. That's a picture of God's brain. We're all in there, don't worry."

I sat on the porch railing and it was still wet with dew; the spiders' necklaces dangled everywhere and the spiders themselves rose and fell, rose and fell, filled with heavy liquid. "I wasn't worried," I said, and you whirled around, outraged.

"Well, you should have been," you said. Then you grinned. "Maybe I'll erase you."

"You can't," I said.

"What do you mean, I can't. Of course I can."

But I was patient and perfectly serious. "You can't erase crayon," I said. "Everybody knows that."

I never knew what to expect, Willie. My life was like that of an assistant at a magic show, wondering whether it would be a red flower or a skull that would pop, next, from the hat. Because, of course, sometimes it *was* a red flower: something lavish and beautiful, like a peony.

At about the same time that I found the drawing on the wall, you planned a family trip for all of us. "We could ride the cog railway up Mt. Washington," you said. "Please?" A boy in your class had described for you the weather station and restaurant at the top; the plaque commemorating the deaths of hikers and climbers; the excitement of being drawn, like a toy on a string, upwards. In those days, you might recall, we were not a family given to such outings. But the specificity of your request—the fact that it named a desire he was capable of fulfilling—made Daddy spring into action. "Mt. Washington, here we come!" he said.

The car we had then was a two-tone Chevrolet: mint and forest green. In front of us we could see the backs of our parents' heads—the black curly hair of Daddy's head, longer than the hair of the fathers in magazine pictures, longer than the hair of the other fathers who stood helping charming wives and children out of cars in the parking area. And there was the gray fuzz that Mama had arranged in what she referred to as a "Psyche knot," pretending to be playful as, I suppose, she thought a mother should be at the outset of a family expedition. They disagreed, as usual, about the radio. "For crying out loud, Constance, it's just the news," Daddy said, as Mama twirled the knob to find music—any music. It was spring and the branches of the trees were dark red, clustered with buds, and there was a heat coming from inside things that had nothing to do with wind or air but was like the heat you feel in the palm of your hand when you exhale into it. Mama's hands were always cold, because she had poor circulation. "The girls," she hissed at Daddy, twisting the radio dial back and forth, as if it was a shameful thing for him to let us hear the voice of the newscaster describing Ike's golf game, or the confusing politics of Berlin, or the presence in our milk of strontium-90; as if it was on our account that the car had to be filled with the sad voices of the Everly Brothers, whose music made me feel worse than anything the newscaster might have said.

The cog-railway car was charming in the manner of things from the last century, frail and outmoded. Mama gasped when she saw it. As the descending passengers, their faces lit with relief, climbed out of the car, we watched a big youth in a blue knit stocking cap, his hair cut in that Dutch-boy style that makes the whole head look like a peasant hut with a thatched roof, jump down from the engineer's seat and begin furiously squeezing oil from a can into the engine's working parts.

"Look," you said to me. "You can see his crack."

"Shh," I said.

In the car we sat two abreast. You sat next to Daddy; he had his long arm looped across your shoulders, across your bright red braids, drawing from the other passengers admiring, approving stares: the handsome father and the delicate, beautiful daughter. Behind you I sat next to Mama: a large, bespectacled girl beside a tiny, gray-haired woman. No one paused to admire us, although I was certain that we aroused curiosity—a nurse and her charge?—and that no one, seeing us, linked us with you and Daddy.

You could have maintained that illusion. I realize that. I think if it had been the other way around, I'd have made the denial aggressively, like Peter in the Bible. "Nope," I would have said, "those weirdos? Never saw them before in my life." But you were kinder.

Mama pressed her hands to her face during the earlier part of the ride, before we hit the higher elevations, where the trees grew smaller and smaller, more and more lopsided, eventually vanishing, to be replaced by huge damp stones, out of which shelves of ice stuck, all in the same direction. Then she hid her head in her lap. It was the only way to avoid seeing it: the terrible vertical track of our ascent, unimpeded, as we neared the peak, by any upright object on which a falling body might catch. We were flotsam being carried to the crest of a wave miles high. We passed the alpine meadow and it diminished, the lake in its center becoming a small blue circle of water, like something left out for a pet.

At the top we climbed onto a wooden boardwalk, where we could see the machinery and cables responsible for our well-being. The weather station was festooned with wires and slowly rotating disks, and a man in camouflage fatigues leaned against one wall, chewing gum and grinning.

"Kitty!" Mama said, wildly gripping my arm. She presented a variety of aspects, our mama, but the one which predominates in my recollection of her is the one which took over there on the mountain, as we made our way slowly to the restaurant. We were like figures in some unsettling fable from a foreign country that honored neither good deeds nor a pure heart; we were a giantess and a mantis, companions in a quest filled with tricks and obstacles.

You danced towards the restaurant. I'm sure you knew that the man in fatigues was watching you, watching the way the wind caught your braids and flung them straight out behind your head, as if frozen, pointing. "Willie!" Daddy yelled, but he couldn't keep up with you either. We found you standing inside the building, transfixed by the plaque, your arms respectfully folded behind your back, your leg *tendu*.

"Look at this," you said. "A little kid died up here in 1931. She was only eight years old."

We both ate up this piece of information: children are interested in the deaths of other children; they hold those deaths up to the light and then align the contours of their own lives against them, looking for similarities. That's why the part of *Little Women* that gets reread is Beth's death; maybe that's why we decide that too much goodness is a dangerous thing.

Mama found our glee shocking. "Girls," she said. "I'm surprised at you." Her hands were shaking and even though she was inside a familiar structure, through which wafted the smells of coffee, fried food, and that steam-table aroma so impossible to assign—who knows if it is exuded by the thing we will eat or the people who will serve it to us?—it was obvious that she hated being up so high. "The poor mother," she said.

You stared at her, then you stared at me. I guess you made a choice. It was a good one, too: at the very least, with my big, heavy bones, I could provide ballast. Gravity as well, although my skills there were still undeveloped. "C'mon, Kitty," you said. "C'mon. Let's see what there is to see."

And then you took my hand. Do you remember that? Sometimes I think it was that memory which, four years later, pulled me right back from the actual edge of the world. You led me outside to where the wind hit our faces, making my glasses fog up, and you stood there, the soul of patience, as I wiped them against my sleeve and put them back on, so that I could see how the man standing by the weather station raised one arm, languidly, to wave at us. His face rotated in our direction like one of the disks and he winked. "Some guys," you said, "are pretty rude."

And so, for the rest of that wintry afternoon, while all around the foot of the mountain spring's modest flowers opened in warm sunshine; while our parents sat in the restaurant drinking coffee; while Daddy made the necessary small adjustments in his behavior to calm Mama down, you devoted yourself to me. We jumped from rock to rock, and the rocks wobbled under our sneakers; we followed a group of Cub Scouts partway down a trail marked by cairns, listening as their leader pointed out geologic features.

"Sound off," you mimicked. "Stokes, it's going to be KP for you if you don't shape up."

Stokes, who overheard, turned around, and you rolled your eyes and stuck out your tongue. Your arm was around my shoulders and I was so happy that I laughed out loud. There we were, you and I, high on top of a mountain, the blue air's wild currents all around our bodies, the rocks shifting dangerously under our feet, but we stuck!—we didn't fly away or fall, even as the world spun like crazy through outer space—we adhered to each other and our density was miraculous.

On the ride back down the mountain you insisted on sitting next to me. Your breath smelled like mint, from the colorless Life Savers you adored; your pupils were fully dilated because, at least for that moment, you adored me more than anything else in the universe. "Stokes," you intoned, "consider the *awe*some power of the glacier. Consider the *awe*some sight of all that ice."

From behind us came the sound of Daddy's voice: "Consider the awesome mess if you two fall out of this contraption."

You jabbed me with your elbow and we both giggled hysterically. Our conspiracy was complete. It should have lasted. Why didn't it last?

That must have been late April or early May. In June
you left us for the first time in pursuit of your career; with
the sly urging of the woman who'd given Mama her card,
you accepted a scholarship at a special camp in Vermont.
This woman, Marina Protzeroff—who insisted on being referred to as "Madame," and who called our house every
single evening for a month, just at dinnertime, until Mama
gave in to your pleas and her own exhaustion—swept you
up one morning into her black Mercedes, like a scene in a
school nature movie about predators and prey. In the
presence of Madame you became limber and cool; you
became something that one ought not touch. Each of us,
in turn, approached the passenger seat window, which
Madame caused to roll down at the touch of a button, and
you offered the sharp edge of your cheek to our lips. Had
you seen one of your heroines, possibly Garbo, make the
same gesture in a movie?

"Take good care of our girl, please," Mama said, and
Madame, without turning her head, blinked once, the lids
rising and lowering with exaggerated slowness, as if signaling accomplices hidden in our bushes. *Now!* that blink
seemed to say and, as the dark car bore you away from us,
I waited for the thugs, their faces mashed to a smooth
marbling beneath nylon stockings, to tie us up and stow
us away forever in the cellar.

"I don't care what anyone says," Daddy said, "that
woman is a complete phony."

"She studied with Nijinsky, Nick," Mama said.

"Yeah, and I'm Albert Einstein. You know what the
trouble with you is? The trouble with you is, you always
fall for the phonies."

"I married you," Mama said. And then she stamped up
the porch steps and into the house, where she began knitting, casting on stitches and humming frantically.

Daddy followed. I could tell he was headed for the
cabinet behind the wing chair where, among Chutes and

Ladders, and decks of cards, and a partly assembled cuckoo clock, he hid his bottle of Scotch, as well as the several dusty bottles of liqueur we kept for company.

"Kathleen!" he yelled, and I went to him immediately. These days, the minute he had the bottle in his hand he was already on his way to being irrational; I didn't want to take any chances. "Did she say anything to you?" Daddy asked.

"Who?"

"Willie. Your sister. Did she say anything . . ." And then he stopped, flustered. "Do you trust that woman?"

"You mean Madame?"

"I mean Mrs. Protzeroff." He was impatient now, trying to hurry our conversation along so that he could make his getaway to the kitchen, land of ice cubes and tumblers.

"I guess so," I said. "Why? Do you think she's a crook?"

Daddy laughed, a single *ha*, and patted the top of my head. "I think she's a piranha, Kathleen." Then he walked out of the room.

That summer was a bad one. I'd gotten a Brownie camera for my birthday, and most of the pictures I took showed great masses of brush: the romantic decrepitude of softwood forests. If you looked closely you might be able to make out the small whirring blot that was the bird whose image I was trying to capture.

Willie, among all those photographs there is one so sad that, no matter how many times I've tried, it will not allow me to throw it away. Mama is sitting in her wing chair, her cold profile bent over her knitting. To the right of her, in his matching chair, Daddy sits, glass in hand, staring at her with disbelief and rancor. His notebook is open in his lap. And what about the photographer? What about me? Even the sudden light of the flashbulb has not been able to rouse them from their solitary gnawing. It's as if I was never there.

Of course, they took me along at the end of the summer, when they went to pick you up. What else could they do with me? I remember how they tried to turn this occasion into an expedition, trying, I suppose, to duplicate that last happy adventure up Mt. Washington. We made side trips to local museums, where elderly curators showed us displays of dolls with dried apples for heads and replicas of the American flag devised entirely of bugs. We stopped at a diner for apple pie, and the waitress smiled at me out of her wide, friendly face; she had a white hankie tucked into her breast pocket, and she took our orders as if we were the most ordinary family in the world. We were so cautious with each other! It was as if, by avoiding contact, we could actually ensure each other's happiness.

The camp was hidden at the end of a dirt road bored through huge shade trees; a long road filled like a subterranean passageway with viscid heat, it was illuminated, from time to time, by a yellowish downpour of sunlight. Once, we saw a glittery cloud of dust on the road ahead of us which, as we drove closer, turned out to be a tan girl in a white bathing suit, her long legs clamped to the sides of a tall white horse. She raised her hand in greeting and the horse shied—that was when the rock flew up and left a tiny, cone-shaped hole in the windshield. "Great," Daddy said. "Great."

Eventually, we found you in the canteen, seated cross-legged on a picnic table, leaning back into the arms of a blond young man—Ernie, was that his name?—whose pink lips were pressed to your ear, whispering or kissing. At first you didn't notice us. "I bet you would," you were saying. "I bet you'd like that a lot." Then you looked up. "Well," you said, laughing, "look who's here."

"Willie," Mama said. "Sweetheart."

We all stood positioned on the black-and-white squares of linoleum like chess pieces, watching as you gracefully lifted the young man's hands from your chest and then jumped down from the table, landing softly on the balls of your feet. "Isn't this nice," you said. "The whole family:

Mr. Noodle, the Mouse Queen, and Little Kitty. They've come to take me away from all this," you said, over your shoulder, to the young man.

"Hello," he said. He was trying to be polite; I think I remember you telling me that he came from a wealthy family on the Main Line, that the extravagant red convertible in the parking lot was his. Whatever his hopes were for romance, they were not so strong as his urge to be mannerly in the presence of adults.

"Have they been taking good care of you, sweetheart?" Mama asked. She walked over to kiss you, but you held up your hands like a traffic cop.

"Whoa, there," you said. "Let me refresh your memory. I am Willie Mowbrey, the one kid in this camp who never received so much as a single brownie from her loving mom and dad." Your lips were painted with bright red lipstick, and it looked as if all the color in your body had gathered there, leaving the rest of you empty and white; an empty white page on which those two lips opened and closed, mysteriously, like a symbol.

"Honey," Mama said, but then Daddy nudged her to one side.

"Perhaps," he said, "it's not too late to rectify that situation?" He held out a round tin box, on top of which was printed a picture of Santa and Mrs. Claus. "Some of your mother's famous sand tarts," he said. "Just for you."

"Oh, well," you said, taking the box and putting it on the table without looking at it, "that changes everything. Mother's sand tarts."

"Maybe you'd like to offer one to your friend?" Mama suggested. "Would you like a cookie?"

"Thank you," the young man said, getting up. He pried the lid off the tin and peered inside. "They look delicious."

"She makes them with real sand," you said.

"Willie, that's enough," Daddy said.

"When she can't get real sand, she uses plaster dust. You can hardly tell the difference." You began to move across the floor in a complicated series of movements—the upper part of your body fluid, as if under water; your legs and feet jittery and rapid, the swiveling eyes of birds.

"Oh!" Mama said. "Sweetheart, that's beautiful."

"She's really good," the young man said, chewing on a cookie. His eyes were vague with lust. "Willie's the best."

"Shut up, Ernie," you said. Then you looked at me. "Some things should be kept private," you said.

The canteen was low-ceilinged and long, with vending machines along the far wall; it smelled like pine needles and cigarette smoke and, because the trees grew so close to the few small-paned windows, it was dark inside, and cool, like the inside of a church. Nothing was happening. You were leaning against the screen door, your hands shoved into the pockets of your blue jeans; your hair was hanging in a single braid over one shoulder, and I thought that your neck looked too fine to bear the weight of all that hair. You were waiting for me to say something, and I knew that, as usual, I was going to disappoint you.

"We've missed you so much," Mama said.

"You're looking good, Willie," Daddy added. He was wearing one of those short-sleeved shirts that men wear in the summertime, out of which his arms extended, like two sticks, more or less in your direction. A mosquito landed on his wrist and drank some of his blood.

"The nonsense continues," you said.

I was the awkward and dopey version of the younger sister, standing there in the middle of that mean, damp room on my black square; I was a giant wearing glasses. I looked up, feeling the ceiling's sneaky descent towards the top of my head, and looking down at me was a teacup-shaped light fixture. Heaven, I thought, that's heaven. Just about the size of a teacup, hovering over my head.

Suddenly you lunged forward and grabbed my arm. "Kitty," you said. "Let's get out of here. Let's go get my stuff."

"Why don't you let me give you a hand?" Daddy asked.

You whirled around and, for a minute, I thought you were going to say something terrible to him. I heard you draw your breath, so that all the bad air in that room flew into you, turning your eyes the color of our cellar walls, flat and moist. Then you changed your mind. You smiled a tight, cool, little smile. When you looked so much like a lizard, did the angels still love you? "It's all right, Dad," you said. "We can manage. Besides, I want to show Kitty my bunk." You turned to the young man who stood brushing cookie crumbs from his lips and chin. "I'll see you later, Ernie," you said. And I felt your arm link through mine like a loop of fire.

"They drive me nuts," you said, once we were outside, walking along a narrow footpath through fir trees. The ground under my feet rebounded with each step, composed, as it was, of years and years of fallen needles. I wondered if this was how you felt, dancing: even the hardwood stage floor, like the skin of a drum, yielded at your toe's touch, springing you into flight. "How can you stand it?" you asked.

"Stand what?"

"Just being with them." You led me into a small cabin, empty except for six built-in beds, their mattresses thin and stained with suggestive rust-colored faces. In the corner I saw your bags, packed and ready to go.

"Is Ernie a dancer?" I asked.

You laughed and sat down on one of the bunks. "Ernie couldn't dance if his life depended on it," you said. "He's the swimming instructor." Then you lay down and folded your arms behind your head. "Kitty," you said, "I don't want to go home. I don't think I can take any more of that shit."

"Are you in love with Ernie?"

"It doesn't have anything to do with Ernie. It's *them*. They're like ghouls. They give me the creeps."

"But what about me?" I asked.

"I'm not talking about you." You paused and rolled over on your side, staring at me. Gradually the room was falling into darkness, like a bucket being let down a well. Somewhere there was a world filled with electric lights and ticking clocks, but this wasn't it. "Listen," you said, "when we were little, things were different. Remember? We were as close as peas in a pod. We told each other everything. And then something happened. I don't know what it was, but something happened and you stopped loving me."

"I can't remember," I said. The air blowing in through the window was fresh, as if we were surrounded on all sides by a meadow. I thought I could smell new-cut hay, that sad smell which always made me wish I was a burrowing animal, curled up and safe in a little dark hole.

"Let me refresh your memory," you said. "There was that fat-faced doll with red braids. Just like mine. There was a tea set of some kind." Your eyes were closed but the skin of the lids was so thin I thought that you could still see me.

"The Saucy Walker doll," I said. "And the silver tea set!"

The edges of your lips curved up in a smile. "She was my doll," you said, "not yours."

I didn't understand, and I felt frightened. Was it possible that your heart had been broken earlier than mine? Your birthday, I wanted to say, what about your birthday? And then I began to remember: I was little—maybe five years old—and I was sitting on the floor playing with your doll. A half hour earlier you'd stood balancing against the back of the sofa, raising first one foot and then the other, so that Daddy could cross-hatch the soles of your new spring shoes —white patent leather with ankle straps—digging into the slippery soles with the key to the Chevrolet. This was so you wouldn't fall down the stairs. I could see the bones of your ankles through your white scalloped socks, your calves, your beautiful oval knees, and then the skirt of your white piqué dress—a bell to the waist—and your hand fiercely gripping your white straw purse. I couldn't see your face. You were high above me and then you were gone. I could hear the gravel crunch in the driveway as you and Daddy and Mama went off to visit Nana in the nursing home. I had a cold; I could make Nana die, you'd told me. One single germ and it'd be all over. Mrs. McGuire was in the kitchen presiding over a pot roast, thinking her usual gluey thoughts.

"I think it was Easter," I said. "Was it Easter? And then you came back."

"Mr. Noodle and the Mouse Queen were fighting," you said. "Their usual technique. You know, the silent stuff. She was sighing, and he had his hands clenched on the steering wheel. It was something the Mouse Queen said." You shook your head. "Kitty," you asked, "have you ever wondered whether Dad plays around?"

"Daddy?" I thought what I was feeling was my soul, like a white sheet on a wash line being flapped around by the wind. There I was, sitting on the floor, playing with your doll. When I heard footsteps on the porch I looked up, and I saw your face in the window. Your mouth was opening and closing, but I couldn't hear what you were saying. It was spring; the wind was from the north—it was fists beating at the walls and windows. "You were beating on the window," I said. "I remember that. And I got up and undid that lock on the door we never used and let you in. You were mad at me because I was playing with your doll."

"You pretended you couldn't hear me, you know that? I just wanted to play with you, Kitty. It was such a little thing, but you just sat there making that dumb doll walk up and down on the rug."

"And then you told me how babies get made. I hadn't even asked, but you had to go and tell me."

"I forgot that," you said. "What did I say?"

"You said that Daddy put his thing up Mama's hole. And then a bean came out and wriggled into her belly. You told me it was called fucking."

"I did?" You opened your eyes now—they were pale and large, printed with the spoked wheels of your irises. "I spent too much time with Jojo Melnicoff," you said. "All of his worst stuff rubbed off on me."

"You told me that even though the bean was very small, there was enough blood in it to make you, with a little bit left over to make me."

"And you believed me?"

"Sure," I said. "I always believed you." But then I remembered an amazing thing: you had been crying! You were sitting there on the floor beside me, and you were crying.

"You shouldn't always believe me," you said.

"Oh," I said, "but that was *then*." I watched the cabin windows fill up with dark red light, as if the whole world was swimming along within an enormous vein. "I remember," I said. "You were crying really hard, asking me to let you play. And then you wet your pants. And the puddle spread out and touched my foot. So I got up and went over to the sofa. I sat down and took off my sock."

"You were really disgusted, weren't you?"

"No," I said. "I wasn't disgusted."

"Don't lie, Kitty. I'm not a complete idiot. I can recognize disgust when I see it."

"Well, you're wrong," I said. It was very dark in the cabin and I could hear the consistent and sexual rhythms of tree frogs and crickets. I wondered where our parents were—if they had found a place to sit down outdoors and if they were, now, discreetly sipping tall drinks, as they did at home, beneath the tall and billowy sails of shade trees.

"And then Rogni came in," I said. "And he held on to you and kissed you."

"Rogni?"

"The angel."

You moved your body over so that it was right on the very edge of the mattress. "There were never any angels, Kitty," you said. "There were lots of other things, but never angels." A tear jumped from the corner of your eye, from the place where the tiniest of lashes grew. "Besides, that was you. You were the one who kissed me. How could you forget that?"

"Cut it out, Willie," I said.

"Cut it out, Willie," you mimicked. "You're doing it again, and you don't even know it. You're still disgusted. You're so goddamn judgmental, Kitty, it drives me nuts."

I didn't know what to say. Outside, I could hear the sound of voices approaching, far off through the trees.

"Then the Mouse Queen took away my underpants, so she could wash them. And she hung them up to dry on the porch. They were the white kind. That's important, because when the spider landed on them it really stood out. It made you scream. You could scream louder than anyone. And that was when we made the pact. No more underpants. Never."

"I can't remember," I said.

"Well, I can. It was a secret pact. And *I* kept it. Did you?" Then you unzipped your blue jeans and pulled the two flaps of denim back, so that I could see the pale skin of your belly and the top of a red triangle of hair, pointing downward into shadow. "Did you?" you whispered.

"No," I said.

Maybe now, secure within the future, I'd be able to yell back at you that it's the secret locked intact within a sister which exudes light, and that that light is like the erotic nimbus all around her body, like St. Elmo's fire around a church steeple. The secret shines like something holy, which it is not. That's why I reached out to touch you, Willie. I was reaching out to see if I could touch the secret, when Mama and Daddy walked into the cabin.

"Kitty!" Daddy said. "What in God's name is going on here?" He pulled me roughly to him, and his arms and hands were wet. Then I heard the persistent dripping of water from the eaves, and I realized that it had started to rain. The chain of my spine fit into the hollow groove between the two halves of his rib cage, locking me in place. After all, I was his daughter—night was moving in with its winds and rain, like a coach full of desperate travelers through the woods—and, however impossible his impulse to protect me, I relaxed into the tense bow of his arms.

Mama handed you a wadded-up piece of tissue, pale blue, drawing it out from under the sleeve of her jersey. She always kept a piece of tissue there. "We ought to be starting back," she said. "You girls know your father doesn't like to drive in the rain."

"Then why don't you drive?" you asked. "You know how to drive."

"I'm not even going to bother answering that," Daddy said. He was still holding on to me.

"I didn't ask you," you said. But Mama was preoccupied with trying to figure out how to close the cabin windows; because she lived in a constant symbiotic state with terror, all events took on, for her, equal weight. Your unzipped jeans and the rain, beading now in the rusty meshes of the screens, impelled inward by the hysterical puffing of the wind to splash on the floor—she acknowledged no difference. "For God's sake, Mom," you said. "Leave the fucking windows alone."

Then Daddy let me drop. At first I thought he was going to hit you. But there were his fingers, long and yellowish, Chinese almost, against the white skin of your belly, fumbling to snap closed your jeans, tugging to pull up the zipper.

"Ouch!" you yelled. "You're hurting me!"

His upper row of teeth, crooked and strange, bit down on his lower lip, as if he was so hungry he had started in on his own body. The order of the natural world realigned itself: the wind's source was now somewhere deep inside him, and whatever the emotion was that pressed it forth, I knew that I would always be afraid of him from that moment onward.

"Get up," he said, when he had finished. He straightened, pushing his glasses back onto the bridge of his nose. "Come on, Constance," he said. "We've got a long drive ahead of us."

In the car you sat as close to the window as you could, your legs bent at the knees, drawn in towards your chest, where you cradled them tightly because they were reliable and you loved them. When I tried to slide up next to you, you shook me off. "At least give me room to breathe," you said, so I moved away and curled up in a ball. The upholstery was gray and scratchy, its exhalations confusing, combining the friendly smell of woolen sweaters with the dangerous smell of vertical rocks in a gorge. You rolled your window down and stuck your face into the opening, filling the car with the tearing sound of its own tires spinning across the road's watery tarmac. "It's really pouring out," you said, turning to face me; your cheeks were moist and shining.

"Put the window up, Willie," Daddy said. He leaned over to switch on the radio, but whatever it had to tell us was interrupted at intervals by static, synchronous with the *ka-thunk ka-thunk* of the windshield wipers.

"See what I mean," you said to me. Then you stuck your face back out the window. "This must be St. Johnsbury," you said.

"Now!" Daddy slammed on the brakes and we skidded wildly to a stop against the curb.

A woman in a yellow slicker looked up at our approach,

and I could see, in the vague light cast across the sidewalk by a restaurant's windows—behind which a solitary cashier in pink picked something from between her front teeth with a toothpick—the resigned expression on the woman's face. She leaned over to pat her dog, a large one, drenched to sorry thinness by the rain.

"We're not going anywhere," Daddy said, "until that window's shut."

"Okay, okay," you said. The car sprang forward and a wing of water closed down over the woman in the yellow slicker and her dog. "Who died and made him king?" you muttered, leaning back and closing your eyes.

Then the heater took over and we were all like separate charms nestled in cotton wadding: intricately shaped little surprises within a box, waiting for the face to lower over us, wide as the sky itself, waiting for the informed hand to lift us out, one at a time, and assign meaning. A circle; a rectangle; a forked thing like a nerve; a knobbed wand. The heat blew into my nostrils and filled my ear holes; it trickled through the tiny openings in my eyes and wadded itself like a fist in my mouth. I fell asleep.

When I woke up we were driving through Crawford Notch. The mountains were black around us and, although it had stopped raining, the wind hauled its silvery vestments overhead, snagging occasionally on the moon's thin hooks.

Luck and disaster are the same thing, Willie, and that thing is the gift of motion. We moved. We rode home in our dark car as if we all understood the meaning of destination.

I think, now, if you'd really been crazy, if there had been a name we could have assigned to your behavior, it would have been easier for me. After your summer away you spent as little time as possible in the house, and yet even your absence assumed disquieting contours: I would pick up the phone almost every afternoon and hear your voice, very faint, as if you were in another country—a land where piano music was always playing, and where I knew that a woman with a black bun and green streaks over her eyelids encouraged you to believe that you had been born into the wrong family.

"Kitty," you would say, "tell them I won't be home tonight, will you? Madame is having a few of us over for a late supper and then, who knows?"

I'd seen you, though; I knew that you weren't always where you said you would be. Once, driving through Conway with Daddy, I saw you walking past the old railway station with Peter Mygatz. His hair was longer and he'd shaved off his beard; still, I knew it was him. He no longer worked at the school, because Miss Mullen had fired him after he'd walked into the auditorium during the Pledge of Allegiance, carrying a Ban the Bomb sign on a stick. Daddy didn't notice you—he was too busy looking for a parking spot—so I kept what I saw to myself. But I was astonished. Peter Mygatz was a grown-up.

Sometimes I rode my bike out past the cranberry bog and, if there was no telltale plume of smoke rising from the bread truck's crooked chimney, I would lean my bike against a cedar tree and peek in through the little window cut in the truck's side. The first time I did this I actually gasped out loud: the room inside was tiny but immaculate, the narrow bed fastidiously made with mitered corners, a pale blue sleeping bag spread out across the sheets. There was a card table and two ladder-backed chairs with rush seats. The table was empty, except for a beautiful terracotta candelabrum, the figures of women forming its branches, holding white candles in their hands. On the wall was a picture of a man with a drooping mustache and a hat something like the ones the Shriners wore for their conventions; you told me, later, that his name was Gurdjieff, and that he was Peter's idol.

"See," you told me, "it was because of the way I moved— Peter wanted to get to know me better because he thought there were things I could teach him. Can you believe it? He said that dance is a really good way to start waking up."

I would look in through the bread-truck window and try to imagine you in that tidy room. I would begin by placing you on one of the chairs, the soles of your feet pressed together, your legs bent at the knees, sticking out, perfectly straight, on either side. The candles would be lit, their heat licking away, little by little, the icy surface of your face. And then, no matter how hard I tried—I couldn't stop it from happening—you would be on the bed, a white star in a blue sky. And he would lower himself onto you; then your face would whip over to one side, staring right at me, as the line of his spine stirred over and over, like a single insistent wave lapping at the lake's edge.

It was *my* vision, Willie, but I could not keep it chaste.

Labrador

One afternoon in late October, following what had, by now, become a routine side trip to the bog, I rode my bike up the driveway and then, when I saw you leaning on your elbows, looking out the living-room window, I turned around and rode back down towards the highway. I was ashamed. As I rode away from the house I felt it behind me, getting bigger and bigger; I felt you watching me, your face a pansy, the features bunched together in one dark scowl. From out of the pine trees to the left of me crows flew up, all at once, as if the air's molecules, thickening and dimming to signal nightfall, had likewise grown so large that they'd acquired wings and voice. The crows were cawing and furious, their fury directed at something I couldn't see. An owl, I thought; for some reason crows hated owls. When I got to the foot of the driveway a tractor-trailer zoomed by, showering me with gravel.

Then you were behind me, out of breath. "Kitty," you said, "Dad told me to come and get you. He said he wanted you inside the house immediately."

"I'll come in when I'm ready," I said, courting your approval, but you shook your head.

"I don't know what's going on," you said, "but he's really upset." And then, when I remained standing there, balancing my bike carefully between my legs, you turned your head to one side, in that way you had, leading with the chin, to let me know that you would not tolerate refusal. "He isn't faking it," you said. "I'm scared."

Daddy was sitting in the west room, his whole body bent forward towards the seductive light of the television set. He almost never watched television; we were, on the whole, not a television-watching family, although there had been a time, not all that long ago, when you sat enraptured by the image of Bishop Fulton Sheen, whose piety interested you less than his appearance. I wasn't fooled, nor did it escape my notice that he bore a striking resemblance to Daddy.

"Kathleen, come here," Daddy said, patting his bony lap and, even though I was still wary of him—of the possibility that at any moment he would change from his grudging self into a monster of purpose and epic fury—even though I was much too large to do so, I sat down where he indicated. His arms folded around me and he held on tightly, as if I was the only substantial piece of flotsam to come his way.

At first I thought that he was laughing, because of the way his body jiggled under me. His breath smelled like Scotch, and I noticed the empty glass on the table beside him. "I've always loved you, you know that, don't you, Kathleen?" he said, and I wanted to kill you, because I thought that you'd brought me back from the isolating darkness of the driveway to even the score, to see whether I could tolerate, as I'm sure you thought you had, the advances of his difficult soul. But then I realized that he was crying. "We've really done it this time," he said.

On the television screen I saw a tiny man walking alongside the trunk-like legs of a woman in high-heeled shoes, lifting from the floor a napkin the size of a circus tent.

"Done what?" I asked.

"We'll get the fallout from Boston," Daddy said, "first. It's only a matter of time. And the idiots responsible for all this will be sitting pretty somewhere underground. Turn it off, Willie," he said. "I don't want to hear any more."

You jerked yourself to an upright position from where you'd been lounging against the wall. "It's just *American Bandstand*, Dad," you said, walking over to flick off the switch. "It's just a bunch of nice teenage kids from South Philadelphia pretending that they know how to dance."

But, for once, he didn't take the bait. "Girls," he said, "there are Russian ships, right now, on their way to Cuba. They're carrying missiles."

"Atom bombs?" you asked. And I saw your eyes darken, saw the pupils' rapid dilation—it was the avidity I remembered from the nursery—and I had an inkling then of how for you desire and fear were the same thing. "But Cuba's pretty far away from here, isn't it?" you asked.

"There's no such thing as far away anymore, Willie," Daddy said.

I got up out of his lap and walked over to the window. Like someone signaling to us through the trees I saw the lights of cars moving from east to west, from west to east, on the highway. I thought of Amy Gertner, spooning soup into her mouth in the rectory dining room, and I wondered whether the holiness of that household precluded despair. "Is there going to be a war?" I asked.

"I don't know, Kathleen," Daddy said. But it was horrible—he had his head in his hands and he was weeping. "I've tried to be a good man," he said, "for all the good it's done me."

You came over and stood beside me. "Kitty," you said, "where's Mom?"

"Do you think we should get her?" I asked, and you shrugged.

"It's just like him," you said, "to turn the end of the world into an excuse for sentimentality."

Mama, it turned out, was upstairs taking a bath. She had filled the tub with hot water and then emptied into it an entire bottle of scented bath oil, so that when she appeared downstairs, her gray hair stuck to the top of her head with a butterfly-shaped barrette, she smelled overwhelmingly of gardenias. "I suppose you're all hungry," she said.

Did she know what was going on? If she did she gave no sign of it, and if her hands shook a little as she cranked open two cans of Scotch broth—that soup you hated, because you claimed it smelled like sweat—it was only her usual tremulousness. Mama stirred the soup lovingly, over the gas flame, and we all sat at the table, listening to the irregular chinging of the spoon against the sides of the pot. "Who wants sandwiches?" she asked. All of us!—our hands shot up as if we were in a classroom. Mama's apparent obliviousness to the fact that at any moment the engines of our destruction might spring forth from the earth's surface lulled us into inactivity. We let her wait on us.

Meanwhile, on its shelf near the refrigerator, the radio played its happy music, music to which we were attentive in the manner of patients hooked up to life-support machines, waiting for the moment when the regular beeping would resolve itself into a single strand of noise. The kitchen looked different to me and I could hear a mouse's sporadic movement in the pantry; a little, separate life was going about its business and I realized that I was seeing the kitchen from the mouse's point of view: a great, yellow carton in which gigantic creatures of flesh and blood appeased their hunger.

After we ate, Daddy instructed us to carry canned goods from the pantry into the cellar. Tomatoes, lima beans, corn: the fronts of the shelves were stocked with the foods we ate regularly. It was only when we began reaching in deeper that we came upon the dust-covered cans with their exotic, faded labels.

"Look at this," you said to me, as we stood side by side in the cellar. You held up a can the size of a walnut.

"What is it?" I asked.

"A truffle. 'Le diamant noir de la cuisine,'" you read. "'Use the juice and appreciate the taste to the utmost.' It must be a million years old." You shook the can daintily between your thumb and index finger. "Well," you said, "when the end is near, we can open this up and cut it into four pieces. It's probably really *bad*."

"Willie," I said, "do you think we're going to die?"

"I don't know." You set the truffle down on top of a can

of Mary Kitchen roast beef hash. "Peter says this world is so fucked up, the only way to fix it will be a war."

"But what do you think?"

"Kitty," you said, "remember me? I'm Willie, the girl who doesn't ever want to die."

I sighed, thinking things over. "There's the angel," I said. "There's Rogni." I looked at you and saw that your mouth was curved in a little smile, like the moon high above the perfect boat of your collarbones.

"Rogni again," you said. "Who, exactly, is this Rogni?"

"I don't think he'll let us die," I explained. But you shook your head.

"Don't count on it," you said. "Besides, if this Rogni is so hot to help us, why doesn't he do something about them?" You pointed to the ceiling, across which the feet of our parents paraded in short bursts of movement.

"You shouldn't say that," I said. "He might be listening."

"So what if he is? Face it, Kitty, we're stuck with them, believe me. Even when we die and go to heaven, they'll be there. Along with Abraham Lincoln and Jesus and all the other people we're supposed to be looking forward to seeing."

"You're the one he loves," I said.

You ran your shoe along the base of the cellar wall, mashing to a bluish-green smear a colony of delicate, umbrella-shaped fungi. "I don't get it," you said. "I mean, if you're going to go to all the trouble of making something like that up, why me? Fantasies are supposed to give you what you want. They're not supposed to make you jealous."

"It's not a fantasy," I said.

We slept in our own beds that night, although Daddy insisted that we sleep in our clothes. And, of course, we slept in those beds for many, many nights after that, because the crisis ended as abruptly as it had begun—the ships turned around and went home to Russia, while our good-looking President was able, once again, to sit beside his pretty wife on a gilt chair in the White House, listening to cello music. Still, I remember that night: how I lay there on my bed in my red sweater and brown wool slacks, itching to death. My feet were encased in heavy oxfords and they felt like they weighed a ton. If I have to get up quickly, I thought, I'll never be able to do it.

"Rogni," I whispered, "where are you?" I remembered that time, long ago, when he had swept me up so fast into the place where the future had already happened. If he wanted to, I knew, he could be there, in my bedroom, in the twinkling of an eye. Then I heard what you had described to me—the chiming of the grandfather clock downstairs—and I thought of how behind its glass door the brass weights were slowly falling, and how the face of the moon was slowly making its way across the curve of blue sky, painted with tiny golden stars. What do I want, I wondered. And then it came to me, like a surprise: what I wanted, I realized, was *not* to want. I wanted to be the object of desire. I wanted to be the precious, frozen stone that a world would die for, its light severe and unattainable. I wanted to be you.

Instead, I turned into what is called a "young adult." As a young adult I moved around the house like a thing made out of stumps and wires. Some of my classmates had begun to date—the boys' fathers drove them into Conway, where they'd sit and watch James Bond movies, and go to first base or second, depending upon the diligence of the usherette.

Amy Gertner and I pretended to have nothing but scorn for such behavior. On my fourteenth birthday—in honor of which she had presented me with a box full of madras-plaid cummerbunds, stolen, as she confessed to me later, from Carroll Reed—we sat together in my bedroom and Amy, who was a talented caricaturist, drew pictures of our peers locked in passionate embrace, wearing diapers or gym bloomers.

"Mowbrey," Amy said, "don't you just hate the immaturity?"

I nodded my head in agreement but, needless to say, I was green with envy. I dreamed about love. I wrote letters to myself:

My darling Kathleen,
 I long for your kiss. I cannot describe to you the torture I feel every time I see you in third-period English class. This hidden passion tears at the very fibers of my soul! It will not be long, my darling. Mrs. Tulkington's horrible disease gets worse and worse. Soon she will be completely covered with pustules. And then it is just a matter of time. I know it is wrong of me, but I think with joy of the day when we will be joined in holy wedlock. Until then, my darling! Be brave!
            Love, Paul.

"He was looking at you today," Amy told me. "When he didn't think anyone else was watching."

"Are you sure?"

"Yeah." And then Amy shook her head up and down energetically, making her blond curls dance like little yoyos. "He was suffering, Mowbrey. It was written all over his face."

The man in question was Mr. Paul Tulkington, our English teacher, the victim of his sad marriage to Mrs. Tulkington. This tragedy in his life, we were sure, explained those unsettling moments when he would stand at the blackboard, chalk in hand, and then fall into a trance.

From downstairs came the sound of ice cubes clinking in Daddy's highball, and the rising pitch of his voice, almost as if he were about to break into song. "Don't pay any attention to him," I told Amy. "He's just had a hard day."

"My dad never drinks," she said. "In our family my mom is the one who drinks. Vanilla extract, rubbing alcohol, you name it. Once, we found her trying to fry a hamburger right on the electric burner. When she's really drunk she calls Dad 'Heathcliff.' "

"But doesn't it make you feel awful?" I asked.

"Mowbrey, they're jerks," Amy said. "What else can I say?"

We could hear Mama sniffling, moving down the hall-way, slamming the door to the bedroom. Then the porch door creaked open and we could see Daddy moving stiff-legged, like an old dog, through the meadow where saplings now grew, crowding in on the house. When he got to the middle of the meadow he turned around and looked back: there were our faces in the lit window and he began waving his arms and yelling.

"Don't do it," Amy said, but I ignored her. The window was stuck and I had to pound on it to get it loose.

"Maybe he needs help," I said.

"Sure," Amy said, backing away from the window and rolling onto the bed. "Maybe he needs someone to freshen his drink."

I got the window up and pressed my face to the screen. The air was cool and fresh and smelled like mock-orange; I could see the thick clustering of those blossoms, hanging in the darkness like sweetly deceptive ghosts.

"Kathleen!" Daddy yelled. "What're you doing cooped up in your room on a night like this? Life is for the living! Why don't you and your little friend grab your sweaters and join me?"

"Amazing," Amy said. "He didn't slur a single word. My mom should take lessons."

"Come on!" he continued. "Throw caution to the winds!"

"No thanks, Daddy," I said. Then I slammed the window back down, sending a shower of dark green paint chips across the bedspread. "I don't believe it," I said, and Amy shook her head.

"How many times do I have to tell you, Mowbrey?" she asked. "When they're like that, you've got to ignore them. It's the only way."

One day, not too long after my birthday, I woke up to find my sheets stained with blood. Of course I knew what this was, having been instructed by all the other girls at school about the process—as the school nurse put it—of "becoming a woman." I knew, as well, that I wanted to wash out the sheets myself. This was a Wednesday, the day on which Mrs. McGuire assumed control of the house: cleaning, ironing, and introducing me to the rules of a queer and sneaky universe.

The washtubs were in the cellar, set against the far wall, adjacent to the shelves on which we'd stacked the canned goods. No one had bothered to bring those cans back upstairs: they remained there in their jackets of dust, and I couldn't avoid noticing the truffle, that tiny harbinger of doom. It was August and the world outside was hot and filled with the chirping of birds, while, in the cellar, the clinical odor of bleach mixed with the smell of mold, making me think of the laboratory in which the egocentric scientist created his monster out of cast-off body parts.

I began to fill one of the tubs with hot water, and then I poured in an enormous quantity of detergent. As soon as I dumped in the sheets the water turned pink but, no matter how much I sloshed them around, the stains wouldn't go away. In fact, if anything, they seemed to get bigger. The detergent stung the places where I'd bitten my nails to the quick, and my pain, as well as my frenzied scrubbing, preoccupied me, so that I didn't hear the footsteps on the cellar stairs, nor the footsteps moving towards me across the dirt floor.

"Ah, there you are! Such a darling child to be help-ing out her poor sainted mama with the washing!" Mrs. McGuire nosed up, close and confidential, as if she was about to hand me a religious pamphlet. "What's this?" she exclaimed. "Can it be that the female sickness is upon my own darling child?" She peered at me out of her rheumy round eyes; it was like being looked at by snails. "And the pangs?" she asked. "Are they very strong?"

"What?"

Mrs. McGuire reached down and poked at my stomach. "Here," she said. "I suppose the pain must be unendurable. How well I remember my own dear mama helping me through the suffering." She paused. "That is why it is called the curse, Kathleen, and it's the curse of all woman-kind to go through their lives at the mercy of their bodies. Ah, but it's a lucky thing for you I have a trick or two up my sleeve."

It was impossible for me to connect Mrs. McGuire with anything remotely *female*. "I feel all right," I said. "Really."

"The child is so brave," she said. "Leave the sheets be, my darling." She thrust her bony finger into the small of my back and propelled me up the stairs. "If this were the wintertime we'd have some red-hot coals on hand. That is by far the best cure for the pain, but we shall have to make do." She filled the kettle with water and set it on the stove. "Just sit down, my precious, while I boil up some ginger tea. Do you know where your mama keeps her garden trowel?"

"Coals?" I asked. Panic sat inside of me: large and white and shaped like myself, covered with thorns.

"Ah, if only we had some," Mrs. McGuire mourned. "Then we could put them into a bucket and you could pee onto them. It's the steam, you see, that works on the organs." She grated ginger root into a teacup. "We shall have to go out and buy you napkins, I suppose," she said.

"I found some in Willie's drawer," I said.

"A belt?"

"That, too."

"Kathleen, you must never, under any circumstances, burn up your monthly cloths. Do you understand me, my darling? When I was just a slip of a thing in Sligo, I knew a girl—my third cousin, I think. Edna was her name—and she always burned her monthly cloths, and she got so thin and sick they had to call for the doctor. 'Do you mean to tell me,' he told Edna's mama, 'that you don't know what is wrong with this child? Well, she is burning up her cloths every month and she is just burning up her life. If she doesn't stop, she will die; and I can't do a thing for her as long as she does.' Do you understand, Kathleen?"

"Sure," I said.

After she made the tea we went outside to where the garden used to be, and Mrs. McGuire handed me the teacup. "Don't drink from it yet," she warned. Then she got down on her hands and knees and dug seven holes in the dirt, in a row. "We need grapevine, not yet one year old. Ah, it's a sorry thing, my darling, what has become of this garden." Eventually she found what she was looking for; she put a length of vine in each hole, ceremoniously lit a match, and set the leaves on fire. Finally, she made me take the tea and sit by each hole and drink a little, until, at the seventh hole, I was instructed to say: "Let me recover."

"The relief," she said, "is so sudden as to make your poor head spin, is it not? How well I remember." She took the teacup and checked to make sure I'd finished drinking all the fiery shavings. "Now we must go back into the house and tell your mama the news."

"Oh," I said, "not now. I don't have time. I have to meet Amy at the lake."

Mrs. McGuire stood up very straight: the posture of pronouncement. "There are, Kathleen, five important events in a woman's life. There is, of course, her own birth;

there is her marriage to her beloved husband; there is the birth of her first precious baby; there is her death. These are four—the fifth is, my darling, the day on which she becomes a woman."

Willie, this synopsis made me want to go right out and kill myself. "I'll tell her later," I said. Then I got on my bike and rode as fast as I could to the lake. In a way I think of that ride as the first leg of my impending journey—the one about which I knew nothing at the time—into the world of men.

I slept late the next day and, when I finally woke up, the bedclothes were damp and wrapped around my arms and legs like the snakes around the man and his sons in the reproduction of *Laocoön* which Daddy kept on his desk. I understood, momentarily, the horrible density of stone, and I smelled a smell which I thought I was giving off myself: slightly sour and hinting at pathos. Then, through the bedroom door came Mama, bearing in her hands the pale green metal tray on which was set a pink bowl filled with farina. I knew that this was not intended as an ironic gesture. Of all the members of our family, Mama was the only one incapable of irony.

"How are you feeling, sweetheart?" Mama asked.

"I'm fine," I said. "Why shouldn't I be?"

"I thought you might like to have your breakfast in bed today. As a special treat."

"I don't want a special treat," I said. "I told you, I feel fine."

Mama unfolded the legs of the tray and put it in place over my stomach. "Mrs. McGuire told me," she said.

"Told you what?" I hoped my nastiness would drive her away, before the word "menstruation" could drop like partly-chewed cud from her mouth, mortifying us both.

"About your period, sweetheart," she said. "If you have any questions, don't be afraid to ask me."

Oh, sure, I thought.

Mama didn't move, but stood there looking at me, baffled and hopeful, as if waiting to see settle over me the transfiguring mantle of womanhood. "We're leaving now," she said. "Your father and I are going to town to pick up Willie, and then we're going to do some shopping. Will you be all right?"

"Of course I'll be all right," I said.

Still, she didn't move. "I remember the day you were born," she said. "I remember how the nurse put you in my arms. It was dinnertime, but it was still light out. All you wanted to do was eat. You were so little!"

And now look at me, I thought. I could see the big bumps of my knees on the far side of the tray.

"I was the happiest woman on the face of the earth," Mama said wistfully.

I put a spoonful of farina in my mouth: she had sweetened it with honey and sprinkled it with nutmeg, and I felt such a longing to be a new thing—was it possible that time could bang up against a wall and start inching backwards? Without swallowing the cereal, I removed the spoon carefully, and set it back in the bowl, trying very hard to duplicate, in reverse, all of my movements. Had the small handprints of light on the blanket slid back a notch? And I waited for her to say it again: "I was the happiest woman on the face of the earth." I held my breath. Then Daddy began beeping the car horn and the moment was over—the planets in their slots sprang forward, and a large round cloud appeared in my window, across which a robin flew with a worm in its beak.

"We'll be back soon," Mama said. "Mrs. McGuire's downstairs, if you need anything."

After she was gone I sat there, perfectly still, as if a spell had been cast over me. I looked at the pictures of birds taped to my walls: scarlet tanager, yellow-shafted flicker, American golden plover, hermit thrush. Maybe if I could fly, I thought. But I knew it would make no difference. Even the birds—so high up that the only sign of their passage was the restless, minute shadows wavering through the grass or across the walls of buildings—even the birds couldn't leave this world.

Even Kathleen Mowbrey, a fourteen-year-old girl in a bedroom in New Hampshire, could be changed by the simplest thing—her body's sloughing off of the red tissue in which a tiny egg was hidden—into one figure among many in the common landscape. I thought of the women sitting in the Conway laundromat, their babies drooping out of strollers or packed into dark carriages; I thought of the sleek women in the magazines, staring up from the laps of those other women, oblivious to the banging of the washing machines or the tumbling prattle of buttons and metal snaps against the insides of the dryers. And each one, I thought—the sleek and the exhausted alike—had inside her body a chamber the size of a fist, into which an egg was falling, was about to fall, had fallen.

Nor did it stop there. I thought of the men, busy with their particular jobs and strategies. I thought about how it might happen that, one day, from high up in the sky, as if in a shower of gleaming spears, penetrating the fragile network of birds, clouds, the nethermost twigs and buds of trees, would drop the bombs. And then it would be, for everyone and everything, the same end—just hoods of light where the bodies had been, where the hand had been turning over the magazine page, or setting into place, like a lozenge on a tongue, the coin that would make the machine fill up with water.

The farina turned to a cold lump in the bowl. *She* was there, Willie, in the corner of my room, her body hidden by the open closet door. I could hear her breathing and hear the way the floorboards shifted under her weight. Perhaps the iron had been too hot, pressing the fabric of her housedress flat, pressing flat the cabbage roses, like those tokens of long-ago love that fall out of old books—she smelled burnt.

"It's all the same pudding," she said. "I ought to know."

"Go away," I said, and she laughed.

"Eat, eat," she said, and my eyes leaped backwards into my head, to stare at the black folds of my brain.

And there he was, fanning his wings, a white thing like a moth. "You can't get me," I said. "Because of the angel."

"Ah," she said, "the angel. How could I forget?" I heard the jingling of hangers, like sly ideas forming in her head. "Of course, the angel. Tell me, Kathleen, which came first, the angel or the nurse?"

I suddenly felt relieved, because I knew the answer. "The angel," I said. "You were just a thing in his story."

Now the hangers were crashing into each other, and the noise they made got louder and louder—I could hear my shoes beating against the walls of the closet. "I wouldn't be so sure, Kathleen," she said. But she couldn't hide the anger in her voice and I thought—believe me, Willie—I thought she was lying.

The night before you moved out, Mama prepared a special dinner in your honor: all of your favorite foods, although we could barely afford such an extravagance as a leg of lamb, since Daddy was out of work. Do you remember? We were waiting in the west room, Mama knitting in her chair, Daddy feeding split lengths of applewood into the first fire of the season; I lounged across the rug with boyish diffidence, rolling a marble back and forth between my two index fingers. And then you walked into the room.

When I shut my eyes I can see you as you were then—very grown up, I thought—with your hair arranged in a French twist; your lips painted with opalescent lipstick, pale like the inside of a seashell; your eyes outlined in black, so that they appeared lidless, unblinking. You were wearing a very short black velvet dress, its square-cut neckline revealing a fullness of cleavage belied by your lean arms and legs. I could not get over how beautiful you were.

"I'll be going out later," you said. Then you reached your arms way up over your head, stretching, so that we all could see the entire length of your body from the waist down, reticulate and snaky in black-patterned tights. "Madame's throwing a going-away party," you explained.

Daddy could not take his eyes off you. You sat down on the love seat, your spine customarily straight, as if to brace yourself against the assault of his longing. Did you feel it? Is that why you shivered a little?

"I was hoping you'd spend your last night with us," Mama said, her fingers busy, busy; the bone needles oscillating. She was making you a sweater, and I thought of the poor girl in the fairy tale, spinning flax from nettles, her whole heart bent on denying her brothers the gift of flight.

"Can I get you something to drink?" Daddy asked.

"Some Dubonnet would be nice," you said.

"You're going to be so far away," Mama said. "My little girl."

"For God's sake, Mom, I'm almost eighteen years old." You sighed and leaned over to tap me on the shoulder. "I want you to promise to come and visit," you said. "We can go out and do the town."

I wasn't sure if you really meant what you said, or if you were just trying to upset Mama. "Sure," I said.

"One of these days you'll understand, sweetheart. One of these days you'll have a little girl of your own and you'll know just how I feel."

"Don't hold your breath," you said. Then you turned to Daddy, who was standing in front of the fireplace, brushing wood chips off his trousers. "Dubonnet," you reminded him, "with a twist."

"Isn't that some kind of sweet wine?" he asked. "I don't think we have any, Willie. How about a little crème de menthe?"

"Forget it," you said. You got off the love seat and sat beside me on the rug, braiding through my dirty, spatulate fingers your long white ones. "Kitty," you whispered, and I thought I would burst into tears, because your breath still smelled the way it had so many years ago, as if you had just finished lapping milk up from a saucer—as if the next thing I would feel would be your tongue lapping against my cheek. "While I'm gone," you whispered, "be careful. Okay? Don't let them turn you into a ghoul. Don't let them trick you, no matter what. Do you understand?"

"You used that word before," I said. "I don't think I know what it means."

Daddy cleared his throat. "I could crack some ice, if that would make a difference," he said. "Crème de menthe over cracked ice is very refreshing."

"I said forget it, Dad." You squeezed my fingers tightly. "Flesh-eaters," you hissed. "The first symptom is, you start to feel sorry for them. And the next thing you know, they've got their teeth sunk in your skin. Believe me, I know what I'm talking about, Kitty. They go straight for your heart."

I lost my appetite. By the time we were seated at the table, all I could do was tug a leaf or two from my artichoke, pricking my fingers on the spiny tips. I watched Mama and Daddy as they cut into their slices of lamb, raised their forks to their mouths, and chewed.

"I hate to tell you this, Constance," Daddy said, "but the lamb is underdone."

Mama looked at you, supplicating, but you merely smiled and continued lifting to your parted lips a goblet filled with wine.

"Lamb is supposed to be served pink," Mama said, "according to Willie. Isn't that so, sweetheart?"

You swallowed and patted your mouth daintily with your napkin. "Madame says that Americans always ruin lamb. She says that no one in America knows how to cook."

"Oh," Daddy said, "Madame. Oh well, that's different."

"Nick," Mama said.

"Nick," Daddy mimicked. "Perhaps we should get Madame to move in and cook for us. How does that idea appeal to you, Kathleen?" he asked.

"It doesn't," I said.

"Too bad." Daddy picked up his artichoke and, for a minute, I thought he was going to throw it, but he merely regarded it with a look of tragic amusement. "And I was just beginning to get excited by the idea of shelling out fifty bucks every night, so that we could chow down in style."

You let your fork fall from your hand, so that it clattered onto your plate. "Maybe I should just leave now," you said. "Is that what you want?"

"Of course not, darling," Mama said. "You know if it were up to me, you'd never leave. I think we're all a little upset," she said, staring down the length of the table at Daddy. "Let's not spoil our last evening together, shall we?"

The dinner proceeded: we assumed an extremity of politeness in our discourse and manners; we employed the cutlery as if it were the tools of a difficult art form; we chewed exquisitely; we questioned each other about the details of our lives and smiled pleasantly at each reply. Meanwhile, Mama and Daddy sat like children passing an interminable graveyard in a car, holding their breath, on the verge of expiration, *wishing*.

Of course, no amount of wishing changed the fact that the next day Madame showed up in her shining car to whisk you off to Boston, where you caught a plane to Philadelphia. It had been at Madame's urging that you'd finally decided to audition for the Pennsylvania Ballet and, when you were accepted into the *corps de ballet,* it had been Madame who arranged for you to rent a room in the home of one of her friends, now married to the first clarinet in the Philadelphia Orchestra.

"Ozzie is a peach," you wrote to me on the back of a postcard showing the Liberty Bell. "Lucy is okay but more interested in baby Daniel than anything else. I'm meeting lots of people, but mostly I'm glued to the *barre*. If you don't come down here for my birthday, I'll never speak to you again. Love, Willie."

I, for my part, was miserable. Amy Gertner had become, over the summer, gorgeous: tan and zaftig, her braces removed, her blond hair drawn back from her noble brow into a tortoiseshell barrette. I would see her at school, lounging against a senior boy's car in the parking lot, smoking a cigarette and laughing. She was not such a creep that she no longer said hello to me when we passed each other in the halls, or when we happened to find ourselves in the same class—but I had become, there was no doubt about it, a liability.

When I wasn't in school, I spent most of my time in the woods, my binoculars around my neck. In the woods I was not tall and ungainly but, rather, soundless and agile, leaping from rock to rock across Stony Brook, sitting crouched on my haunches at the very edge of Heron Pond—a round blue jewel in the center of which the refracted light resolved itself into the shape of a great blue heron. It unfolded its body and took to flight as I watched. When I stood up I could feel that the air was in layers: warm and smelling of algae and frog spawn near the ground; cold and metallic, as if it was about to snow, higher up. By the time I got home it was usually dark, and I hated the heat inside the house and I hated the way my arms and legs banged against the doorjambs when I walked through the downstairs rooms.

"Don't forget to take off your boots, Kathleen!" Mama would call out, and then, no matter where I was, I would stop and stoop down, undoing the laces, picking off them the globes of burdock, which I would pack into a ball and toss into the air, whistling to myself. Later I would be scolded for leaving my boots in the middle of the floor.

You wrote, this time in a letter:

Dear Kitty,
   I'm assuming the reason I haven't heard from you is that you were in a car wreck and are in a body cast.

———————

Allow me to extend my condolences. I suppose now you won't be able to come down for my birthday. Oh well, such is life.

Living with the Brezinskis is not always easy. Lucy seems to think I'm their private built-in baby-sitter. She's one of those earth-mother types who always look like they know some secret about you. Ozzie, on the other hand, really seems to enjoy my company. Usually we eat breakfast together, while Lucy is off somewhere doing who knows what. Probably taping some of my hairs from the drain in the shower to the head of one of Danny's stuffed animals.

We're putting together a production of the Nut-cracker for Christmas. Remember when I danced Clara, back home? This time, believe it or not, I'll be waltzing with all the other flowers. But Madame tells me I should be honored.

I have to stop now and try to get some sleep. The kid wakes up at all hours of the night, screaming his head off. I hope you've remembered what I told you before I left. All I ever hear from Mom is that everyone's "fine."

Love, Willie.

It was October: soon it would be your birthday and, with its approach, I knew a general mood of recrimination and atonement once again would sweep through our house like weather. It always did. I was sitting on the porch, rereading your letter, trying to eat an orange as slowly as possible, breaking it up into segments and then removing the membrane, sucking on the tear-shaped sacs of pulp one at a time. Mama and Daddy had gone to the nursing home to visit Nana, and I had been left alone with Mrs. McGuire. I was thinking of what my math teacher had told us: that if you imagine the distance you're about to cover, and consistently divide that distance in half, then you will never get to your destination. I wondered whether it would be possible to spend the rest of my life eating this orange. I wondered whether, by dedicating my life to that task, I could keep the world from blowing up. To accept that idea, I thought, would be like deciding to believe a lie. According to Daddy, all organized religion was based upon such a premise—it was called faith.

The day was unusually warm for that time of year, and the smell of rotting apples drifted up from the orchard, where the trees had gone wild, raising knobby fists to hurl their fruit everywhere. Soon the hunters would come, and the cars would drive slowly southwards, the bodies of deer lashed to their trunks—the deer's eyes were always wide-open, as if even in death great watchfulness was called for, and their tongues lolled out. I thought about how these hunters in their red hats would walk through the woods all around our house, never suspecting what was going on inside, while they raised their rifles to their shoulders, their mouths dry with excitement.

At the very end of the driveway I saw a black truck pull in, a cloud of dark exhaust uncoiling from its rear end. It proceeded a short distance towards the house, and then stopped. As I watched, a man got out—he stood perfectly still for several seconds, and then began walking up the drive. His carriage was erect and stately, that of the representative of a foreign monarchy; when he got closer I could see that he was actually walking with a cane. From time to time he stopped and looked up at the house. Through the window behind me, propped open with a rock, I could hear the high-pitched and choked sound of Mrs. McGuire's voice raised in song, like music wrung from a wet sock. If you speak to strangers, she'd told me, they can bewitch you, so that you will spend the rest of your life unable to speak, clucking like a hen or barking like a dog.

The man stopped when he got to the porch steps. "Hello,

there," he said. "I'm looking for Nicholas Mowbrey." His voice was thin, although the impression was of a resonance locked within his chest, releasing only a piping echo. He was wearing a parka made out of something like blanket wool, dark blue and embroidered over the pockets with Canada geese; his body looked as if it had been whittled, late at night in the light of the moon, by an absentminded sailor who did not know when to stop.

"My father isn't home," I said.

The man leaned over, balancing on his cane, and brought his face very close to mine. I could see the hairs in his nose twitching with his breath, and the smell he gave off was thick and smoky, like bacon. "Well, well, well," he said. Then he straightened back up and reached into his pocket. "How about a Life Saver?" he asked.

I shook my head and, as I did so, the window behind me flew all the way open and out popped the upper torso of Mrs. McGuire, her expression cunning and delighted. "Who're you talking to, Kathleen?" she asked. Then she rotated within her frame to confront my seducer. "Whatever you've got, we're not buying," she said. "Go away before I call the police."

The old man stood there, sucking on his candy. "Who's she?" he asked me.

"You're a wicked, wicked man to think you can sweet-talk a poor little child. If I didn't know better, I'd say you were old Malone, the tinker man, cursed by a lifetime of sin to walk this earth, up hill and down, tempting good Christian folk like ourselves with your lying promises. Come in the house, Kathleen."

I hesitated, and the old man smiled at me. "It's all right," he said. "You might as well do what she says. At least it'll shut her up." Then he sat down on the porch and sighed. "Who would've thought they'd get so tall?" he said under his breath, wonderingly. I think he was talking about the trees.

I went inside, where I found Mrs. McGuire engaged in sprinkling salt on the surface of the wood stove in the kitchen. "I only hope it's not too late," she said. She put on an oven mitt and began arranging the granules into a pattern: three concentric circles, like a target. "It will be, my darling, as if all the fires of hell are burning right within his evil shoes. He will not be able to move fast enough! Go on," she urged. "To the window. Tell me what you see."

The man was still sitting on the porch, his back very straight, his nut-like head balanced neatly on the thin pole of his neck. Do I have to tell you, Willie, that this was a posture with which I was familiar? I knew who he was. This was Jasper Mowbrey, our famous missing grandfather—I ran into the dining room and checked to make sure. The face in the portrait had more flesh on it, but the eyes were the same: that lucent blue-green which pooled in your own bony sockets, the surface hard and sharp, beneath which glinted bits of mica dust, hanging suspended in layers and layers of lake water. The man in the portrait looked more sure of himself than the man on the porch, but disillusionment was an imperfect disguise—I knew they were the same person.

I went over and tapped on the window. When he glanced over his shoulder—expectantly, like the dogs tethered by their leashes to parking meters in town—I motioned for him to come inside. "Mrs. McGuire," I said, "it's Grandfather." I went into the kitchen, where she was sticking skewers into a loaf of bread. "The man outside," I explained, "I figured out who he is."

"Kathleen," she said, "you are just a child." Then she yanked open the wood-stove door and hurled the loaf into the fire. "It is the Evil One's greatest talent," she said, "to take on, in the twinkling of an eye, the appearance of a vanished loved one." Her conviction was so great that when, moments later, he walked into the room, she began crossing herself over and over, with such rapidity that I saw her hand turn first to liquid, then to gas.

The romantic sensibility despises the prearranged and is, consequently, despotic. Grandfather walked over to the stove, where the beskewered effigy of himself was in the process of burning down to a lump of black toast, and rubbed his hands together. "I could do with a cup of something hot," he said, and I felt very strange, as if he'd just stepped from some secret room in the house where he'd been sitting all this time, while we—fools that we were— had thought him dead.

"Begone!" Mrs. McGuire said, but it was no use. The house was *his*: the walls and floors and ceilings all shook themselves into wakefulness and, when I went into the pantry to find the tin of Lapsang Souchong—that tea I assumed he would prefer because it smelled just like him— I saw the porcelain duck's bill swing open from its place on top of the tureen we never used.

"It's about time," the duck head said. "Now, when the men go out at dawn into the marshes, he will be among them. Then I will be just a speck up in the sky, and it will be his shot which will bring me down. I will lie there in the rushes, waiting."

"Pride, pride," said the mug shaped like a man's head. "If you get eaten, it will be your own fault."

The diamonds of glass in the cupboard doors hummed and shone; I grabbed the tin of tea and ran from the pantry, but eyes and mouths were springing open everywhere, clamoring for attention. Grandfather was sitting at the table, his hands folded politely in his lap. Opposite him, her arms crossed, bunching up her dull, tan cardigan, sat Mrs. McGuire. "The water is boiling, Kathleen," she said, but she kept her eyes fixed on Grandfather's face, as if to catch it in the moment when its molecules would begin shifting; when the little tips of horns would begin sticking up out of the thick silvery hair on top of his head.

"Thank you," Grandfather said, after I handed him the cup of tea. Then he removed the top of the sugar bowl and dumped spoonful after spoonful of sugar into his cup. "I've picked up a lot of bad habits," he said. Mrs. McGuire let out a little snort and he laughed. "But at least," he said, "*I've* still got all of my own teeth." How did he know, I wondered, because I had seen those dentures lying on a saucer—the clenched teeth of an invisible watchdog Mrs. McGuire left to guard her territory when she thought she was alone in the house.

"Willie doesn't have any cavities," I said, and Mrs. McGuire reached across the table and stuck me with her finger.

"Shhh!" she hissed. "We must remain silent now, Kathleen. His craving for power is great, but he cannot take possession of us so long as we remain silent."

"You have a brother?"

"No," I said, "a sister." I heard Mrs. McGuire let out a moan, the sound a mummy might make, muffled in cerements. "I told you," I said. "It's my grandfather. It's not the Devil." I paused; I thought I could hear a showering of skewers against the grate in the wood stove. "See," I said, "it didn't work."

By the time Mama and Daddy returned, cranky and introverted from the nursing home, Grandfather was snoring softly on the love seat in the west room. I had gone in to look at him when I heard the car pulling up outside—the car doors banged closed, but he was sound asleep; his mouth moving a little, as if he was tasting something very nice. I picked up one of the hundreds of afghans with which Mama had filled our house and I tucked it in around my grandfather's narrow body. I had already decided that I loved him; my heart flew all around inside me at the sight of the afghan's pink, scalloped rim, just touching the whiskery skin stretched across his tilted-back jawbone. "I love you," I whispered and, for a moment, the snoring got louder, as if in response. Then I tiptoed out of the room.

Once, at a fair, I let go of my balloon on purpose: I watched it being drawn upward into the sky, until it was just a tiny dot of green and, then, nothing. In this way I knew that my relationship to it could never be violated; do you remember how Daddy hit his fist up against his forehead? I thought about keeping Grandfather's presence a secret, but I knew that the house would give me away.

At first Daddy didn't believe me. "It's not a very funny joke, Kathleen," he said.

"I'm not joking."

Daddy shook off his shoes and kicked them into a corner of the kitchen. "Listen," he said, "I just spent the better part of the afternoon trying to convince a senile old lady that the reason she never hears anything from her husband is because he's dead. Never mind the fact that he supposedly left her to live with some Eskimo."

"Your poor nana isn't very well," Mama said.

"He's asleep in there," I said, pointing. "Why don't you go in and see for yourselves?"

"She asked about you," Mama said.

"Christ, Constance!" Daddy pulled off his sweater, as if he was trying to shed himself of the burden of his own skin; the electrical noise of wool touching hair was like the tearing loose of capillaries. "What's wrong with you? Why don't you just tell Kathleen the truth? She doesn't even recognize me, for crying out loud."

"Well," Mama said, "we did notice that truck at the end of the driveway, Nick."

"She thinks I'm her brother Lloyd. Lloyd must've died sixty years ago. He got struck by lightning, believe it or not. He was out taking a walk, when *zap!* That's the kind of family you come from, Kathleen."

"If you don't believe me," I said, "why don't you go look?"

"Where's Mrs. McGuire?" Mama asked.

"I don't know," I said, and it was true: she had vanished, although I could hear across the ceiling the scraping sound of rearrangement. Was she cleaning, or was she still engaged in the complex mechanisms of exorcism?

Meanwhile, Daddy left the kitchen and, when he didn't come back right away, Mama and I followed to see what was going on. We found him standing in the middle of the west room with his long arms hanging at his sides, staring at the dreaming face of his father. I didn't think we should be watching—whatever the nature was of the transaction taking place, it was private, as if the old man's presence could call forth, not only from the house itself, but from Daddy's mute and pinched soul, such soliloquy as I'd heard in the pantry. I grabbed Mama's hand and tugged. His mouth was opening; language was swimming upwards. But Mama wouldn't budge.

"You're right," Mama said. "It's him." She sounded terrified. It took me years to understand her terror—how in some way Grandfather's absence was the secret element whereby their marriage achieved its sad balance of guilt and tyranny.

"He looks so old," Daddy said. "The last time I saw him, he was standing right here, sharpening his hatchet. The bastard." Daddy walked up closer and bent down— Grandfather's eyes were darting back and forth under his closed lids and his legs wiggled a little as if he was dreaming of escape. "I never thought he'd have the guts to show his face here again. Kathleen," he said, turning to me, "what did he tell you? He must want something. In all these years the only times the bastard's gotten in touch is when he's *want*ed something."

"I don't know," I said. "He was looking for you."

"Money, probably," Daddy said. "Well, he's come to the right place. All this money's just burning a hole in my pocket." He reached down and drew forth a handful of change, which he tossed onto the floor at Grandfather's feet. "More?" he asked. "Well, of course." And he pulled out his wallet from his back pocket and threw that down on top of the coins, where it landed with a *thunk*. "The key to the safe-deposit box is upstairs, but if you can hold on a minute, I'll go get it for you." Then he stormed out of the room.

Mama was whimpering—the strange dry noises she made in place of weeping. I never actually saw her cry; even later, when good reasons presented themselves one after another—that cloaked retinue which passes relentlessly through the landscape of adulthood—all she could do was place her face in her hands and move her shoulders up and down. "What are we going to do?" she asked.

But I was only fourteen years old, Willie. I didn't have a clue.

Later I was sitting at the kitchen table, trying to memo- rize the principal imports and exports of European countries for a test the next day. Mama and Daddy had disappeared upstairs, and Mrs. McGuire's nephew—a fat man with freckles and a merry demeanor, reminding me of the Ghost of Christmas Present—had arrived to drive her home to her apartment over the Tamworth post office. "I have done what I can, my darling," she'd told me, as she stood fixing her black straw bonnet in place on her head, jabbing in hatpins energetically, through hair and cranium alike.

"Come along now, Aunt Rose," the fat man had said, and he extended his arm, which she'd seized upon, col- lapsing against his bulk in an unconvincing version of delicate old-ladyhood.

"Be careful," she'd intoned, and then they were gone.

"Liechtenstein," I was saying, "grain, fruit, grapes, wood; cattle, pigs, chickens; cotton, wine, leather; false teeth, pottery, woodcarving," when Grandfather walked into the room.

"I thought I heard voices in here," he said. "Is your father home?"

"He's upstairs," I said.

"Oh." Grandfather sat down with me at the table and picked up my book. "Geography," he said, companionable, turning pages. "Did you tell him I was here?"

I nodded my head, wondering what to say.

"This is Labrador," Grandfather told me, pointing to a blue wedge sticking out from the northeastern coast of Canada. He ran his finger down the coastline, tracing the intricate ins and outs of the fiords. "Nain," he said, pausing on a small black dot. "It's all right, Kathleen," he said, smiling at me. "You don't have to make excuses. I've known your father for a long time."

"What's Nain?" I asked.

Grandfather closed the book and looked around the kitchen. "Some things never change," he said, "you know that? Nain is where I live. You'd like it there. And your grandmother would be crazy about you. You look just like her. She's getting old now, but she's still strong as an ox." He reached out and felt my upper arm approvingly. "You spend a lot of time outdoors, don't you?"

"Uh huh," I said. He was still smiling; his teeth were neat and shiny, like yours. "But I thought Nana was my grandmother," I said.

"You call her Nana? She probably eats that up. Lessie was always big on things like that. When your father was a little boy she tried to send him off for his first day at school in a velvet suit."

"She's in a nursing home," I said. "That's where they were when you got here. Mama and Daddy. They were out visiting Nana."

Grandfather rubbed his knuckles into his eyes and blinked. Something happened then to his body: the skin softened as the whole skeleton snuck inwards to hide itself —a pronged fork of lightning concealing itself in a cloud.

"I haven't been honest with you," Grandfather said. "When I said she was strong as an ox, that wasn't the truth. The truth is, Bella's sick. This whole thing was her idea. She's not like other people, Kathleen." Grandfather took my hand and held on to it tightly.

"I'm sorry," I said.

"It's not your fault," Grandfather said. Then, suddenly, he let go of my hand and stood up. "What in the name of God is this?" he asked. He picked up the brown teapot nestled within a quilted tea cozy—one of Mrs. McGuire's gifts to our household. "How can you live in a place like this, Kathleen?" he asked.

I shook my head, because I didn't have an answer. Red light welled out from between the trunks of the pines and a gusty wind set all the windowpanes in the house to rattling. *Kitty Kitty Kitty Kitty*, they chattered, seductive, implying that I might have some choice in the matter. But their voices were drowned out by the water pump switching on in the cellar—that liquid and eruptive note, a prelude to regurgitation. *Fat chance*, it said.

Much later, after I'd been sent to bed earlier than usual—my dinner a solitary communion with one of Mrs. McGuire's stews, out of which I'd fished with my fork the kind of gelatinous tube you find in canned dog food—I was awakened by that same dialogue: the windowpanes now hysterical; the water pump far off and malevolent, its message rising on its stalk from the bottom of the house, prodding against the underside of my mattress. I lay there stiff and miserable, listening, and eventually I heard the other sound: human voices this time, raised to a high and nasty pitch. At first I told myself, Ignore them, but then I heard my name—Mama was saying my name loudly—and I pulled on my robe and tiptoed down the stairs.

They were sitting in the west room on their opposing chairs; a fire was burning in the fireplace: this might have been a picture in a magazine promoting the good life, were it not for their faces, the features a hasty application of plasticine. I thought if I shook either one of them they'd rattle, the pods of their bodies filled with dry seeds.

"What are you doing up?" Daddy asked coldly.

"I couldn't sleep," I said.

"Go back to bed, sweetheart," Mama said. She didn't look at me but, nobly, at the far wall—a version of St. Joan on the tumbrel.

"This is between your mother and myself, Kathleen," Daddy said.

Kitty Kitty Kitty Kitty—the windowpanes would not shut up, and my desperation emboldened me. "Where's Grandfather?" I asked.

"I'm hoping he's asleep," Daddy said.

Suddenly infused with dangerous warmth, like a log on the verge of combustion, Mama opened her arms to me. "Kitty sweetheart, come here. Give me a hug, sweetie. You've gotten to be such a big girl, you hardly ever hug me anymore."

But I stood my ground. "Daddy," I asked, "Nana's your mother, isn't she?"

"Of course."

"And her name is Lessie?"

"Celestine." Daddy swallowed down the last of his high-ball and stood up. "Constance," he said, "the kid should be in bed." He walked out of the room and, in no time at all, I could hear the musical fall of ice cubes into his glass.

"Kitty, please?" Mama whined. "Come sit here with me. Let's not pay any attention to him. Sweetie?"

I moved closer and kisses began flying up out of her like moths. "Stop it! Stop it, Mama!" She smelled slightly sour and powdery, like a baby.

"You're all the same," she said. "I don't know what's wrong with this family."

"Mama," I said, "listen. Grandfather said something. I don't think Nana's my real grandmother. He was talking about a woman named Bella."

"Your grandfather's an old lush. He's probably hallucinating ninety-five percent of the time."

"I like him," I said.

"You haven't known him as long as I have. You haven't had to put up with what I have. He broke your poor nana's heart, not to mention the misery he's caused your father."

Daddy came back into the room. "You want to see misery?" he said. "I'll show you misery. Kathleen, my patience is wearing thin. Do you hear me?"

"Yes, Dad," I said.

I think it was then, Willie, climbing the stairs back up to my room, that I decided I wanted to go away with Grandfather. I wanted to get away from the creaking ship of our house; from the embarrassing scrutiny of Mrs. McGuire, her damp little eye trained, as if through a spyglass, on my female organs; I wanted to get away from our parents' nibbling, restless souls; I wanted to get away from all of you. The air in the house felt thick, as if there was a storm approaching, yet when I looked out my bedroom window I could see that the sky was clear—the Big Dipper marking the place above the pines, the bushes extending their shapeless shadows across a lawn the color of verdigris. Grandfather's truck, canted to one side at the end of the drive, was radiant in the moonlight.

I looked at my face in the mirror. I removed my glasses and peered in close. The cheekbones were high; my hair, straight. Otherwise, there was nothing of the Eskimo about me. Did Grandfather live in an igloo? I opened my geography book and looked up Labrador. "Part of the Labrador-Ungava peninsula," it said, "Labrador forms the northeastern tip of the Canadian mainland. It is bounded on the east by the Atlantic Ocean down to the Strait of Belle Isle, and on the south and west by Quebec. Cape

Chidley, Labrador's northernmost point, is on the Hudson Strait. The province is almost completely unpopulated." And that was all, except for a small photograph of a bear reared up on its hind legs—some past prisoner of the Conway school system had drawn trousers on the animal and given it a beard and a mustache. Under the photograph was the caption: "The King of the North. Polar bears are essentially aquatic and get their food from the sea."

I dreamed that night about white things. I dreamed about the downstairs of our house, all the furniture sheeted, drawn in away from the walls. I was sitting at the little rosewood desk in the living room, staring down at a piece of white paper and, when I looked up through the window, I saw that it was snowing. Animals like reindeer were walking into the meadow, in the center of which was a round blue pool. The animals approached the pool; they bent their necks to drink. They were very beautiful and their horns were long, twisting intricately outwards; their horns locked together and then I saw that they were not animals at all, but small children, their hands joined, making a circle around a reflecting pool in a formal garden. Thin white sunlight coated over their fingers, over their faces. They held on to each other's fingers tightly—they could not let go. In their white clothing they bent over to look at their reflections.

In the morning I woke up very early—the word "destiny" kept forming on my tongue, and each time it did I imagined a cowboy's lariat spinning through the air, its loop about to close down over *some*thing. I sat up in bed and looked out my window but, of course, the pool was gone and the meadow was bare of snow. A narrow pinkish cloud hung in the sky on the other side of the pines and I could hear, as they gathered thickly on the branches of the apple tree, the screams of grosbeaks fighting over the seeds in my feeder. A truck shifted gears as it hit the curve in the hill just east of the foot of our driveway; I imagined the driver pulling down his visor, momentarily blinded by the first rays of the sun as it rose up, far away, out of the ocean. He was probably listening to music on his radio—a long song with guitars that told a story about the wages of love. From downstairs came the sound of water drumming against the shower stall, and then the sound changed as a body inserted itself there.

Now I saw a man made out of cracks in the ceiling. A stick man with a wobbly nose and a squashed bug for an eye. As I lay back and looked up at him, he began to change shape: the cracks momentarily radiated outward, like the lines we used to be taught to place around our drawings of the sun, to show heat. Then, suddenly, these lines flew together and knotted into a tight small ball, which pulsed crazily, before assuming the contours of a face, with tiny white wings sticking out on either side. The face's lips were pursed and the blue eyes stared down at me coolly, dispassionately. I stared back, frightened that if I looked away, even for an instant, the face would move closer.

"Kathleen," the lips said, and I heard a clattering sound on the floor—a small object hit the wood. When I twisted around to see what it was, the voice got louder. Rogni's voice. "Leave it be," he said. "It's just the ring; I don't need it anymore. I made a mistake, it was the wrong thing." I could see it glimmering in the corner, lodged against one of my socks.

"You're scaring me," I said.

It was only a face—there was no body attached to it—but the impression I got was of a hand reaching down towards me. "I've watched her dancing," Rogni said. "She practices in the attic of a house on Lombard Street in Philadelphia. Up on her toes and around and around." I felt the lightest pressure: light itself, in the shape of a finger, brushing across my cheek.

"Go away," I said. "She isn't here."

"I've touched her, Kathleen."

"Why're you telling *me* this?" I asked.

A long time ago we began trying to capture the images of angels, painting them into borders of manuscripts, or carving them across tympanic arches, their garments falling in rigid folds along their flanks. What we didn't know is that they have been doing the same thing with us. This is what Rogni told me as I lay there on my back, my eyes squeezed shut, my fingers plugging up my ears. But I couldn't keep him out. The angels see us as snakes of light, plotted against the dark backdrop of eternity. We can be differentiated, one from another, only by our shapes, and it is these upon which the angels seize, inventing stories. Our lives, Willie.

Only, sometimes, the wash of sunlight across a particular set of features—of that woman named Mary, for example, whose baby forms the centerpiece of our greatest story of hope and despair—such details will undermine detachment, and then an angel will well up from out of a slot in the solid angles and curves of this world, assuming a form that is, at least, partly human.

"But we can't understand mutability," Rogni said. "Our stories have to have endings."

"Go away," I said again, but the face dropped down, closer to my own, so that I could feel the fanning of the wings across my skin, like light falling through beech leaves.

Sometimes the angels fall in love with us. But I don't have to tell *you* that.

"Listen to me, Kathleen," the angel said.

"Once upon a time there was an old woman who lived in a small house in the middle of the tundra. She was huge and fat and she got fatter by the day, mysteriously, because all she ate was spring salad—the partly digested lichens and mosses she scraped from inside the intestines of caribou. She never touched their flesh, but piled carcasses up behind her house, to tempt the predators. She was lonely. She was a million years old and what she wanted more than anything in the world was a child on whom to lavish her riches. Because, you see, she was very rich, this old woman. Inside her house she had boxes and boxes of jewels and gold, which she'd stolen over the years from out of the pockets of the men who came north to map her kingdom. They starved to death, or they froze, resorting to boiling their own clothing, choking, naked, on the tongues of their boots.

"This old woman knew that for the purposes of breeding these men were less than useless, even if she was lucky enough to find one of them alive. They were too tender and thin, like the shoots of cotton grass that came up in the early summer. And besides, they would have found her repulsive. She knew that. But she also knew that the King of the Bears was her designated mate; she'd planned it that way herself, in the beginning. So she waited. It took a million years, but eventually one day, when the snow was blowing around her—a glamorous effect, she thought, like a cape, and then, again, it felt so good—he appeared. He was tall and white. He was whiter than snow, which is where that cliché got its original meaning. Their congress was brief: he mounted her from behind, leaving the marks of his claws across her breasts. And when he was done he left her panting in the snow and lumbered off to the carcass pile, where he chipped off whole frozen chunks of meat with those same claws. He ate and he ate and he ate. The meal had been waiting for him for a million years. And as he ate, his hide began to strain; it began to get thinner and thinner, thinner than membrane, thinner than the wall of a single cell. The old woman could scarcely contain her merriment; never before had she seen such a sight. And then—*boom!*—he exploded. Pieces of him flew off in all directions. It's been suggested that this is how the land animals were made, but that's just wishful thinking.

"The old woman crouched down to shield herself from the putrid fallout: his privates, with a remote and mindless irony, hit her in the rump. Finally, when she thought she was safe, she looked up. And there, where only moments before he'd stood gorging himself, was a child. The old woman was filled with rapture! Here was a beautiful girl-child—as beautiful as the old woman was hideous. Here was a creature of flesh and blood to keep her company throughout the millions of years to come. She made her a dress out of fur and sewed to it jewels and gold: it was so heavy the child couldn't move, but stood fixed to one place like a statue. The old woman worshipped the child; she pricked her own finger and fed her the blood.

"One day, after many years of silence, the girl spoke. 'Mother,' she said, 'I am discontent. I would like a sister with whom to share my thoughts.'

"This took the old woman off guard. After all, the King of the Bears was dead, and she saw no further suitors on the horizon. But the old woman was cagy. 'Daughter,' she said, 'you already have a sister. She lives far south of here in a place called a city.'

" 'Then I must go and find her,' the girl said.

" 'But she's a useless piece of trash. Hardly worth the effort.'

" 'Nevertheless,' the girl insisted, 'she's my sister.' And she slipped out from under the heavy garment and fled.

"The old woman tried to run after her, but so many years of inertia had taken their toll. She was dense as pudding, intricately marbled with fat. Under a vast and starry sky she put her head in her hands and wept.

"Meanwhile, the girl made her way southward. After many weeks she came to a road. Of course, she didn't know what this was, but after toiling through alder swales and muskeg, she could not believe her good fortune at finding such a pleasant surface on which to walk. Perhaps this leads to a city, she thought.

"She had walked several miles when suddenly a horse-drawn carriage pulled up beside her. The driver motioned for her to get in and so she did. She was a tender morsel, stark naked, and the driver's eyes glowed like coals in his tidy, round head. 'Giddyap!' he shouted, and the horses sprang forward into a canter. There was no one else in the carriage and the girl curled up on the plush red seat and fell asleep.

"When she awoke it was dark and the carriage was rolling through the streets of a city. She pulled back the curtains and saw the graceless stone buildings of government agencies arranged around a central square; street lamps exuded a vague, yellowish glow. The driver pulled the carriage up outside a three-storied house, its entrance partly obscured by the protruding arms of potted boxwood, clipped to resemble human figures.

"The girl stepped out of the carriage and into the house, whereupon she was taken by an elderly servant—either a man or a woman, she couldn't tell—into a huge ballroom. Here a small orchestra played waltzes, as gentlemen cupped the ladies' waists with their gloved hands, guiding their partners expertly across the polished floor. Upon her arrival the most beautiful of the ladies, whose yellow hair rose up high above her forehead, and was crowned with stephanotis, left her partner and approached the girl. 'Come with me,' she said, leading her by the hand down a hallway and then up a flight of stairs, the banisters of which were carved out of whalebone. At the head of the stairs stood the host, a tall man with heavily-lidded eyes. 'Look what I've found for you,' the lady said, pointing to the girl. 'This is my body, exact as to every detail. You will have to take my word for it. Under the circumstances, it is the best that you can hope for.' Whereupon the hoods of the man's eyes lifted. 'You narcissistic bitch,' he said, laughing. Desire divided and branched as the man ran his hands along the girl's body. For several minutes the beautiful lady stood watching; then she gathered her shimmering skirts up and swept away, trailing her thin fingers along the banister.

"Far to the north the old woman was looking through a whale's blowhole. It was like a little window through which she could see the bone-colored flash of one of the girl's arms across the man's dark back; the sharp peaks of her knees, the triangle of her throat and chin. 'Go ahead,' she whispered, and she dropped an emerald ring into the blowhole. 'For you, my darling,' she whispered. The ring fell and fell and when it hit the bottom a tiny spark of light jumped out of it. This tiny spark of light rose up, higher and higher—high up into the air—and eventually it lodged in place. It was heaven. The old woman stared at it—it was so pretty, she thought, winking down at her. But it was so far away; it justified nothing!

"She called out then, and the empty garment lurched

towards her across the ice, raising its empty sleeves. Its hunger for love was now insatiable. On this account it had learned the rules for motion. And, one day, after much effort, it learned the rules for speech as well. 'Mother,' it said, 'I would like a sister.'

"And then, from deep inside the earth and from under the oceans the angels rose up, their flanks shining and hard. And all traces of the future evaporated—like wet footprints on a wooden floor, marking the lover's passage down a corridor towards the beloved, who wakes screaming in a bath of light. And all that was left was a dark imp, hunched in the corner, sucking on a marrow bone. And the imp's name was Romance."

Oh, it is true—as I came to understand in time—angels are avid for their stories to have endings. But it is also true that as storytellers they are unencumbered by the idea of motivation. Motivation is a purely human invention and, if I was oddly qualified to accept Rogni's stories, it is because I grew up in a household similarly devoid of that quality—a household where explanation was reserved only for the most trivial matters. "Don't eat your soup while it's hot," Mama would say, "or you'll burn your mouth." I don't have to tell you this; you lived there, too. "Wear your hat, Willie. Most of your body's heat escapes through the top of your head."

The angels' stories, on the other hand, are about desire, for which there is no good explanation. Their stories always begin in the same place, with that old hag in the housedress, cooking up something on her stove. Do you know what she smells like? Salt and mercury, Willie—she smells like sex.

And that is what the angels love about her; without her there would be no stories. It would all just be more of the same thing: God poised, holding the world in His big hand, admiring His work. How could such a thing—a precious, frozen stone—yield any surprises? Of course, God is watchful. Some people have said He is a voyeur. I swear to you, even as He saw fit to punish Rogni, consigning all of that desire for you to a bodiless head, it is ultimately His own doing that the stone cracked open, revealing inside a nest of worms. After all, He is the one who made the angels.

Not too long after Grandfather's arrival, you came home for the weekend. Do you remember? You brought me a pair of golden shoes with pointed heels and then stood there watching as I struggled to squeeze my big feet into them. "You look just like a hooker," you said, delighted. "Dad'll die."

I paraded from one end of the house to the other. *Click click click*—the sound of the heels on the bare floor made me feel like a small horse with neat, polished hooves. I loved those shoes! I thought about how I would wear them to Mrs. Wick's ballroom-dancing class—a torture I was made to undergo every third Thursday of the month—and how I would become, in them, finally, the object of passion. At Mrs. Wick's, trim and understated Capezio slippers were the acceptable footwear, whereas these were the shoes of legend; these were shoes whose heels could pierce a young man's heart.

"Of course," you said, when I returned to the kitchen, "they'll look a lot better with a dress. You *do* have a dress, don't you?"

"Sure," I said. "Thanks, Willie."

You yawned and walked over to the refrigerator. "Where is everyone?" you asked, yanking open the door and looking inside. "I don't believe this," you said. "This is the same fucking leftover stew that was here when I left."

"They've gone to town," I said.

"All of them?" You poured yourself a glass of milk, smelled it, and then dumped it in the sink. "The Mouse Queen tells me the family's gotten bigger since I left."

"I don't know where Grandfather is," I said.

Suddenly I felt uneasy, wondering what his reaction to you would be. Yours to him, I thought, was more predictable: that combination of amusement and scorn you usually reserved for anyone whose objectives were so clearly different from your own. I looked at you where you stood, staring out of the window, absently rising up onto your toes, and then settling down onto your heels. Routinely, my jealousy unfolded. Could you see it? I thought it must be as noticeable as ostrich plumes, agitating the room's air.

"What's he like?" you asked.

"Oh," I said, "he's very nice," and you spun around to face me.

"Christ, Kitty, you sound just like Mom."

"Well, he is," I said. Then I sat down and removed the shoes, because it had occurred to me that if Grandfather saw me wearing them he would think it a kind of betrayal. "These shoes smell funny," I said, to get back at you.

You bent your small head down to sniff. "You're right," you said. "They smell like meat. The guy I bought them from had a whole pile of shoes right there on the sidewalk. It was in the Italian market—you know, goat and pig bodies swinging from hooks in the breeze. Maybe something *dripped* on them." You grinned. "If Mrs. McGuire was here, she'd tell you to take those shoes off the table. In case it's slipped your memory, shoes on the table are bad luck."

In Labrador, Grandfather had told me, everything is filled with light: the mountains rising straight up out of the sea; the sky; the sea itself. He told me it was like a land carved out of crystal. How could he fail to fall in love with you?

"When he goes back north," I said, "he's going to take me with him."

"Kitty, wake up. You're just a kid. You should be out having fun with people your own age. Besides, he's Dad's father. You know what they say about how the fruit never falls far from the tree?" You reached out and touched my shoulder, making me shiver. "Can't you do something about your posture? If you keep sitting like that, you're going to have a hump on your back when you're an old lady."

I melted down farther into the chair. "I don't remember you being so crazy about people your own age," I said.

And then the back door swung open and they were inside: Mama and Daddy with their arms full of grocery bags, the expression in their eyes—before they had a chance to make the quick adjustments essential to conveying a spirit of delight at your presence—haunted. We have been to hell, their eyes suggested, and we are none the wiser for it.

"Willie darling! Let me look at you." Mama set the bags down on the table and hugged you. "Those people aren't giving you enough to eat," she said. "You're just skin and bone."

"Have you ever seen a fat ballet dancer?"

Daddy, meanwhile, stood hanging on to his bags for dear life, as if they might protect him from his urge to embrace you in a way that would embarrass us all. "Don't listen to your mother," he said. "I think you're looking just fine."

As it turned out, my worries were groundless: Grandfather was, apparently, immune to your beauty. He appeared in the kitchen when he smelled the bacon Mama was cooking to make sandwiches and, although he was cordial enough, I didn't hear the quickening of breath that would have signaled conquest. In fact, if he was attentive to anyone, it was to me. I was so relieved I almost burst into tears. The truth is, Willie, that since he'd been staying with us, I'd felt my loneliness draining out of me. Sometimes I could almost see it: the dark spoor of an ungainly beast courting extinction; the matted trail by which Grandfather and I would trace our way back to the house, after a day spent walking through the woods. On these occasions we would sit in the moist V between two glacial erratics the size of houses, eating the lunch Grandfather made for us—sharp cheese and onion and hot mustard sandwiches—chewing in companionable silence and breathing in the thin blue air. For a little while after our return I'd be able to smell it on me, that air by which I was distinguished from all other people in the world.

"This is for you," he said, handing me a package wrapped in brown paper. "It just came in the mail."

Everyone watched intently as I tore off the wrapping paper: as you probably recall, the opening of gifts in our family was always a drawn-out procedure, releasing us all from the burden of conversation.

"Thanks, Grandfather," I said. It was a book: *A Woman's Way Through Unknown Labrador*. I opened it and immediately came upon a picture of a tall woman staring gravely into the camera, lifting her long skirts as she stepped out of a canoe. "Who's this?" I asked.

"Mrs. Hubbard," Grandfather said.

"Let me have a look at that," Daddy said, reaching out and grabbing the book. "What's she doing? Getting her poor dog a bone?"

"Grandfather gave it to *me*," I said, trying to get the book back, but Daddy drew it in close to his chest, peeking down at it and then looking up slyly, like a poker player.

"The writing style leaves a lot to be desired," he said.

"It's Kathleen's book," Grandfather said. He picked up a paring knife and jabbed it once, lightly, into Daddy's lower arm, making a tiny incision out of which a drop of blood welled up, and when Daddy yelped, he smiled. "Just checking to make sure you're human," he said. Then he drew a large plaid handkerchief out of his breast pocket and dabbed at the cut. "When you were born, the midwife swore you were made of wood. She said when she held you up and hit you on the back, you didn't cry like most babies. You just made a hollow sound. Like knocking on a door, she said."

"I don't have to put up with this," Daddy said.

You sat with your face propped in your two hands, your eyes moving from side to side, bright with the faint sheen of moisture that I knew indicated pleasure. "You didn't tell me things'd gotten so lively around here," you said.

"Ah, but you do," Grandfather pointed out. "You do, Nicky. Or have you forgotten that this is my house?"

"Of course we haven't forgotten," Mama said. "Can I get you something to drink, Father?"

Daddy slammed the book down on the table. "That's right, Constance. Go ahead and grovel. The old bastard's got us right where he wants us, as usual. What do you want, Dad? Dom Pérignon? If I leave now, I think I can make it to the liquor store before it closes. How about you, Willie? Anything I can get for you while I'm out?"

"The milk's sour," you said. "The cow it came from's probably been dead for about a year now." You opened up your sandwich, set the bacon off to one side, and began picking at the lettuce.

"Milk," Daddy said, shoving his chair away from the table and standing up. "That's simple enough. And you, Kathleen? You haven't said a word."

I felt Grandfather's fingers close around mine: warm and rough, they squeezed gently, and my body, which had been swelling outwards—the skin thinning, just like the beast's in Rogni's story, as if I had been feeding on something unspeakable—fell back into its normal shape.

"All Kitty wants," you said, "is one red, red rose."

But Daddy didn't hear you; already he was out of the room, although it became clear to all of us that he wasn't planning to leave the house. We could hear him upstairs, stamping down the hallway; when he slammed the bedroom door, something fell from a shelf in the pantry, breaking into pieces on the floor.

The next morning I slept late. By the time I came downstairs the kitchen was empty; dishes were stacked in the sink, their various patterns smeared with egg yolk; the Sunday paper lay across the table, portions of certain articles circled, as usual, and marked with arrows or exclamation points—this was, as you will recall, our father's method of accumulating evidence against the world. The windows were all open, and a mild breeze turned the pages of the magazine section, as if, even in his absence, Daddy's quest continued, his invisible eyes trained on pictures of women in evening gowns, or pictures of immaculate living rooms, their glass coffee tables supporting bowls filled with unblemished fruit. It is true, I guess, that the evidence might have been found in these pictures—if anywhere—for a universe in which the idea of entropy had not yet been invented. I shook some cereal out into a bowl and then, remembering what you'd said about the milk, I ate it dry, with my fingers.

Grandfather was in the barn, bent over the front end of his truck, staring into the engine. When he heard me approach he looked up, smiling, and called me over. "We've got a little work to do," he said, "before we can take off. Nothing major. I think I've narrowed it down to the generator." He pointed, with a screwdriver, at a dark object nestled in among wires. "How do you like the book?"

"It's great," I said. In fact, it was because I'd stayed up half the night reading that I'd slept so late that morning.

"Mina Hubbard was a remarkable woman. They don't make them like that anymore. Big and strong and adventurous." Suddenly he straightened and stared at me, speculatively. "The wilderness is hard on women," he said. "The wilderness is a female spirit and, as we all know, the female of the species is inclined to jealousy. That sister of yours, for instance—it's eating her up. If she doesn't watch out, there'll be nothing left for the crows."

"Willie?" I couldn't believe what I was hearing. "Willie isn't jealous of anyone."

"Hold on to this," Grandfather said, indicating the generator. "I'm going to see if I can't loosen these bolts. Get a good grip, Kathleen—once it comes loose the sonofabitch weighs a ton."

I wrapped my hands around the cylinder and stiffened my shoulders. Above us, in the eaves, swallows swept their iridescent bodies through the dust-speckled air; the air in the barn smelled of humus and old hay—the pony's legacy —mixed in with the truck's smells of gasoline and rust.

"Okay," Grandfather said, "hang on tight now. I've almost got it."

For a moment I felt my body being drawn down into that complicated, metallic mouth—like a person bent on suicide, her dive accelerated by the mass of the stone held between her hands. And then Grandfather's hands were on top of mine; together we lifted the generator out of the truck.

"There used to be a man in Tamworth—Brian Stenk— who knew how to rewind these things. A real ladies' man. You wouldn't happen to know if he's still around, would you?"

I shrugged. "What did you mean," I asked, "about Willie?"

"He's probably dead by now. Shot by an irate husband." Grandfather set the generator down on the barn floor and walked over to the door. "I'd guess it's about eleven o'clock, wouldn't you say?" He no longer used the cane, although he still limped—his right foot had been badly mangled when he'd stepped, unsuspecting, into a trap. "What I meant," he said, "is that your sister is so jealous of you she can hardly see straight."

"That's crazy," I said. "Why would Willie be jealous of me?"

But he didn't answer; he merely waved his thin, dark hands around, agitating dust motes, as if the answer was too obvious to require language—as if, God forbid, I was actually fishing for a compliment. "Kathleen," he said, "you *are* planning to come with me, aren't you?"

I nodded my head. This was the same question he had used one week earlier, exacting from me a promise to accompany him to the nursing home and, as much as I hated the place, I'd acquiesced. In this way I had found myself, one drizzly afternoon, wandering at his side down that dark hallway, through which the bodies of very old people moved with excruciating slowness, their hands drawing them, by inches, along the varnished railing that ran the length of the hall or wrestling into motion the big rubber wheels of their wheelchairs. As we'd passed a gleaming stainless-steel cart piled with clean towels and bed linen, an old lady—her acorn eyes impassive, her mouth yanked in on a thread and knotted at the very back of her head, so that the lower part of her face puffed out like quilting—removed a pristine washcloth from its pile, blew her nose into it, and carefully replaced it.

You might say that this incident had set the tone for the entire visit. Nana had been sitting in her bed, propped up by several pillows; the auburn hair of which she'd been so proud was dull white, and cut close to her skull. If we hadn't known who she was, we might have mistaken her for a very old man. "Hattie," she'd said, when I walked towards her, "the well is dry, the well is dry, the well is dry." Her voice rose and fell, issuing from her tiny chest like sounds squeezed from an accordion by a monkey. "And who is this?" she'd asked, looking at Grandfather. "Is that you, Marcus? I hate to be the one to tell you this, but you've shrunk."

"It's me," Grandfather had said. "Jasper."

"And I saw a door open in heaven," Nana exclaimed, "and He who was seated there appeared to me like a jasper and a sardonyx!"

You see, it had been Grandfather's intention to "set things right" with his wife; whether the mission had been Bella's idea or his own no longer mattered. At least, this is what he'd told me, as we drove back to the house. "She was a beautiful woman, Kathleen," he'd said, "and look where it got her. She was the apple of her father's eye. History repeats itself—don't think I haven't noticed the way my son looks at that sister of yours."

But I found myself wondering—even days later, as I stood nodding my head in the barn, agreeing to travel in his company to that place where danger and magic, by all accounts, appeared interchangeable—whether Grandfather had been right. It seemed to me then that it *did* make a difference whose idea it had been that he come back to see Nana. My moral vision was unformed and hazy: because I loved him, I wanted to believe that he embodied all goodness. My usual mistake.

"Here," Grandfather said, reaching into a pack in the bed of the truck. He handed me a wonderful small boat, fashioned out of some animal's skin stretched over the thinnest of bones. "I've got to see about getting into town," he said. "Why don't you take this down to the lake—see if it floats?"

"Did you make it?" I asked.

"You don't happen to know if your father's home, do you?" A sprinkling of dead leaves, heated by the sun, flew in through the open doorway. "No," he said, "a friend of mine made it. Jobie Aleeki. Once we get this thing working again, you'll be able to thank him in person."

Indian summer, Willie—the world was blown up full of thick air. It was just about noon as I walked by myself to the lake, holding the boat against my new breasts, saying to myself, over and over, "See if it floats." When I thought about the conversation I would have to have with our parents, convincing them to let me go north with Grandfather, I pictured it this way: I stood breathing the gray fluff off the tops of dandelion stems, watching the fluff drift away. If I had any doubts about his reliability, I dealt with them similarly, although it was hard for me to forget the morning, not long ago, when he had insisted on taking me to see the night-heron rookery at the edge of the property: we'd stumbled around and around a boggy meadow, our clothing catching on broken cedar limbs, until finally he gave up.

I took the shortcut past Bellmans', where the hedge made way for me before compressing into stone. In front of me I could see the lake, a white lens, in the middle of which floated the wooden raft built by the summer people. The mosquitoes were out! You must remember. When you got home late that afternoon, wandering vaguely into the kitchen, Mama set down the block of frozen chops she'd been trying to pry apart with a knife, took one look at you, and said, "My God, you've been eaten alive."

The mosquitoes landed on my arms and legs; it felt as if they'd started their sucking while still in midair, so that my skin was drawn up, by just a fraction of an inch, to meet them. The sun was orange and appeared imperfectly round—everything in the landscape was being pulled this way and that. I set the boat in the shallow water at the lake's edge and tapped it with my finger. It rocked a little, then moved in a semicircle, impelled, likewise, by an invisible current: one of the frigid springs that fed into the lake. I tried to focus my vision on the boat; I tried to imagine a tiny man, a double-bladed paddle, such as I'd seen in photographs, balanced in his two tiny hands, dipping first one blade and then the other into the water. But I couldn't concentrate—no matter how hard I tried, I felt the range of my vision moving outwards, past the boat and the wriggling reflection of it on the lake. There were two figures on the raft. For once, I could see with great precision, as if I was looking through one of those viewers that provide an unnaturally three-dimensional look at, for instance, the Grand Canyon.

You were sitting on the raft, Willie. You were wearing that blue two-piece bathing suit Mrs. McGuire called "indecent." Your hair was pulled back and onto the top of your head, fastened in place with a barrette. As I watched, you removed the barrette and handed it to the person who was sitting there with you. I squinted to see better, but I wasn't wrong—it was Rogni. His whole body: how had he gotten it back? Such white skin, whiter even than yours—together the two of you looked like a hole cut in the landscape.

Rogni took the barrette, and your hair fell, all at once, down your shoulders and back. Then you stood up very straight and dove into the water, your body disappearing into the dent it made, sending out small waves in circles. You swam towards the opposite shore, your arms lifting and curving rapidly—I had no idea you were such a good swimmer.

You swam for maybe five minutes, out and back, until I could see Rogni bending over to lift you onto the raft; it was as if I was seeing your thin white soul slipping from its silver sleeve. Rogni turned, finally, so that his torso blocked my vision; even so, I knew that he was leaning forward to kiss you.

"Hey!" I yelled, but I'd been on the raft myself, and I knew how the *plit plit* of the water against its sides obliterated all other sound. I knew how the shoreline receded into tenuity, so that the trees and houses became as hard to see as the people on the other side of the earth, in China, raising grains of rice to their mouths with chopsticks.

Rogni's body folded down over yours, and then I saw

that fluctuation of spine I had imagined so long ago, staring in through the window of Peter Mygatz's bread truck.

I ran off into the woods, cursing as I ran: Fuck, fuck, fuck—that word Bobby Hallenbach had taught me on the school bus, diffidently, as if it carried the same weight as "tree" or "cloud." Of course, I thought. That's why the emerald ring hadn't been good enough. I paid no attention to where I was running; by the time I found myself in an unfamiliar softwood stand, the angle of light was closing in on the world, the shadows around me getting longer and longer, moving towards the single, thick line of nightfall. I sat down at the base of a wolf-tree—an old, useless maple, the trunk of which twisted into the forest floor, like a giant's arm imprisoned in the act of seizing treasure. Grandfather had told me that there were no trees in Labrador. I thought of that, and I thought, as well, of how a land inhospitable to women might not be such a bad thing. I thought of *you*. "Mother," I said out loud, experimentally, "I would like a sister." But nothing happened. I could see the first star in the sky, through the heavy net of branches overhead. I drew in a deep breath, and the air, entering me, surprised me: cooler, now; serous; it filled me up, finding its own level at the place just behind my eyes.

When I got home, Grandfather was sitting on the porch, drinking a cup of coffee. The light was on in the kitchen, illuminating him from behind; he sat perched on one of the decomposing wicker rockers like those harvest figures we used to make with Mama's help, in the old days, before she decided it was no longer fun to stuff Daddy's clothes with dead leaves. "We've seen the last of the warm weather," he said. "Tomorrow it's going to snow." He pointed to the moon.

Suddenly I remembered the boat—I'd left it behind when I ran off. I'd forgotten it; I thought of it floating out towards the middle of the lake, solitary and small, and I wanted to kill you. "Grandfather—" I began, but he interrupted me.

"I was right," he said. "Stenk's dead, but his son's taken over the business. He says he'll have the generator fixed in a couple of days." He leaned forward and stared into my face. "That's supposed to be good news, Kathleen. You're not upset about Stenk, are you?"

"The boat," I said, and as I said it I felt like I was about to cry.

"What happened? It sank? Come on, Kathleen, it's not the end of the world."

"It didn't sink," I said.

"So it floated off where you couldn't get it. Kathleen," Grandfather implored, because now I was weeping loudly, "listen to me. Nothing would make Jobie Aleeki happier than to hear that one of his boats took off on its own."

"But I forgot it," I said. "I forgot all about it."

"Here," Grandfather said. He handed me the same plaid handkerchief with which he'd wiped up Daddy's blood; as I held it up to blow my nose I could see a little brown stain, shaped like a boat. "Why don't you sit down here and tell me what's bothering you?"

"I told you," I said. I couldn't bring myself to tell him about you. I thought of that game called Parcheesi where, at any moment, one player could stop another from climbing their little ladder and going home.

"By the end of the week," Grandfather said, "we'll be on our way. We'll be sleeping under the stars, Kathleen. And you'll see birds you've never seen before. Puffins. Ptarmigan. You've never seen a puffin, have you?"

"No," I said.

"Well, you will. I promise you, we'll get Jobie to take us out in his trap boat, and then you'll see puffins to your heart's content. How does that sound?"

"I'd like that," I said.

And then you walked up, from around the side of the house; you were wearing one of Daddy's sweaters over your bathing suit, picking your way through brush and stubble, your legs like the ivory points of a compass, defining white arcs in the darkness. "Look what I found," you said. It was the boat, which you held up casually between your two hands.

"Where did you get that?" I asked, as if I didn't know.

"Down by the lake," you said. "It was caught in some weeds."

"That's Kathleen's boat," Grandfather said, and you laughed.

"Finders keepers, losers weepers," you chanted, but you handed it to me, anyway. "Aren't you two freezing out here? I'm going in. Does anybody know what's for dinner? Road kill, as usual?"

After you walked into the kitchen, we sat a little while longer on the porch, rocking back and forth in our separate chairs in silence, like the crazy people I had seen on the porch of the halfway house outside Conway, staring into the night. "Why do you let her get to you like that?" Grandfather asked, finally.

"I don't know," I said, but of course I was lying. I waited, hoping Grandfather would catch me in my lie; I thought of how consoling it would be to be *seen through*, as if there were such a thing as clarity. Instead, he stood up slowly—his bones and the wicker making the same noise—and took my hand.

"Come on, Kathleen," he said. "If you're going to be going to Labrador with me, we've still got one big fight ahead of us."

Inside the kitchen you sat at the table, scratching the welts on your skin. "You're in luck," you said. "Pork chops."

I sat down beside you, pulling my chair up close. "Why did you do it?" I whispered.

"Do what? Take the boat?" You widened your eyes, presenting the perfect image of innocence affronted.

"That's my question," Mama said. "I don't care how warm it was, October's no time to be going swimming. You could catch pneumonia, sweetheart."

"It was seventy degrees out, Mom," you said, sighing.

"Why don't you answer me?" I asked.

The pantry door swung open and Daddy walked into the room, joining us at the table. He had a pencil stuck behind his ear and the pleased look on his face that signified discovery. "It's just possible," he announced, "that we've got the whole thing backwards. I mean, who's to say which way the arrow is pointing? What about spontaneous generation? What about proud flesh?"

"Let's hear it for proud flesh," you said, standing up. "I'm going to go change, and then I'm going out." You held up your wrist and I saw, for the first time, a small silver watch held in place by a black velvet band. "Madame's coming to pick me up in about fifteen minutes."

"But your chop!" Mama wailed.

"Give it to Kitty, she's still growing."

You leaned over and kissed me, elaborately, on the cheek. "Where did you get the watch?" I asked.

"It was a present from an admirer." I realized I'd never seen you blush before: your ears turned dark red, the color smudging outward from them across your face.

"Willie," Daddy said, "as long as you're up, could you get me a beer?"

I sat there, thinking things over, as you walked to the refrigerator, scratching the damp place behind your knee. Rogni would never have given a watch as a present; I remembered what he'd said to me in the third-floor room, so

many years ago, about angels and time. Nor could I picture
him walking into Mr. Booker's jewelry store and pulling a
wallet from his pocket. "Who gave it to you?" I asked.

"You're suddenly full of questions." You stood looking
into the refrigerator. "I don't see any beer," you said, and
then you walked back over to me, and stuck your lips right
up against the side of my head, so that I could feel how
moist they were. For my part, I was like ice, and it occurred
to me that your lips might freeze in place there, the way
my own lips used to freeze to the steering mechanism of my
sled. "Peter Mygatz," you whispered. "Satisfied?"

I nodded. Maybe, I thought, I was wrong. Maybe it had
been Peter Mygatz on the raft. I tried reawakening the
image in my mind, but because I was fooling myself, it
proved invulnerable to alteration—if anything it grew
more damning, replete with new details: from the man's
back I saw wings unfolding, the feathers fanning out and
extending downward, gathering you in.

"Sweetheart," Mama said, "there's some calamine lotion
upstairs in the medicine cabinet."

You drew away from me, looking at me curiously.
"That's great, Mom," you said. "But I think what Dad
wants is a beer." And then you danced out of the room,
laughing.

I suppose it is just as well that you weren't home for
dinner that night. Certainly, with your love of family
drama, you might have jumped into the discussion of
Grandfather's and my plan, fiddling around with my sense
of purpose, re-forming it into something more closely
resembling guilt. And if I hadn't gone? Who knows
whether that would have changed the course of events.

Meanwhile, Grandfather was persistent. He pointed out
the educational benefits of such a trip. "Kathleen's a born
naturalist," he said, "in case you hadn't noticed."

"That's great," Daddy said. "Correct me if I'm wrong,

but don't naturalists study *living* things? I don't want to disappoint you," he said to me, "but I don't think you'll find much alive up there."

"You're wrong," Grandfather said. "The tundra is teeming with life."

"He means flies," Daddy said, "don't let him fool you."

"I want to go," I said. "Besides, there won't be any flies this time of year."

"But, sweetheart," Mama said, "what about school? What about your friends? What about us?"

"I hate school," I said. "I don't have any friends." Then I paused, because I didn't know how to finish my statement. "You'll be here when I get back." I poked my fork angrily into a Tater Treat. "Willie always gets to do what she wants to do. And don't tell me it's because she's older. She's been taking ballet lessons ever since she was born."

"Kathleen, listen to me." Daddy reached out and tried to take my hand, but I pulled it away.

"Leave me alone," I said.

"All right, you don't have to be friendly, but I want you to listen, just the same. I think it's commendable the way you've developed a fondness for your grandfather. Only, I've known him for a long time. He's not the easiest person in the world to get along with, believe me."

"I think he's easy to get along with," I said.

"When he left here, Kathleen, he never told a soul he was going. He just took off, as if he didn't have a care in the world, as if he didn't have a wife and a family. The closest thing any of us had to advance warning was the fact that he'd suddenly begun buying camping equipment."

"You're wrong," Grandfather said. "I told Lessie. She knew all along. If she didn't choose to tell you, then I'd say that was her problem."

"See," Daddy said, "that's just what I mean. He can't take responsibility for anything."

I pointed out that I would be gone for only two months.

I pointed out that I'd never asked for anything. What I didn't realize then was that, if I were to leave, Mama and Daddy would find themselves alone together; even if they were oblivious to the fact, that was the fate they were trying to forestall.

"Sweetheart," Mama said, "you're used to certain things. You're used to a warm house, and running water, electricity. You take things like that for granted. You don't have any idea what it would be like, living in a house made out of ice."

Grandfather laughed. "Kathleen wouldn't be living in an igloo," he said.

"Well, then, where would she be living?" Daddy asked. "In that tent you were so excited about?"

"Don't knock the tent, Nicholas. It's held up better than this house. No, Kathleen would be staying in the Nain Hotel." Grandfather became expansive, conjuring up visions of luxury: an outpost of civilization, such as one might read about, in which the guests wore formal attire for dinner, stopping to pick up their mail in a lobby lavish with potted ferns and velvet-covered furniture. In the Nain Hotel, he suggested, one might recline in a tub among scented bath salts, while beyond its walls the tundra extended until the rock gave way to ice, and walruses inched along on their bellies like enormous garden slugs. "A friend of mine owns the place," he said. "Curtis Hastings, from the Concord branch of the family? You probably know Angela," he said to Mama.

She nodded her head, even though I felt certain she didn't know Angela Hastings from a hole in the wall. Grandfather had her pegged: as socially inept as she was, Mama was a climber. Think of how proud she was of the fact that Daddy's family came over on the *Mayflower*. Why else did she make me go to that ridiculous ballroom-dancing class, except that there—if anywhere—I could meet the right sort of little ladies and gentlemen?

By the time I went upstairs to bed that night, I'd extracted a promise from our parents that, at least, they would "think about it." And I knew, from past experience, what that promise meant: it heralded capitulation. I could hardly sleep. One o'clock, two o'clock, three o'clock—I counted the hours as they struck on the grandfather clock; I listened as a voice swam into the wall behind my head.

"I can tell you about the wind, Kathleen, when it is from the north," the voice said. It was Rogni.

Traitor, I thought. Go away.

"It is heartless," Rogni's voice said, "it makes me tremble. It is *her* breath. She is breathing on a small green stone, shaping it into something else, polishing it on the hem of her housedress. And she is very patient. She knows that it is just a matter of time before *crick crack cree*, the walls fall down. She is hateful, Kathleen. Keep your wits about you."

"But I'll be with Grandfather," I whispered. "As long as I'm with Grandfather, I'll be safe."

LABRADOR

Listen, we are going to begin. When I am at the end of the story you will know more than you do now, for she was young and inhospitable to the facts about her life—do you think what you have been hearing are *facts*? If you do, you are wrong, just as you are wrong to think that there is a place called Labrador. So what if you can set the blue globe of the world spinning with your hand, if you can stop it with a simple pressure of your finger, obliterating a town called Nain, a portion of seacoast? Do you really *know* that there is such a place as Labrador? Have you ever been there? Have you ever seen the harbor water turn red; the sun filling the dent between two black mountain peaks with liquid? Have you ever ridden in a trap boat back with Zoar, watching the phosphorescent disks of tiny sea creatures revolving in your wake, while across the sky the northern lights erect their blue-and-green fences? Have you ever tasted seal meat?

Once upon a time, a young girl traveled to a place called Labrador in the company of her paternal grandfather. She was not yet fifteen years old, tall and ungainly in the manner of certain large birds when landbound, strutting across wide beaches—if she'd possessed the potential for flight, she might have been considered beautiful. Her eyes were wide-set and intelligent; even with her perpetual slouch, it was impossible to overlook her gravity, that quality without which flight would be meaningless. The old man loved her. He did not think, until he met her, that his blood had managed to find its way into anything worthy of being called kin. He was a romantic old man and, consequently, single-minded. He was, in fact, a kind of demon—a low order of that form, to be sure, but a demon nonetheless. These are the ones which we have all encountered, masquerading as toys, pinching our fingers in their metal joints, rolling their eyes, unbidden, from the recesses of our closets. They are the ones we will not let out of our sight, contributing to our parents' belief that we love them above all our other possessions.

Of course, the young girl did not know this. She had been warned, years earlier, that the world is filled with traps, but she was haughty in the way of most misfits, and skeptical, as well, that she might snag on anything so random in its intention. And so she rode along beside her grandfather, looking out through the windows of his black truck, watching the unfamiliar seep into the landscape— those gray, fishy shores, for instance, of the Bay of Fundy, where a middle-aged woman in a tartan-plaid shawl walked bent over a metal detector, slowly, slowly, as if in the act of vacuuming up all the sand. The young girl was dreaming about the future. At least, this is what she thought she was doing. She didn't know then that what she was really dreaming about was her sister, because she thought she had left her sister behind. She thought that her sister had betrayed her, that she had wandered into the dark and sexual folds of a forest, without so much as one backward glance.

And, indeed, if the truck had not been moving so quickly, she might have seen the woman in the tartan-plaid shawl suddenly stop and get down on her hands and knees, digging in the damp sand; she might have seen that woman reach into a hole and pull out a miniature shape cast in silver—a miniature dancing woman, a treasure from Ceylon lost in the wreck of the trade ship *Persiflage*, over one hundred years ago.

If this had happened, our story would have ended right there—it is not as if the young girl could have ignored such an artifact's emergence. But by the time the woman dug up the dancer, the young girl was far away, sitting by a fire. She was watching the bearded shells of mussels swing open on their hinges, revealing, inside, the pearly flesh, speckled with sand. Her grandfather ate greedily. Juice dribbled out of his mouth, dribbled through the stubble on his chin. He asked her if she believed in love at first sight, and she told him that she did; we might assume that they had this belief in common, if we were not aware of the fact that he was speaking of love between a man and a woman, whereas she was thinking of the first memory she had of her sister's face. The moon shot up into the air like a clay pigeon and stuck there. Out came the stars, larger and brighter than she had ever seen them, so that it was possible for her to accept the existence of other lives, hitched in unimaginable ways to spinning worlds.

The seawater, as they drove up the coast, was warm and strangely clear. The old man explained that this was because it was the Time of Change: that time when the wind shifted from east to west, and the whole ocean assumed a transparency, showing off the terrible deeps in which fins flashed and toothed mouths swung open, swallowing whole schools of tiny rainbow-colored fish in a single gulp. Sailors, he told her, had been known to leap from their ships, tricked by visions of wrecked galleons, enticed by the hope of scooping up sunken jewels and gold pieces, as if such riches were at arm's length, and not miles below on the sea floor.

As they traveled, the young girl was happy. She wrote letters home, in accordance with her mother's instructions.

She enjoyed the idea that she might be shocking her parents; she imagined them passing her letters back and forth.

One morning she woke earlier than her grandfather; the mist lifted its wet body off of the sand, uncovering the rough grass of the dunes, sharp as knives and coated with frost. She slid out of her sleeping bag and stood like a young giantess—like famous Anna Swan, the Giantess of Tatamagouche, whose wedding dress had been a special gift from Queen Victoria, a woman who took pleasure in discrepancies of scale—stretching and yawning. As she stood there, a female cormorant flew from her nest of seaweed and landed, in the upright and military posture characteristic of her breed, on a rock beside the young girl. She was very proud of her plumage, running the tip of her beak down through her black chest feathers. "To look at me," she said, "you would never take me for a grandmother. How the little ones love me! They bring me the smallest, choicest fish, wriggling in their beaks. My son is the bravest one of all. He flies far up the coast, where the only trees that grow are no bigger than your finger, where the whole ocean freezes, and the men go hunting on the ice for seals and walruses. It is a dangerous place, Mother, he tells me. There are bears there that walk on their hind legs, like humans. You would not like it there: every day the old women put on their mourning clothes and weep in their houses, until their tears melt the ice. Then it is spring and the ice cracks open. The cracks are so deep you can see all the way down to hell, where the young devils play with the bones of the dead hunters; they think they are their dolls. The flowers of the cloudberries bloom on the mountains, like small white stars, and they are the souls of the dead hunters."

Then a fish jumped up, all at once, from out of the water beyond the breakers, and the old bird's eyes grew sharp and alert. "You must pardon me, my dear," she said. "The little ones are off amusing themselves, forgetting that their poor grandmother is hungry." As the girl watched, the cormorant took flight, her curved wings shining in the first light of the sun.

Why, that is where I am going, the girl thought, and she imagined falling in love with one of those hunters—the strongest and the most handsome—so that in time her life would be given the perfect, lucent shape of bereavement. How the people she had known back home would envy her white, sorrowful face! How they would speculate, among themselves, about the hidden sources of her sorrow!

The farther north they traveled, the more involved the young girl became in anticipating her destiny. If her anticipation made her shiver, she was able, at least, to warm her hands and face every night over the huge fires of driftwood the old man built. On one such night, after they had pitched their tent on a promontory called Cow Head, a furious wind flew down at them, blowing through the grommet holes of the tent fly, transforming itself into the high-pitched wailing of a ghost cow, into whose forehead they'd driven their pegs. The old man was in a melancholy humor, filling and refilling his cup with whiskey, reminding the young girl, as a smooth pole smoked and burst into flames, that it was a ship's spar—that they took their comfort from the misfortunes of others.

But she remained oblivious to this information: in a sled, with the hunter's hard arm around her shoulders, she rode behind a pack of dogs through a field of radiant snow, while above her head the stars circulated in their whorls of light. When the hunter turned to kiss her, she discovered that there was another star, wildly spinning at the base of her spine.

Is it possible to infect the air with one's private dreams of erotic intention? Certainly they are very powerful; perhaps it is for this reason we are warned against them by those among us who have chosen God's love, which is chaste and immutable, as their fate. For whatever reason, it was on that night that the old man told the story of the first time he met the woman named Bella: how she had picked him up, like a sack of potatoes, to carry him from the bar where she found him, and dumped him on the floor of her shack. As he described it, she had removed all his clothing and smeared his body with red hematite. This is the substance with which archaeologists find the bodies of the dead smeared in late-archaic burials. It is compounded of pigment and bear grease—it makes the body appear to shine within the grave.

With the perfect seriousness of the confirmed narcissist, the young girl's grandfather began to enumerate parts of his anatomy: the nipples, the navel, the thighs, the penis. Although the young girl did not realize it, such narcissism is a distinguishing characteristic of the lesser demons. Instead she realized, suddenly, that his hands were dappled with those spots her mother was so afraid of getting—liver spots, they are called—and she thought, Why, he's just a very old man. I am sitting here at the edge of the world with a very old man who might die at any moment, leaving me with a truck I don't know how to drive, and a skinny, pathetic corpse to bury in a place apparently without dirt. Indeed, she was very tired, and it occurred to her that maybe he was already dead. Certainly he was obsessed by his narrative, like a ghost.

Meanwhile, far to the north, the town of Nain was assembling itself for their arrival. In the garden kept by the reverend's wife, outside their tidy rectory, cabbages wrapped themselves in layers of tough leaves, protecting their yellow, foliate hearts from the first snow. Large snowflakes gleamed and then melted on the furry backs of a pack of dogs, snarling over a pile of viscera behind Root's Fried Chicken Shack, crunching the thin bones of *pitsulaks* —those sea pigeons which Root breaded and sold as chicken—between their jaws, swallowing the slippery gobbets of feather and bone that would, eventually, kill them. As the snow began to accumulate, four brothers strapped rifles over their shoulders and drove on their snowmobiles, down the town's only road, past the rectory, where the reverend's wife pulled her curtains closed; past the place behind Root's shack where, only moments earlier, the dogs had been fighting, leaving the snow dented with paw prints and streaks of blood. They drove across the bridge that led to the gasoline storage tanks, accelerating now, climbing the first of a series of hills that would take them to the interior—hill after hill stretching endlessly northward, into regions where glacial erratics perched at the top of sharp peaks like eyeless heads presiding over the migration of caribou and the quick unknotting of ravens' bodies into flight. At any moment the snow might thicken into the shape of a carnivore; then, over the sound of their engines, the brothers might hear the rustling sound of panic, the dull fall of a body that signals its transition into meat.

Of course, the young girl was unaware of these things. She and the old man were stuck in a town to the south, waiting for that same storm which adorned, indifferently, the four brothers' eyelashes and hair with glittering snowflakes, to let up, making passage across the Strait of Belle Isle possible. They stayed in a decrepit hotel; after the daytime succession of hours, through which the young girl had drifted, as if through the rooms of a museum filled with tedious clockwork objects, she lay, at last, on her bed. From downstairs she could hear the swilers—the men who killed seals—laughing as they danced in the purple light of the lounge, sticking their big hands up under the backs of their partners' mohair sweaters. The sound of their laughter was water rushing into a sea cave; the smell of fish filled the hotel. So the young girl came to understand that she was being lowered, bit by bit, in the orange box of her room to the ocean floor, where her hair streamed out around her head on the pillow, and she was beyond rescue.

This was wilderness, believe me, without margin, beautiful and predatory.

The plane which carried the young girl and her grandfather to the town of Nain was bright red; when it touched down, its pontoons sent up wings of frigid water. From their squat, fragile houses the townspeople came to gather around the harbor, to see what the pilot would do, since the dock had detached itself from its moorings during the night and now floated—free at last!—into the open sea.

How did such things happen? The townspeople, it must be admitted, clustering together, turning their faces this way and that as they discussed whether the passengers would be able to get off the plane, found the pilot's predicament exciting—in the same way they had found it exciting the day the iceberg glided into the harbor, scuttling several trap boats. On that day they could not contain their laughter: the boats were so small, the iceberg so queenly and oblivious, the blue light emanating from its frozen heart so beautiful! Still, it was a lucky thing for the young girl and her grandfather that the Aleekis' trap boat had not been among the ones destroyed. It would have taken only a single sharp knock: trap boats are delicate in their composition, assembled out of the parts of other boats; they are never named, because they are too unreliable to love.

Now the four Aleeki brothers rode on their boat right up to the side of the plane. They were the sons of Appa Aleeki, who had drowned when his snowmobile tumbled into a rattle—one of those places where strong tongues of current lick the icebound sea to mush. All four of the Aleeki brothers were fine to look at, but each of the younger three was flawed in a way impossible to ignore. Obiah was gun-happy, shooting at things which remained invisible to other people's eyes; Mooli was insane, obsessed with the notion that he would one day become a rock-and-roll star; Ben, the baby, was a thief. Only Jobie, the oldest, was perfect—about this fact the residents of Nain were in agreement, although they kept to themselves the uneasiness they felt in his presence. Even the cold-blooded Bella Tooktasheena, a woman capable, it was claimed, of turning herself into a narwhal, a raven, a walrus—even Bella was a little afraid of him. Perhaps this was because she suspected that one day she might find herself, while not in her human guise, caught in the silver teeth of one of the traps with which Jobie laced the landscape. His genius for concealment was legendary, as was the wealth he had accumulated by selling his furs to flaccid and insatiable dealers from the south.

It was Jobie Aleeki who steered the boat, as his three brothers lounged on the deck like courtesans, charming but useless. And it was Jobie Aleeki who lifted the young girl off the plane: he lifted her into air so cold it made her face turn to crystal, mirroring in its facets Jobie's dark eyes, the four bone buttons stitched to his cap—three white and one black. Do I have to tell you that she fell in love with him then and there? It was all she could do to keep herself from reaching out and touching the smooth convexity of his cheek, that skin the color of *café au lait*. On either side of his head she could see the line of the horizon drawing itself across the harbor's mouth, and she thought it was the first morning of the world. She thought that, and she sighed, because the expression in his eyes remained serious, impassive.

What she did not understand was that he had never seen anything like her before, with the exception of those pale creatures scurrying like fish in a weir, trapped within the television set in Nain's only bar. There had been a woman with hair the color of a fox's winter pelt, splashing water up onto her face out of a white basin! Jobie Aleeki was only nineteen years old, and he was as susceptible to desire for the unfamiliar as any of us.

Hadn't it been on account of such desire that Lucifer

himself had chosen to drop like a plumb, straight from heaven to hell, rather than sacrifice his talents for invention and imagining the impossible?

The young girl, I am sorry to say, was too much caught up in her own desires to be aware of any of this. She wanted to be the heroine of a story out of which rapture radiated; she wanted that story to float southward in a glass sphere, distracting her sister at the precise moment when she lay, avid, beneath her lover's body. But the young girl did not understand the law of rapture. She did not understand that, in order for there to be rapture, she must first love her soul more than her body. If she had known to ask him, Jobie Aleeki could have told her, for it was just such understanding which informed his genius as a trapper. He could have explained how such an artful creature as the fox might be snared, tricked into thinking hunger took precedence over freedom. Still, even if he had told her, I suspect the young girl would not have believed him.

"Impossible," she would have said, and then the Devil would have laughed out loud, recognizing evidence of his first, and favorite, invention. "I think I'll have a little fun with this one," he would have said.

And so he did.

To begin with, he made Bella Tooktasheena's heart wither into a jealous, many-pronged root. If it was true, as the children of the town agreed, that Bella was over three hundred years old, then she had probably been jealous before. Hadn't there been an explorer from Jutland—a tall man with a red beard whose misfortune it had been to whisper *Julla, Julla*, as he was drifting off to sleep? And what about the young missionary who had confessed, under pressure, that his first passion was for Jesus Christ? Whether Bella had actually caused the explorer to be buried in an avalanche, or split open the missionary's skull to pluck out and eat that tiny gland shaped like a pine cone which is said to be the seat of mystical vision, we cannot know for certain. What is important, for the purposes of this story, is that the root of Bella's heart sent out its tentacular, star-nosed tips everywhere within her body: she could not hold on to anything without feeling them there, waggling through her palm's flesh.

How could she keep her Blue Willow plate—that most prized of all her possessions—from leaping out of her hand when she bent down to serve the old man his supper? She wasn't blind; she could see the way he never took his eyes off the young girl. It made no difference that she had given him the choicest cuts of caribou meat, nor that she had kept the meat from the hock, through which ran cartilaginous and rubbery tissue, for herself. To the young girl, finally, she handed the tongue. Eloquent, Bella thought, but the young girl's sense of etiquette was strong: even when the tongue curled up from the plate to lick the length of her forearm, Bella could not overlook the fact that she did not cry out in disgust.

Nor could Bella overlook the girl's impressive size and strength—those collarbones the size of juggling pins! It was as if she was seeing herself, before the skin around her eyes had puckered into crevices so deep that the old man, if he'd wanted, could have slipped his fingers through, extracting her foul, squirming thoughts, holding them up for everyone to see. Bella enjoyed a reputation for indifference, but, the truth is, she was vain. And despite her gift for transformation, the one thing she could not change into was a younger version of herself. That was not allowed.

Still, it is possible that the old man's betrayal, alone, might not have been enough to make Bella vengeful. Capricious, she might have caused a wen to rise from his forehead, the usual sebaceous matter replaced by a hatching of flies. Something simple—playful, even. But there was the additional betrayal of Jobie Aleeki. And this was much worse, betraying, as he had, nothing so basically unreliable as another person's trust. Jobie, Bella thought, had betrayed that natural order whereby a frail link exists between decorum and magic. Together, she knew, they made compartments which couldn't be seen—compartments without which all things would run together into a primeval pudding, comprehensive and deadly.

Circling and circling high in the air above them, Bella-the-raven watched Jobie's and the young girl's small bodies —their prints in the snow infinitesimal and stained red where they trod on hidden cranberries—join at the hands. How she screamed, *Cree! Craw! Cree! Craw!* making them look upward, encouraging them to see it as beautiful: her black wings flapping across the wide sky, flapping across the moon, the moon's face swimming slowly to the sky's surface, like the face of the boy's own father, just before his sons pulled him from the sea.

And so it came about that Jobie Aleeki asked the young girl to ride with him on his boat, far up the coast past Aulatsivik Island where, on sunny days, the puffins liked to perch, watching for fish. He told her that he would show her the locations of his most cunningly hidden traps, but only after she had tried to uncover them herself. Did the Devil have a hand in this invitation? I doubt it very much, although I suspect it was his voice the young girl heard, pleasant and matter-of-fact, chattering inside her head. "Such glory!" the voice said. "He has singled you out, my dear. It is a pity that your only spectators will be the rocks and the sea and the sky." No one can deny the fact that the secret life of a romance is enhanced when it is observed by those from whom its secrets are withheld.

As it turned out, this was not a problem. Bella insisted that she and the old man be included in the excursion. She became, suddenly, maternal. "And who will remember that your feet must be kept warm and dry?" she asked. "Who will see to it that you have nourishing things to eat?" Fulsomely, drawing herself up in her bundle of clothing— so that the girl thought, if only for an instant, Why, now she is turning herself into a walrus!—Bella alluded to future events of great magnitude, in which it was essential that she play a part.

Nor were she and the old man the only other passengers: Jobie Aleeki's three brothers wheedled and cajoled. "Let us come with you," Ben said, "and I'll give you this shirt." It was the color of labradorite—the native gemstone, iridescent-blue and gabbroic—printed all over with the noble heads of dogs. Ben had stolen it from Nain's only store, in which it was possible to buy a can of Spam, or a sofa, or a clarinet; he had stuffed it up under his anorak when no one was looking. Jobie refused to take the shirt; he refused to acknowledge, as well, the pistol which Obiah held pointed at his face. Still, in the end, he acquiesced. "If the weather turns bad," he said, "I'll be able to use the help."

Of course, he never really believed that that would be the case; the day on which they set out was perfectly clear. Jobie didn't know that far to the north, in the place where the Torngat Mountains rise up straight out of the sea— those huge horned presences looming miles above the little waves—a storm was being born. The Devil tugged, and out it came, from a pocket of air, furiously revolving its many arms and legs.

The trap boat rode low in the water, its narrow decks filled with ropes and bottles of orange soda, a pile of rubber boots, oilskins, and drums containing gasoline. Four rifles stood propped against the cabin: a small, three-walled house as haphazardly constructed, the young girl thought, as the boat itself. But she wasn't scared—not a bit!—because there at the tiller was Jobie Aleeki, smiling at her, eating bright yellow cheese snacks out of a cellophane bag. As they left the harbor she could see all the dogs of Nain arranged along the shore, their plumed tails waving elegantly above the snow in which their legs were hidden.

Now they left Nain behind. They left behind the abandoned mission building, with its rooms storing kayaks, mildewed hymnals, harpoons, old Bibles and their spidery genealogies; they left behind the hospital, and all the tiny houses; they were in the ocean now, so that they could no longer remember the streambeds and gullies choked with debris, with rusting parts of machines, cans and bottles, wires and bones.

The trap boat swung north, past the walls of mountains and the mountainous islands increasing in size on either side; old-mountain rocks, toughened in the early days when they lay hidden under ice. Then, from the earth's heart, burning metals welled up, intruding themselves into the cracks and seams, solidifying into shining black ribs which remained visible, even now, millions of years later. If you stared too long at these mountains, you might begin to forget that there was such a thing as human personality. And once you had forgotten personality, you might begin to forget morality as well.

Gradually, the sky began to fill in with clouds, all that empty space having left God's hand itchy for completion. The clouds were ragged and pearl gray; they occupied the whole tall, darkening sky, as the sea, in turn, became the color of nickel, through which rang chords of silver light. Obiah picked up his rifle and started shooting. *Bang! Bang!* Was he trying to put a bullet into the pillar of the wind, to halt its dancing approach? Or was he shooting at the birds—hundreds of them—beating their wings like crazy, as if they could fly faster than the storm? The wind shoved itself against the boat's prow, mean and hectoring, and all at once a hand of water reached over the rail, plucking Bella's cigarette from between her lips.

It was a very bad storm. It killed a geologist, just as he was reaching up to tap off a chunk of hornblende, tossing his body into the air; it disengaged the wires of the missile-tracking station on the hill above Hopedale; it hooked the trap boat, wildly flapping, to a course that made no sense. Jobie Aleeki might have been a skillful sailor, and his arms, in accordance with the young girl's dream, might have been strong, but he could not control the tiller. The boat was heading towards shore. It was heading towards the cupped fingers of an enormous hand—a wall of rock curved as if about to close down over them all.

The Devil, as you have probably suspected, took pleasure in this situation. But it was not his intention that the boat should crash. His plan was more artful: there, at the very top of the rock wall, he knew there was a raised beach, the thinnest, gray smear of sand. Eons earlier, this beach had provided sanctuary at sea level, but as the glacier released its grip on the land, the beach rose higher and higher, like those visions of heaven designed to torment the sinful. The Devil delighted in imagining the expressions on the faces of the people in the boat, as they sped closer and closer to the wall, their necks craned backwards, their frightened faces looking up. Although not all of them were frightened. The old man, for instance, felt the gloved fingers of Ecstasy—she who prepares the body for Death's inspection—running up his spine, dusting the keys, both the black ones and the white.

Then, at the last moment, the boat's hull dragged itself across a submerged rock and stuck there. The young girl could see, all around them, other such rocks, unnaturally smooth and seductive in their arrangement, appearing and disappearing as the waves rose and fell; even though they were close to shore, the water was still deep enough that a person's body could slip in and be gone.

Jobie Aleeki gathered up an armload of rope. He stood, briefly, one foot pressed into the deck, the leg rising up from it a leg of flesh and blood, recognizable and human, as his other leg extended out into space, a spirit leg, jointless and glimmering. Then he leaped. Would you believe me if I told you that he is leaping still? Would you believe me if I told you that the space between two rocks—the one on which the boat was lodged and the one on which he landed—remains printed with the bright arc of his form? There are places like this all over the world, but they are only visible to those who recognize, in moments of pure transition, evidence of the infinite.

A narrow shelf of rock, small particulate bits in their sheaths of ice, stretched along the base of the wall, and it was onto this shelf that Jobie climbed. I cannot tell you how he did it: pulled and pulled the boat in towards himself; perhaps it was because he had heard the soft splintering noises from where the hull rubbed itself against the rock, because he knew that, at any second, the whole boat might crack into small pieces, just as the porcelain teacup had, in the rectory, when his hand closed too tightly around it. He did not want the young girl to die. And he saw that she was terrified, even as she tried to smile, to let him know that she trusted him, even as he lifted her across the black and convulsive water. How many times had Jobie slept wrapped in skins on a bed of rock or snow, while a storm paraded with giant purpose across the landscape? His sense of peril was constant and familiar, whereas, for the young girl, this was a place without coordinates, an idea in the mind of a madman.

Together, Jobie and the young girl climbed the cliff. The wind set itself to prying their bodies loose; the knobs of rock that were their hand-and-toe holds shone with ice and popped out: the higher they climbed, the more of the wall fell away behind them, rumbling into the water. But despite her terror or, perhaps, inspired by it, the young girl proved to be a skillful climber; she got to the top first, so that it was her reward to be able to reach down and, summoning all her strength, bring her heart's desire right up into her arms, that dark body smelling of wet fur and salt. They lay there, side by side, high above the sea, looking down to where the boat rocked, still studded with pale, upwards-pointing faces. If he had kissed her then, would things have turned out differently? Because, believe me, he wanted to. It is difficult to know, in fact, what stopped him —there she was, so close to him that her warmth made the ice melt from his hair and lashes, running down his cheeks and into his mouth, where it tasted pure and sweet, as he imagined the inside of her mouth would taste, kissing her. Perhaps what stopped him was that most common of all human afflictions—another of the Devil's proud inventions—the great delight we take in the thing imagined, at the expense of the thing itself. For whatever reason, instead of kissing her, he let down the rope and, one after another, up the others all came, huffing and puffing, the expressions on their faces uniformly passive, as if they had decided that getting to the beach was no longer their responsibility. Certainly this would account for the annoying heaviness of their bodies.

At least, the young girl thought, as they struggled to pull Bella over the edge, she could turn herself into a bird and *fly* up. The young girl was exhausted, and it did not make her feel any better the way Bella glared at her, ominously, as if reading her mind. Nor did it make her feel any better that, within minutes after her arrival on the beach, Bella seemed to vanish. Where had she gone? Was it possible that the young girl had failed to notice the precise instant at which Bella slid, a tusked, damp, black sausage, back into the sea? Why had no one called out to alert her when the tufts of fur first began sprouting from Bella's face, and her eyes shrank to the size of raisins?

In fact, the other members of the group all stood together at the farthest end of the beach, where a small hunting tilt had been erected. Tilts are houses of wood and stones and skins, as mutable in their composition as trap boats, and equally subject to revision. Now Jobie Aleeki was engaged in the act of breaking off parts of the tilt, in order to make a fire, and the young girl thought, Those hands have held on to me. Everyone else thinks that those are hands dedicated to the performance of useful tasks, but

I know better. She became smug: she thought this was, finally, the long-awaited story of which she was the heroine; she did not notice the ptarmigan, its body so skillfully hidden against the snow, until it flew up all at once into the air and Obiah shot it.

This should have warned her to be on the lookout for other hidden things as well. But the young girl was too much caught up in her own story's abundant, unfolding details to be watchful. She didn't notice the storm's abrupt passage, the sun slit through by one of the toothed peaks to the west, spilling red liquid all across the sky. She didn't notice when the old man left the group around the fire. Or, at least, she didn't notice until it was too late.

Behind the largest of the rocks with which the beach was ringed, the young girl stood leaning into Jobie Aleeki's arms. Now, at last, he kissed her. She had been waiting so long for this, can we blame her that, for as long as the kiss lasted, she was nowhere but in the small pocket their mouths made? Indeed, it became her curse, forever after, to judge all other kisses by that standard. Jobie held her shoulders lightly; they both kept their eyes wide open, and if it is true that eyes are really windows, then theirs were without panes. What they saw, looking at each other, flowed out into the air between them, distinct and feathery at first, and then pervasive, like ink dropped into water.

It was an innocent kiss, almost chaste—it didn't last very long. And yet, by the time they drew apart and looked out at the world—surprised and enchanted by what they saw, as if they were agents of its creation—the old man had already pushed his way through high drifts of snow and stood beckoning to them. What could he possibly want? There was the safe enclosure of the beach, where the fire spat as juices dripped onto it from out of the ptarmigan's roasting body; there was the endless white plateau, off the rim of which a person could step to fall, endlessly, among the faint blue tubes and cones of eternity. The old man stood there, in the middle of that plateau, waving and waving his arms, pointing.

Jobie and the young girl looked around, confused. From out of nowhere a raven swooped down at them. It came so close that the thick, sharp whiskers of its ruff brushed against the girl's cheek; its smell was sorry and pungent, such as swims forth from an old woman's underthings. The bird cursed once—a terrible word that cannot be transcribed—and then raced off towards that place where the girl's grandfather pointed, its dark body getting smaller and smaller, disappearing like a piece of ice on a hot stove.

"Look!" Jobie said.

At first the young girl didn't know what it was she was seeing—were those disembodied arms and legs of snow, tossed around by the wind, actually the ghosts of doomed explorers? They were so far away! And then, squinting her eyes, they began to come into focus: reared up on their hind legs at the exact place where the snow and the sky came together—great white bears, dancing, swaying their thick torsos from side to side, the pleated fur of their chests and shoulders tapering upwards into tiny heads, the dark tips of their noses. That is where such bears are most vulnerable to attack: the colorless nerve of ice which threads through their bodies is exposed there, frayed and moist.

As Jobie and the young girl watched, horrified, the old man began walking closer and closer to the bears. What could he be thinking of? Slowly, his little body erect, he approached the world's edge; he approached the place where the bears' bodies shifted and revolved, occasionally thinning down at the extremities into single flashes of light.

The largest of the bears stopped dancing and started to move in the old man's direction. The young girl could hear a tiny *click* as Jobie released the safety on his rifle; his long, dark arms were perfectly steady as he raised the rifle to his shoulder, sighting through the scope.

But now the bear was on all fours! Is it possible there was something *familiar* about it? How else can we account for the old man's eagerness, for the way he almost stumbled in his rush to move closer to the thing? He needn't have bothered: the bear's advance was rapid. Soon they could all smell it, its heavy carnivorous stink; and they could see the yellowish cast to its fur—the dense plates of fur separating, as if by fissures, with each step—and they could see the dark holes that were its eyes; they could hear the intestinal churning as its appetite awakened.

It was a real bear filled with the breath of this world, putrid and immense, its tongue a grayish pink, its teeth crusty with green sediment. Believe me when I tell you it was not a story bear; not a legend bear; not a bear preparing to shuck off its skin and reveal itself to the youngest sister as a suitor—the prince, at last, static as paradise and requiring only admiration.

The old man pulled a little gun from inside his anorak. He fired once, and the sound was festive, like a champagne bottle being opened. For a second the bear stopped, poking its dark nose down into the fur on its chest.

"Did he hit it?" the young girl asked, and Jobie nodded.

But it didn't make any difference. The bear kept coming closer and closer. Meanwhile, the old man had stopped moving; he just stood there, firing his gun again and again: *pop! pop! pop! pop!* If anyone could have seen the expression on his face they might have been surprised: he was smiling, even as miniature tears pricked from his eyes.

Finally, the bear's mouth swung open on its hinges and, as it did, Jobie's gun went off. He was aiming into the vault of that ridged and moving throat; that was his only hope, to be able to send his bullet through the throat and into the brain, where the bear worked at turning information into slobber. The gun went off again, but as you might have suspected, it was too late. The bear was eating the old man up.

In many of the tales which we all know, bears ingest human beings whole, making way for the denouement of regurgitation or excision. Jobie grabbed the young girl and held on to her tightly, pressing her face into his chest. The idea was that she shouldn't see what was happening. But, nonetheless, she could hear the crunching. For years afterwards, that would be the sound she remembered—that and the high-pitched coaxing voice of Bella Tooktasheena, which seemed to drain, out of nothing, directly into her ear.

"I don't understand you!" the young girl wanted to scream.

"Of course you don't," the voice replied. "I don't expect you to."

For a single instant the young girl hesitated at that portal beyond which her story did not extend, beyond which the glittering plates of ice stretched themselves to impossible thinness underneath a blue-black sky. She thought she could see her sister, seated rigidly in a wicker chair, combing her long red hair with one hand and reaching out with the other. Some kind of a choice had to be made. *Kathleen*, the young girl's sister whispered, and their hands came together, the fingerbones pliant and a little damp, warmed by the pumping of those two odd, isolate hearts.

"But I don't know what to do," the young girl said.

"There is nothing you can do," Jobie said.

High, high above their heads the raven flew, its wings beating against the air—*flap! flap!*—and, for once, the echo preceded the gesture. At any moment such things can happen. If they did not, it is very likely that the world would have ended long ago.

The bear picked the old man up—what was left of him— it picked what was left of him up in its long, furry arms, with the curved black claws digging into the small of his back, as if carrying forth from the drawing room a tender young thing who had just fainted, from shock or out of a sense of duty to her sex. The old man's heels dragged through the snow, leaving a path marked by surprisingly little blood; a path we could follow if we were stupid enough to want to find all of them—the whole repulsive bear family, devoid of little tables and chairs, of candles dripping tallow onto royal nightshirts—if we were so stupid as to want to track them to the place where they strew their leavings, a few hipbones and the heart, having been taught that the human heart is poison, as we have been taught that their livers are poison, across the ice and snow.

OUT OF THE ICE

It was snowing as we walked down the road together. I saw snow gathering into pinions, pinions into sleek beating wings: white birds, their whiteness chaste and eyeless, settled down all around us, marking our passage, hemming us in. I walked down Nain's only road with Jobie Aleeki. The snow obliterated our footprints. We were so shy, Willie, holding hands, and I don't think that either of us knew whether this gesture was meant to be romantic or consolatory. Perhaps both—perhaps any difference between those two urges is illusory, and this is why the poor, legless soldier falls in love, over and over again, with his nurse. The air was so cold it smelled blue. It was so cold that, with every breath, I expected my body to break apart, releasing a faint thing such as I saw flying out of Jobie's lips.

He was escorting me to the rectory belonging to the Reverend Schwenk and his wife, Lotte, conveniently adjacent to the house of God. It was the only two-story dwelling in a town of shacks and prefab boxes; its front windows glowed yellow ahead of us, and thin skins of yellow light lay across the front yard. I thought of the time when I'd peeled back a skin of birchbark from the forest floor and found, under it, the skeleton of a bird with clusters of small white flowers growing up between its ribs. Then I began to shiver, and Jobie put his arm around my shoulders. The lights of the rectory were arranged in the shape of a face, and as we approached the front door, I could hear the sound of a record player. Guy Lombardo and his Royal Canadians, it turned out—the reverend was a fan. Before he knocked, Jobie bent down and kissed my forehead.

"Why can't I stay with you?" I asked.

Jobie shook his head. "Hey, Kathleen," he said. "Please."

"But I want to," I said. I could feel his hands holding on to my shoulders, the fingers pressing in tightly—the whole weight of his dark head bent towards me. I took a deep breath and blurted it out: "I want to stay with you forever." I knew, as I said it, that it was a ridiculous thing to say; I realized, as well, that I didn't even mean it. What I meant was, I wanted to go home. What I meant was, for the first time in my life, I understood the power of hope. And I understood it, Willie, by its absence.

Then the front door swung open and there was Mrs. Schwenk, the branches of her arms swaying from out of the plaid blanket wool of her bathrobe, a nest of rollers high on top of her head. "Hurry up, child," she said. "You're letting all the heat out."

Jobie stepped back, his hands moving off from my shoulders and into his pockets. Through the open door I could see the dissolving contours of thickly-varnished paneling, the pawed feet of chairs and tables inching towards me across a liver-colored rug. The music was louder now, and two large dogs simultaneously raised their heads—their eyes were golden and frighteningly rational.

"I'm never going to see you again," I said.

"Nonsense," Mrs. Schwenk said. "You can see him tomorrow. The plane never leaves on schedule, if it leaves at all." She took hold of my wrist and began pulling me inside.

"We could write to each other," I said, looking back over my shoulder. He was so far away; the snow fell faster and faster between us, actual and cold, touching my face, as if to distract me from that secret process wherein the sensory details of those we love withdraw into memory.

Only a little while earlier, I could tell, the Schwenks had eaten boiled cabbage. "Welcome to the present"—that is the message implicit in the smell of boiled cabbage. It is the message implicit in such furniture as the dark green horsehair sofa on which Mrs. Schwenk urged me to sit, its insistent fibers sticking into me all over my body.

"He can't write," Mrs. Schwenk said, laughing cheerfully, shutting the door and turning off the porch light. "Well, he *can't*," she said, when I turned what I suppose must have been my sorrowful face towards her.

Lotte Schwenk had been one of the first people I had met that day two months ago, when I dropped from above the clouds straight into the blue eye of the harbor. "I can't imagine what your parents were thinking of," she had said to me then. I remember realizing how much she reminded me of the women who used to come to our house from time to time, trying to interest Mama in community-improvement projects. She had the same way of speaking, breezily, out of the corner of her mouth; the same rectangular smile, when dispensing uncalled-for advice.

"You just sit right there, Kathleen," she said. "I'm going to fix you a bowl of soup."

There were things hidden under the sofa cushions. I found wadded-up tissues—little pink balls—and paperback romance novels, their covers showing beautiful women in cloaks standing alone, as their long hair blew back to point towards the houses in which their fates assembled themselves. Who read these books? I admit, it was easier for me to picture the Reverend Schwenk, with his filamental hair and tenderhearted ways, dabbing with pink tissues at the breaking cloud of his face, than it was to picture the obdurate Lotte similarly affected. I replaced the books and tissues carefully under me and then, like a compulsive eater, I looked around frantically for something to stuff my eyes full of. I was just beginning to discover that if I didn't, what I would see was the white skin of a neck with a bite taken out of it, a pinkish bowl filling in, little by little, with red. On the table in front of me there was a framed photograph showing about twenty Eskimos in dark uniforms, standing near the dock in summer sunshine, playing band instruments. The tuba, as usual, predominated: I was staring into that yawning orifice, trying to see if I could make out, from the liquid and elongated reflection slipping down the tuba's throat, the identity of the photographer, when Mrs. Schwenk returned, tray in hand. Such a close call, Willie! The reminders were everywhere, even in my own mouth's saliva, rising to meet the smell of tomato soup. How often had I eaten tomato soup in the kitchen at home, as the sun came—just at lunchtime—right through the window over the sink, making my spoon glitter? It would heat the ink on the newspaper as Daddy shook out the pages, filling the room with that inky and diligent smell, which mixed with the friendly smell of the soup. I could feel tears burrowing upward from their hiding place underneath my breastbone.

And I could tell by the way that she stood there, the hot air from a vent in the floor ruffling the surface of her robe—exactly as the fur along the backs of the two dogs stood up whenever I moved around on the sofa—that Mrs. Schwenk was waiting. Just one tear! If I would only let drop one little tear, then she would have me. Then there would be nothing else to do but allow it to unfold, the usual tragedy: the changeling child, amoral and potentially disruptive, would be, once and for all, delivered over into the hands of the childless human woman.

I was stone; I was ice. The two dogs came over to breathe

on me while I ate my soup, and it seemed only fair that as punishment for my coldness I should have to endure the sight of those two wide-open mouths, in each of which the tongue draped across the lower row of teeth. Well, of course, I thought—the dogs were waiting, too.

Eventually I fell asleep. When I woke up it seemed to me that it was very late: I could hear the murmuring sounds of human voices, the sound of human shoes walking across the kitchen floor, a great groaning yawn which I knew was human only when it did not finish with that wrenched *click* characteristic of the yawns of dogs. Something was poured down the drain. A light was switched off, and then I squeezed my eyes shut because I heard them walking into the living room; I knew that they were both standing there —the Reverend and Mrs. Schwenk—looking down at me.

"It's a wonder she can sleep at all, poor little thing," the reverend said.

"Well, while you're handing out the sympathy," Mrs. Schwenk said, "don't forget who's got to deal with this mess."

"*Caritas*, Lotte, *caritas*. Look at her. She's just a child. It isn't her fault what happened."

"I'm glad you can be so certain." There was a brief moment of silence, during which some changing of position occurred. "The hosta is infested with aphids," Mrs. Schwenk said. "It's going to need a good soaking."

From its place on the kitchen floor one of the dogs got up, the noise of its toenails disturbingly tiny in comparison with the dog's actual size. I didn't think I could keep my eyes closed too much longer. Already the lids were twitching, so that, in narrow and jumpy segments, I was beginning to see things I didn't want to see: a dark hair sticking, like a scimitar, out of a mole on Lotte Schwenk's chin; a pink eruption at the nape of the reverend's neck; Lotte Schwenk's mouth, out of which she pressed, one after another, bricks of speech; the reverend's hands grappling in the dark around his wife's body, as if he had no concept of its dimensions. Oh no, I thought, he's going to kiss her.

"The eldest Aleeki was here earlier," Lotte Schwenk said. "If you ask me, the whole family's nothing but trouble."

"Lotte," the reverend said.

Was this my punishment? Was it possible that, if I hadn't been so busy kissing Jobie Aleeki, I might have been able to help Grandfather? I wondered whether, for the rest of my life, I would be cursed by my proximity to those sexual events in the lives of others which we are, for the most part, happy to know nothing about: the endless boring conversations; the snagged hooks and eyes; the graceless collapse of limbs onto carpet. In this way, I thought, I would be constantly reminded of the foolishness of my choice; I would be reminded that beneath the flashing wings and musical breezes of romance there always lurks a gloomy, dull, and flatulent resignation.

"The child is awake," Lotte Schwenk said.

The reverend reached into his vest pocket. "How about a lemon drop?" he asked.

Actually, it was only eleven o'clock: as we climbed the stairs to the second floor I heard the hour announced by a cuckoo clock in a far-off part of the house. The upstairs hallway smelled even more strongly than the living room of cabbage, and when Mrs. Schwenk stopped to remove bedding from a linen closet, the odor of camphor sprang loose, making me feel the combined exhilaration and melancholy of summer's alteration into fall, the woolen clothes removed from their trunks, making your eyes water if you got too close.

After Reverend Schwenk disappeared into a large square room—his study—at the front of the house, Mrs. Schwenk led me to a tiny bedroom at the farthest end of the hall. The bed was white metal, like in a hospital, and although I offered to help make it up, she waved me away. I had to stand there, perfectly still, watching her work. A picture of Jesus hung over a washstand and his hands were raised as if he'd just washed them in the basin and was waiting for the scrub nurse to help him put his gloves on. Mrs. Schwenk turned back the top sheet in a neat white V and then set a pile of dark-colored blankets at the foot of the bed. "Here," she said, handing me a flannel nightgown. I understood, by the way she discreetly wandered over to scrape a little hole in the frost on the window and to peek out through it, that I was meant to put on the gown, then and there. If ever a woman had eyes in the back of her head, this was she.

"Charlie McPhillips will be coming for you after break-fast tomorrow," Mrs. Schwenk said. She turned around at the precise moment the gown slipped into place on my shoulders, just as a shiver ran up my spine and burst through the top of my head like a fountain—it had oc-curred to me that Mrs. Schwenk's body had been, before mine, naked under this same tent of flannel. "The Mountie," she explained. "He's going to take you home."

"Oh," I said.

Mrs. Schwenk held my hand and I was shocked to feel how warm and soft her fingers were. "Kneel down with me, Kathleen," she said. "Let us pray together for the immortal soul of your grandfather."

The tone of her voice implied that we had a big job ahead of us. I was fourteen years old, Willie, and not about to argue. Mrs. Schwenk explained to me that there were irregularities in this situation. She had read, in a religious tract, that in the event of atomic war a person at ground zero would lose not only his body but also his soul. Was this true, she wondered, in cases involving digestion? Per-haps, she speculated, lacing her fingers together, getting ready, this might explain our disgust with cannibalism. The Eskimos, of course, would say that Grandfather's soul was in the bear. She made a face, but I thought it was an optimistic approach to an otherwise apparently meaning-less event. I was still in shock, Willie.

"Our Lord Jesus in heaven," Mrs. Schwenk said, "listen to the voices of two sinners raised in supplication. We are as but the poorest lambs of your fold. Have mercy on us. Have mercy on us—"

The prayer went on and on in this vein, establishing relationship and, before we got to the part about Grand-father, I fell asleep.

The next day was terribly cold, although windless and clear. While I stood on the dock, watching the plane fill in more and more of the colorless air in front of me with its red shape—even while I watched the dark body of Jobie Aleeki approaching me—it was as if nothing moved. The Mountie consulted a piece of paper in his gloved hand.

"We'll fly to Goose Bay," he told me, "and if the weather holds we'll catch the plane to Montreal at one o'clock."

I'm going home, I thought. I could see Bella Took-tasheena emerging, momentarily, from the doorway of her shack; it was like seeing the naked body of a turtle as it slid out from its shell. She stood with her arms folded across her chest, staring at the plane as it taxied down the runway —that flat stretch of ground at the end of the town where, on nice afternoons, the young mothers would drive their babies around and around on the backs of their snow-mobiles, shouting gossip at each other over the noise of the engines.

"Okay," the Mountie said, "let's get going." He picked up my pack and began walking away from me, kicking lumps of snow into powder with the toes of his high, polished boots. "Come on," he said.

But the only part of me capable of motion was my heart, red and polished as the plane, tiny and blunt-nosed, its attempts at flight constantly thwarted, as if there was nothing inside my body so vast as a soul. I felt Jobie's arms closing around me; he hugged me hard and I let out a little *oof!*—a little puff of air that he swallowed right up.

"You be careful, Kathleen," he said.

"I will," I said. I could see every single hair growing from out of his head, even the individual hairs of his brows and lashes. If there had been time, I would have been able to count them; I knew that. And then the future appeared to me in the way the future sometimes does, washed clean of desire, repetitive and perfunctory. I saw myself in the kitchen at home, writing in my spiral notebook, my arm reaching out at regular intervals to pluck from the waxed-paper-encased tower in front of me one saltine after another. Jobie's lips tasted like salt. Would I remember that? My own lower lip was chapped and split open in the middle: the kiss stung. "But I'll come back someday," I said. "I promise."

Of course, I never did. For a while I wrote letters—long letters filled with promises and adjectives—and then, finally, because I received no replies, I gave up. I suppose Mrs. Schwenk was correct: Jobie didn't know how to write. In this way he became a character in the story of my life—graceful and silent, requiring no revision.

The Mountie rented a car in Montreal; the only time I saw him smile during that whole trip was when he took the keys from the woman behind the yellow counter and slipped them into his coat pocket. He was a big man, neckless, with a wide flat head, and he looked so much like a wooden clothespin that it surprised me whenever he bent to sit. "Miss Mowbrey," he called me, his manner excessively polite, so that it was impossible to tell whether he was being ironic or sincere.

It was a long drive from Montreal to Conway, down along the dangerous highways where we stopped, regularly, to be directed to windowless washrooms by attendants with their names scrolled over their hearts in red. My stomach was upset. I would race to unlatch those stiff locks while the Mountie stood beside the shining green Buick, smoking a cigarette. To the north, pieces of trash were moved by the wind along the concrete; farther south, the sun dropped down behind fir trees. Now in the houses that we passed I knew there were ordinary families eating dinner; mothers, and fathers, and children seated around tables, handing bowls heaped with mashed potatoes to one another. We rode in silence, moving onto increasingly smaller roads, our passage marked by the ticking of the turn signal. In Conway, the Mountie stopped to buy cigarettes, and I sat catching my breath, as if I'd been running every inch of the way from Labrador.

A young woman walked by the car and then stopped, turned around and came back to tap on the window. I rolled it down and there was her face, so close to mine that I could smell spices in her open mouth; I could see tiny black dots along her cheek where the eyeliner had flaked off. She pointed towards the license plate. "My brother lives in Quebec," she said. "In Three Rivers?"

The early explorers, after months on the open sea, claimed to be able to smell approaching land; then the shore birds would hang in the air over their boats, swooping to grab at garbage—later the dim, round hills would appear. The woman waited expectantly, and I thought, nervously, that what I was smelling was the first whiff of you, Willie, queer and exotic. I had no idea how close to you I actually was.

"I live outside of Conway," I said.

"His name's Warren," the woman said. "Warren Posner? He owns a topless joint in Three Rivers. The Kit Kat?"

I smiled and shrugged, but when I began to roll the window back up, the woman stuck her hand—the fingernails painted dark red—on top of the glass and wouldn't let go. "Hey!" she said. "What's your rush?"

"I'm sorry," I said, "but I don't know your brother."

"That's no excuse for rudeness." Abruptly she let go of the window and backed off; she was still standing there, apparently without a car, when we drove away several minutes later. I could see her in the blue light cast by the windows of the supermarket, her face angry and dramatic, her mouth opening and closing, her arms raised and gyrating, as if she was hurling stones.

"Who's your friend?" asked the Mountie.

This was January; snow was piled all along our driveway, cut off cleanly at the edges by the plow. I'd almost forgotten how many times the driveway curved through the trees before coming out, finally, into the open. January: the world faced away from the brightly-lit rooms in which a father might bend down to kiss his youngest daughter's cheek under the mistletoe. This was the time of year when things were hoarded and forgotten. I felt myself slipping down, lower and lower, onto the seat of the Buick; I felt myself slipping into a little pouch—a receptacle with a slit for an opening, such as you might find in the satin lining of a father's dress jacket, where an old ticket stub, pale blue and rubbed to illegibility and softness, had co-existed since the dawn of time with a foreign coin of mysterious denomination.

The Mountie slowed the car, staring ahead, and I saw, for the first time, his gaze tighten, as if drawn on purse strings—he was looking at our house, and I wondered what it looked like to him. Did the stone pillars holding the porch roof aloft impress him with their weight, or could he see the delicate roots of creeper digging in, loosening the mortar? Could he hear that constant powdering, or the moaning sound as thousands of shingles were pried up by fingers of ice? As we approached it in the dark, the house looked as it must have looked years earlier: big and important, a place where people who had money lived. A shape hurried from window to window, moving towards the back door. Was it Mama? The porch light switched on, revealing her body of twigs and froth—I realized that I didn't want the Mountie to come inside; I didn't want a stranger to watch love's failures flying around our rooms like a shower of needles and pins.

"Sweetheart!" Mama said. "Oh, let me look at you!"

But then she grabbed me and hugged me tight, so that it wasn't me she was looking at but the night behind me, filled with its winds and perilous stars—with saints and crackpots and criminals, all of those people who, in their dark clothing, consumed God's attention.

"We've been so worried about you," Mama said.

The Mountie edged past the clot in the doorway that was me and Mama, and I could hear him setting things down on the kitchen floor.

"Mom, I'm cold," I said.

"Of course you are, darling."

I felt her fingers reluctantly slipping away. Out of the corner of my eye I could see a wire plant hanger padded with sphagnum moss swinging from the porch eaves. "I love you, Mama," I said, as we walked inside. Just for a second I could smell almonds—the hand lotion she had used ever since we were little children, Willie—and I thought my heart would break open then and there, a tight bud exploding into petals.

The Mountie stood near the refrigerator, his hand half-way to his mouth. Was he hiding something? Or was he succumbing to the process of petrifaction, which appeared general? The 1956 calendar, with its picture of a very large horse-drawn sleigh heading for a very small opening in a covered bridge, still hung where I remembered over the plate rail; a ball of gray yarn connected by a strand to an incomplete gray sleeve cast onto a knitting needle, reaching across the table—was it possible that this was the same sleeve Mama'd been knitting three months ago? Was it possible that when Daddy appeared I would notice that one of his arms was a wing, that he'd been unassisted by his wife in making the transformation from animal to human?

"My baby," Mama said. "My poor baby."

"I'm all right," I said. "Really."

"But you're thin as a rail." She lifted her hand and touched my face. "This world is a mess," she said. "Nothing makes sense anymore." Wearily she yanked open the refrigerator door, on which someone had taped the postcards I'd sent back from Labrador—the mission buildings of Hebron, enormous and fanciful as dressage stables; a herd of caribou browsing on lichen; a bright yellow arctic poppy cupping a clear drop of water. She took out a jar of mayonnaise and held it up. "Your nana used to make mayonnaise," she said. "Every afternoon at four-thirty we'd have tea, with cucumber sandwiches. She'd salt the cucumbers first, to draw out the moisture. You and Willie were just little things then. But Willie had to have her tea black, like a grown-up."

"I'm sorry, Mama," I said. And I *was*, even though I didn't know what for.

"But she wouldn't eat the sandwiches," Mama said, sniffling. "She had this idea that the seeds would grow in her stomach. Where did she ever get an idea like that?"

I watched the Mountie watching Mama. His judgment is so harsh, I thought; her narrow, speckled hands shook as she sliced meat loaf.

"Jojo Melnicoff," I said, and Mama nodded.

"He's married now, you know. To some girl he met at Hampton Beach." She turned to the Mountie. "You'll have to forgive me," she said, "for not fixing you a proper supper. These last few days—"

"No need to apologize," the Mountie said, although I suspected that he didn't forgive any of us for anything. He leaned back against the counter on his elbows, his hair lapping down over his forehead in one thick, russet-colored leaf.

"Sweetheart," Mama said, "there's something you should know. Your sister's here."

"Willie?" In the place where the two halves of my rib cage almost met two claws dipped in and pressed down hard. "Where is she?" I asked.

The Mountie was staring intently upward at the tin ceiling. Even though he was standing right there in the room with us, the impression he gave was of an eaves-dropper.

"In the west room," Mama said, and then, when I dropped my fork onto my plate and began walking towards the door—wildly drawn in your direction, as if I were beating my way through alder swales at night, drawn by a faraway pinprick of fire—she stuck out her arm and I caught there. "She hasn't been very well," Mama said. "She's—" And then she paused, confused. "Kitty, she's cut off all her beautiful hair. How could she? How could she go and do a thing like that?"

I found you sitting tucked into the corner of the sofa, your feet bare and side by side on the mossy cushion, your head tipped back, revealing a white channel of skin from throat to neck, the skin rippling and liquid as you swallowed. You were asleep. I stood in the doorway, looking in, trying to make out the details of you, but the room was dark. A fire had burned down to coals in the fireplace, assigning to objects that dark glow that seems to come from the objects themselves, from that secret place inside objects where stored-up heat is transformed into light. You were wearing a pale pink bathrobe and, if possible, you were more beautiful than ever: your hair clung in a cap of goldish-red feathers to your skull; your skin was the thinnest wash of moonlight on snow, the snow across which the rabbit leaps at the sound of approaching footsteps.

I walked into the room cautiously. I didn't want to wake you up. So long as you were asleep, I thought, you were mine, as if I were the one asleep, and you were the dream sister, the one whose love was uncomplicated and durable, bending down to wake me with a kiss. I tiptoed across the rug, being careful not to step on the sheets of newspaper scattered randomly around, nor to set them rustling with my body's light breezes. You made a little noise in the back of your throat, like a stone dropping into water. Why had I ever thought that I'd be happier far away from you?

In the blackest corner of the room something stood up, expelling breath. I remained perfectly still, willing whatever it was to go away. Why was it that every time I caught a glimpse of happiness something had to rise up, unbidden, casting a length of shadow across the landscape? In this case it was Daddy, tall and drowsy; he came to stand in front of me, holding an empty highball glass in one hand. His hair was pressed flat against one side of his head, springing outwards little by little as I watched; lit from beneath, his face was anything but nice-looking, like Godpapa Drosselemeyer's in the *Nutcracker*, on the verge of calling forth infernal life from toys.

"Hi, Dad," I said shyly, and he continued to stand there, shy and frightening, like a boy my own age, trying to figure out whether or not to ask me to dance.

"Kathleen," he said, "stringbean." And holding the glass aloft and to one side, he gave me a short, fierce hug.

"Mama said Willie's been sick," I whispered.

"You might say that," he said, but it was obvious he didn't want to elaborate. "What's important to me is that you're home in one piece. If we'd only known—" He looked at me and then over at his empty glass. "Don't go away," he said, "I'll be right back."

I watched as he wandered off towards the kitchen, blowing tuneless notes from his mouth—the sound that he always made when on the trail of alcohol, as if to make his obsession appear casual. What had I expected? Wreaths on the doors, everyone garbed in black, weeping inconsolably into handkerchiefs? I sat down opposite you in one of the wing chairs and waited.

It took a long time: the coals got cold, unlocking into ash; then the moonlight from outdoors entered the room, like the water that seeps out of rocks, encasing the tables and chairs in glass. At some point Daddy returned to tell me that it was very late, that Mama had made up the bed in the spare room for the Mountie—whom he referred to irritably as Sergeant Preston—and that he thought it was time for all of us to get some sleep. "It's been a long day," he said, but I shook my head.

"I'm just going to sit here a while," I told him. I was wondering what, exactly, was a long day?

There was something restless, like intelligence, circling the room. From moment to moment an object or a face would swell up into prominence and shine: the bright ovals of your fingernails clasped across your stomach; Daddy's glass, from the bottom of which bubbles rose in a string, as if the glass contained something alive; the quick, flat ticking of the clock. When Daddy bent down to kiss me good night, a yellow pencil fell from his breast pocket, landing in my lap. He obviously didn't trust himself to remove it.

"Don't stay up too late," he said, and then he was gone.

Still, I didn't wake you. You moved around a little and your robe fell open, revealing a nightgown thin and grayish as newsprint, with a knob or a paw of the stuff lodged between your breasts. I could see your nipples—dot dot—and, when you raised one arm to rest it behind your head, I could see the tuft of red hair under your armpit, which I understood to be evidence of your strange new life in Philadelphia. Aside from the fact that you slept so soundly, I couldn't make out any signs of illness on your body. Your breathing was regular; I moved closer to peer at the blue vein of your temple, through which the blood appeared to be moving; you smelled sweet, like melon—like a slice of melon sprinkled with a little bit of salt.

"Willie," I whispered. "Hey, Willie!"

And then, like two wings, your eyelids lifted, and there was the flight of your vision rising to meet my face.

"Oh, Kitty," you said. "Thank God. I was beginning to think I'd never see you again." Your arms floated upwards, white and soft from out of the pink sleeves of your robe, and the next thing I knew we were hanging on to each other on the sofa, hanging on so tight that I could feel the sharp points of your bones, the mysterious clusters of bony tissue under the soft flesh of your breasts.

"I missed you," I said.

"Me, too," you said.

Do you remember? My glasses fell off and one of the earpieces broke, so that for days afterwards I walked around looking lopsided and vaguely threatening, like the man with the American flag pinned to his lapel, the one who used to accost us on the streets of Conway with his stories of how he had been cheated by the patent office. But, for now, the effect of my glasses falling was to turn the whole room into a blue and shifty aquarium, where the only thing I could see was you, your face swimming back a short distance from my own.

"You look so pretty," you said. "One of these days you should get contacts." You ran your hand over my forehead, smoothing the bangs away from my eyes. "It's a perfect heart-shaped face," you said. "If I had a widow's peak like that, I'd make sure everyone could see it."

I ducked my head down, so that the bangs fell back into place. "I hate it," I said. "It makes me look like a raccoon."

"Oh, Kitty," you said, and you smiled your off-center little smile. A door slammed shut upstairs, making the walls around us come to life in an internal drizzle of plaster dust; I could hear the crystal droplets of the wall sconces in the dining room softly chime; in the cellar the furnace expelled a single loud *houf!* "No one's told me," you said, "what happened. You don't have to talk about it if you don't want to."

I shook my head. "It's okay," I said. But then I didn't know what to say. For a moment I felt as if I was the one who'd gobbled up Grandfather, and that now, in a lump, he was trying to get out.

"You saw him die, didn't you? God, it must have been awful. I can't even imagine what it would be like to see someone die."

He was there, right at the back of my throat—the pared-down, essential version of Grandfather; a slick, damp finger —negotiating the final bent turn into my mouth.

"All I can get out of Dad," you said, "is that Grandfather 'passed away.' The Mouse Queen's lips, as usual, are sealed."

The two hands of the clock came together like clappers.

"Kitty, are you all right?" you asked.

You bent forward, concerned, just as I jumped up, my hands pressed against my mouth—there seemed to be wavering coronas of green light radiating out from each of the doorways through which I ran, transmitting to me the prickling ice and heat of nausea. By the time I got to the kitchen, you were right behind me. You held on to my shoulders as I leaned over the sink, throwing up on top of the mismatched plates with their smears of ketchup and crumbs of meat loaf, the cutlery white with congealed fat, the saucepans and glasses and the several bloated noodles. Tears sprang from my eyes. I think I really expected to see him lying there, viscous and tiny on his back, his face black and shrunk like a prune.

"I'm sorry," you said. "God, Kitty, I didn't mean to upset you."

"It wasn't you," I said. I straightened up and wiped my face with the dish towel, which smelled sour, like the inside of my mouth. The truth is, I felt much better. "I'm glad I didn't eat a big dinner," I said, and then I started to giggle.

"Listen," you said, "maybe you'd better go to bed now."

"I don't think so," I said. I sat down on one of the chairs, because laughter was forming in every part of me; I pointed at the sink, laughing wildly. "I think what I'd better do is wash the fucking dishes."

I turned on the faucet, and the water, brownish at first, jumped out in separate, noisy bursts, like a companion joining me in my hysteria.

"Cut it out, Kitty," you said, whereupon I selected a paring knife from amid the sink's foul soup, waving it around and around in the air.

"Cut what out? Cut what out?" I thought I was unspeakably funny.

I can't remember how you actually did it: removed the knife from my wet hand, turned off the water, and got me back into the west room, where you made me lie down on the sofa, propping one of Mama's hard little cushions—embroidered with a mean-looking parrot—under my head. In fact, all I can actually recall is your fingers skimming along my brow, the *shh shh* of your incantation, the soft wind of your breathing. I thought it was spring, and that a window was open, the wind, spangled and momentary, a trapeze artist preparing, at last, to leap.

When I woke up you were gone. I could just make out the time on the clock's face. Four-thirty. Little pieces of my dream, two-dimensional and intricately shaped, shuttled through the cold space around me, some of them locking together: a cupped hand held a white ball with blue stars on it; the blue eye of a man stared out at me from between the fingers of a white hand; the marble folds of a robe shivered, quickening, lifting from beneath.

"Where are you?" I said. My body felt very weak and, with each breath I took I felt sad, the way I would after swimming in seawater. I knew that he'd come back; I knew that Rogni was somewhere in the house, looking for you. Maybe he had already found you. Maybe that was why you were no longer in the room with me. And I realized that the whole time I'd been away I hadn't thought of him, not even once. Was it possible that it had all been his idea: that marble shelf on which I'd perched for three months like Nana's goose girl, stupidly imagining that I was at the heart of the story, when, in fact, the real story was going on in another room of the house? A passionate and violent story, capable of disturbing the arrangement of the objects around me?

"How could you?" I asked.

I meant *you*, Willie.

Arms of you, voice of you, face of you, breath of you! You were my sister! How could it happen that my love for you would keep getting bigger and bigger? How could it happen that I would find myself flitting, finned and cool, through the thumping, fluent corridors of the house, as if my love for you were a thing external to myself—as if it were the only substance in which I could move or draw breath? On the second-floor landing I paused for a minute and checked my appearance in the mirror. Vanity is mortality's sidekick. But I don't have to tell you that, do I? Nor do I have to tell you that I caught, out of the corner of my eye, the briefest glimpse of a face, like dough left to rise too long, collapsing in on a bean-shaped mouth.

"Go ahead," a voice said. "It'll serve her right. Why do you think I made two of you, anyway?"

I turned around, fast; all I could see was the empty stairwell, although I thought I could smell the faintest odor in the air, glutinous and porridgy.

The third-floor hallway was intermittently lit with moonlight wherever a door stood open. It was like walking past clipped boxwood and statuary in a formal garden at night, and I felt as if, turning to enter any one of those rooms, I might find stretching before me other long passageways—I might surprise, with my presence, amorous couples, their faces washed clean of personality. Each dark interval, as I walked through it, was like an intake of breath, the suspended moment preceding great activity.

Of course, I found you where I expected to find you: in *our* room, sitting cross-legged on the bed, looking out into space.

"Kitty!" you said. "What are you doing here?" You moved over a little, making room for me, patting the mattress with your hand. Do you remember? The ticking was hardly dented where your body'd been.

"Where is he?" I asked.

You smiled and shook your head. "You know, I've always loved the way you look when your mouth's hanging open. Come here. Have a bowl of gruel for old times' sake."

I saw them then, the two pink bowls, still sitting side by side on the dresser. Why hadn't Mama taken them back downstairs?

"Dr. Chun," you said, "explained the whole orphan thing to me. My shrink," you elaborated, as I continued to stand there, my arms pasted to my sides, staring.

"Willie, where is he?"

"Where is who?" you asked. You got up, arching your back, and went over to the dresser, where you set one bowl inside the other—I realized I'd never seen them that way before. "The part we can't figure out," you said, "is which one of us thought it up. You or me? Kitty or Willie?"

"I asked you a question," I said.

"And I answered it," you said. "Besides, I don't know why you're getting so angry. This is my house, too, in case you've forgotten. I can go anywhere I want to in it."

I looked around. The windowsills were thick with dust, above which, on the panes, plumes of frost arose. A mouse scampered past within the walls, its little feet scrabbling for purchase. Everything seemed to have a moral lesson attached to it, an unfurling scroll such as one sees in medieval paintings. I went over to the northward-facing window and tried to look out. Vaguely, through the frost, I could see the moon, perched like one of the glacial boulders of Labrador high on top of Mt. Chocorua. "He was here, wasn't he? You can tell me, Willie. I know he's been here."

It was a shock to feel your arm circling my waist. "Kitty," you said, "I really don't have any idea what you mean. Really." Each of your fingers, distinct and individual, pressed in on my skin as you tried to pull me away from the window. Miss Pinky, I thought, Pointer, Thumbkin, bearing out the message of one of Mrs. McGuire's endless songs. "Unless it's that hearty fellow in the uniform I saw wandering towards the bathroom? If so, you're barking up the wrong tree. He's all yours, if you want him." Your head came to rest on my shoulder, and then I felt the slow rotation of your face towards my neck, and the pressure of small, wicked kisses where the pulse leaped. "I only have eyes for you," you said.

But I pulled away. "What I *mean*," I said, "is the angel."

"Oh," you said. "That again."

"Don't pretend, Willie. I saw you. I saw you together on the raft, right before I left for Labrador."

Wearily you stretched out, on your back, on the bed. "Look at that," you said, "there's a stain up there that looks just like Africa. I don't remember that. It must be new."

"Don't change the subject, Willie," I said.

"Willie," you repeated. "How did I ever get a name like that? Willie." Then you rolled over on your side, facing me. Your eyes were stitched shut along the seams of your lashes, but there were tears getting out anyway, dripping onto the mattress. "How could I be changing the subject when I don't even know what it is?"

"You and Rogni on the raft," I said. "That's the subject. Before you found the boat, remember?"

"The boat?" Your eyes opened, wet and shining. "No, I don't remember any boat. Listen, Kitty," you said, "I'm not trying to be obtuse. If you want to know the truth, I've been having a rough time myself lately. I mean, hasn't it occurred to you that I'm supposed to be in Philadelphia?"

"Sure," I said. "But I thought, you know, that it was because of what happened." When I was little I had a puzzle composed of cubes, the faces of which each had printed on them parts of six different scenes: the transformation from Little Miss Muffet to, for instance, Little Boy Blue was always gradual and marked by an incongruity of detail, as if the boy asleep under the haystack remained haunted by an earlier memory of an enormous spider, dangling in the summer air above the small and distant cows. My anger began to change into confusion; the confusion into something else. I could feel a fissure opening in my brain, out of which a sleek, fearsome thing dragged itself up to look around. "I thought you were here because of what happened to Grandfather," I said.

"Well, you're wrong. But how could I expect you to know what's been going on? Let's face it, Kitty, our parents are not exactly communicative."

"Mama said that you haven't been well."

I wasn't prepared for your reaction. All of a sudden you sat straight up and punched your fists down, hard, into the mattress, sending forth a surprising amount of dust. My point of view shifted, so that I no longer was focusing just on your face but on your thin torso within the context of the room—a pink stalk wavering, solid and alive, against the blue currents of the walls, above the blue floor where the darker shadows eddied, pooling here and there into the bewitching prints of your feet. "Not well," you said. "Jesus Christ! Can you believe it? For your information, Kitty, I'm in disgrace. For your information, I went and got myself pregnant." You pointed, but I couldn't tell if you were pointing to your stomach or farther down—I couldn't tell if you were indicating cause or effect.

"You mean you're going to have a baby?" I asked.

"That's not what I said." As suddenly as you'd sat up, you flopped back again onto the mattress.

"I knew it," I said. The words had a bitter flavor to them as they came out of my mouth and, with their utterance, I felt strangely purged, as if my heart, without that brackish coating, was now the newest thing on the face of the earth. It was new, Willie, and already there was a little arrow through it.

"You knew what?"

"What I've been trying to tell you," I said. "About you and Rogni."

Then you sighed—such a tender, soft sound. I thought what I was hearing was the voice of the baby. "It's a mystery to me," you said, "why I'm the one in this family who's supposed to be a little *unglued*. Willie's always the one with the shaky grip on reality. God, Kitty. Sometimes I think if it weren't for me—"

"But I saw you," I said.

"Come here." Your arm reached out; in a tusk of light it raced towards me. "I want you to listen to me. I want you to lie down here beside me, and then I want you to listen. Okay?"

"Okay," I said.

Your eyes were looking right into mine, but I knew you were seeing something else. Someone else's eyes? Or an entire landscape, the sun a tiny peephole in the sky through which God's vision poured beneficent and warm, across two bodies rocking together? Rocking and rocking.

"I don't think I can stay awake too much longer," you said, "so I'm going to make this fast. For a while now I've been, well, in*volved* with Peter Mygatz. You remember him, don't you?"

"Sure," I said. "Your birthday party."

"That's right. I'd almost forgotten. He gave me a necklace. I wonder what ever became of it?"

How could I tell you, now, that I'd found the necklace one day where you'd hidden it in the secret drawer of your jewelry box? How could I tell you that, in a private ceremony, I'd wrapped it up in toilet paper and buried it in the woods, digging a hole with a soup spoon—scooping the moist and leafy soil away from the pervasive tree roots, chanting? "What do you mean," I asked irritably, "you'd almost forgotten?"

"Give it a rest, Kitty. Do you want to hear this or don't you?" You yawned so that I could see the whole inside of your mouth, the pink stamen of your tongue quivering.

"Go ahead," I said.

"At first it was just a crush," you said. "I mean, I was a kid and he was this grown-up. It was very pure. Sometimes we'd hold hands, stuff like that, but always in a very pure way. I used to go visit him in that bread truck where he lived. Over near the bog."

"I know," I said. "It had a window cut right in the side. You could see his table and chairs."

"I never realized we were being watched," you said. "I wish you'd told me. At least I would've had a good reason for feeling paranoid."

"But it was always empty. I just looked in. I never saw anything."

You raised your eyebrows, and it occurred to me that even your skepticism was enchanting. "He was into being a holy person," you said. "You know, we spent a lot of time sitting face to face, cross-legged, breathing. Peter wasn't into sex. Or, at least, that's what he said. But then, after I moved down to Philadelphia, he began coming to see me. The Brezinskis were very enlightened; Ozzie, especially—he liked to think of himself as a liberated kind of guy, if you get my drift. And everything changed. Sometimes it was all I could do to remain upright at the *barre*."

I saw, for the first time, a flat, rose-colored mole on your left temple; I wanted to kiss you, right *there*, but I was afraid. "The man puts his penis in the woman," I said, and you looked at me, your drowsiness tightening, momentarily, into interest.

"Well, yeah," you said. "But—"

"It makes her rattle and rattle," I continued, watching you closely. "It spreads out everywhere."

For a second your face was surprised, and then you closed your eyes. "What happened up there in Labrador, Kitty?" Your arms folded lightly around me. "Did you fall in love? You can tell me."

"That's not what I'm talking about," I said.

"You *did*, didn't you? You did fall in love in Labrador. I should have guessed. Why do I always forget how much alike we are?"

"It was before," I said. "Don't pretend you don't know what I'm talking about. He told me he touched you. He was your lover."

"Peter told you that?"

"No!" I shouted. "Not Peter. I don't even know Peter. Rogni told me. When you'd be dancing. I was supposed to keep him away from you, but I couldn't."

"Jesus," you said, "I don't believe this. Kitty, listen to me. The only person I've ever slept with is Peter. Period. Why do you keep harping on this Rogni? Don't you think it's time you grew up? I mean, if there was such a thing as an angel, don't you think our lives wouldn't be in such a big mess as they are now?"

"He's real," I said.

"I wish you were right."

"I am," I said.

Then you shook your head from side to side, slowly. "Oh, Kitty," you said, and as I watched, your face grew liquid,

with recognitions swimming in dim schools under its surface. "Except, you know, it's funny you would say that,"
you whispered, "about the dancing. It's funny you would
say that."

I could see sleep branching through you. "Willie," I
pleaded, "not yet. Wake up. Please."

"I was really good, wasn't I?" Your voice was so soft I
could hardly hear it, extending in silver rings around me,
lapping softly against the far-off walls of the room. "Maybe
you mean that? A long long time ago?"

And then you were gone—your arms slipped, little by
little, away.

I got up and went over to the dresser. The bowl that I
picked up was full of gruel, and I carried it back with me,
carefully, to the bed. Downstairs I could hear people
moving around: conversations with the undercurrent of
nighttime emergency, power failures, sickness, doors left
unlocked, tempting in all things foreign. "Her bed's empty,
too," I heard Mama say.

Soon, I thought, they would be up here, their chests
rising and falling; soon the room would close in on us, like
fingers around a firefly. To the curve of your lips I lifted an
invisible spoon. I could see it: my hand guiding that spoon
slowly through space, bearing that spoon slowly towards
your closed mouth, which, as I got closer, began to open.

"Willie," I said. "That's right. That's right. Now
swallow."

You were sound asleep, the castle of your face lit from
within by secret assignations. Someone had to feed the
baby. So tiny—it was just a tiny human baby and it didn't
know anything! I thought of it, curled up in its moist nest;
I was sure it was a girl. "Open wide," I coaxed, and she
stirred. "Just your mouth," I implored, because I realized
that she didn't know how it might be a dangerous thing to
open her eyes, how the whole room was dancing with shining bits of her mother. She didn't know how it might

happen that a fleck would fly into her dark blue eye, changing the way she would see the world forever.

"Don't worry," the Nurse-of-Becoming said, "I've got a whole pot full of this stuff. Don't you worry, dearest beloved, there's more where that came from."

For the first time I noticed her forearms: muscular and hairy, like a sailor's. I noticed them and I began to scream. That's why I was screaming—screaming and screaming—when Mama and Daddy ran into the room. That is why I was shielding your body with my body. But I wasn't protecting *you*, Willie. I thought that my days of protecting you were over.

The morning was clear. I remember that: how the light seemed to have been diluted to unbearable thinness and clarity; how it seemed to have its source in something farther away than the sun, so that the sun was just one more object illuminated by it. By the time I finally came downstairs, the kitchen was empty, littered with the signs of earlier, purposeful activity. The smell of coffee lingered, mixed with the smell of toast; steam chuffed out of the cast-iron kettle on the wood stove and, on the table, I saw the burnt stems of several wooden matches, arranged by someone—ironically?—in the shape of a simple house such as a child might draw. Where was everyone? I stood still, listening, holding my glasses in place with one hand, as if greater accuracy of vision might help me hear better. But the house was unnaturally quiet. If there were people in it, they were hiding, holding their breath, trying not to laugh.

I scrambled myself an egg, put on my parka, and went out to sit on the porch. I wanted to think things over. The egg was cooked perfectly, just the way I liked it: dry and rubbery. With each bite I imagined the new weight it added to my body. Every little bit, I thought, would be important, if I was going to be able to win the fight about the baby. It had taken me a while, Willie, but eventually it had sunk in—I realized that your own plans did not include motherhood. I kept thinking about a play I'd been in in third grade: a play about the Pilgrims, about lives so innocent that, remembering them, it took my breath away. What a hoax! "Fear not, love," I had recited, cradling the Tiny Tears doll that was my child, as the stage floor presumably tilted up and down beneath us, caught in the large swells of a storm. "Fear not, the strong winds will help us. They will fill the great white sails that carry our ship along."

Where was Rogni? Why had he come to peek at me through the meshes of my dream, if not to tell me something? My brain rose up on a string out of the top of my head. Was there a normal world just a hairsbreadth to the left or the right of the one I was in, where a normal Kathleen sat on a porch glider, chewing? I thought that *that* Kathleen must be a clear thinker, a girl of wonderful substance and insight. If I moved a little, could I make the two Kathleens overlap? I tried but, if anything, I felt lighter, dizzier. There was a layer of snow covering the meadow, and I could see, off to one side, hints of Mama's garden: tomato stakes twined around with black, wiry vines; two Hubbard squashes, burst and pearly, at the foot of the bean poles.

A blue Rambler pulled up in the driveway and lurched to a stop by the back door, sending forth a spray of gravel. The impression was incongruent and romantic, as if a galloping horse had been suddenly reined in—from the driver's side my heart sank to see pop out the fat body of Mrs. McGuire's nephew. He saluted me briefly, and then floated, with surprising grace, around the car, to open the door for his aunt. She emerged, feet first, her shoes protected from the snow by transparent rain boots, her skinny legs encased in long johns gray from many washings.

Wobbling, she clamped on to her nephew's arm, adjusting with her free hand the placement of some undergarment, the image of which I did not want to entertain.

"I will be ready to leave at four o'clock, Patrick," she said. "If it is not too great an inconvenience, I would appreciate it if, for once, you could be on time." Then she looked up and saw me. "Kathleen! My darling girl! Ah, your poor mama and daddy have been beside themselves with grief." Picking up speed, as if the mere sight of me had caused to surge through her crisp bones fresh new marrow, she approached. "I have done what I could, my precious," she said significantly, crossing herself. "The blessed Virgin and her own sweet Son have been with you, night and day, even while the Evil One filled your mortal soul with foul longings."

As she folded me in her swift pincers I could hear her intestines whining, a protracted squeal as she broke wind. "Hello, Mrs. McGuire," I said, pulling back.

"Ah," she said, "of course. I am forgetting how long it takes for the evil to work its way out. My slightest touch is like fire, is it not, Kathleen? We must be patient. We must search the house from top to bottom, my darling, for if I'm not mistaken, there will be a darning needle working its way through the feathers of a mattress. There is no end to the trickery!"

This torture might have gone on indefinitely, had not the kitchen door swung open, revealing Mama, a rolling pin in her hand, a hand-shaped print of flour on her baggy chino trousers. Was it possible that she was wearing Daddy's pants? "Thank heavens," she said. "I've got a house full of people and Nick is down with some bug."

Sure, I thought. Some bug.

Mrs. McGuire hefted the straw beach bag in which she carried the smaller tools of her trade—a genuine chamois cloth, a can of Pledge, the skull of a snapping turtle, a Bible —and walked into the house. "It was a full moon last night,

Mrs. Mowbrey," I heard her saying, "but I shall see what I can do."

The kitchen had become, as if in the twinkling of an eye, a populous place. The Mountie stood in the center of the room, his arm raised and bent, a quarter balanced just below the elbow joint. "Steady, steady," he was saying, and then he jerked his whole arm forward, catching the coin as it swooped through the air, neatly, in his hand. I could see how he blushed with pleasure at his accomplishment, casting glances in your direction, hoping against hope for some sign of admiration.

You sat impassive in your sea-green sweater and blue jeans, with your feet looped back around the legs of the chair, your cheek resting in the palm of one hand. "Bravo," you said, rolling your eyes, "bravo."

"It's not so hard," the Mountie said. He sat down at the table beside you, crossing an ankle over a knee. "All it takes is a little practice. Here, let me show you." Then he made the mistake of reaching out for your arm—for a moment I thought you were going to punch him right in the middle of his wide, thick lips.

"I'll stick with dancing," you said. Slyly you looked at me, grinning. "There's always a thicket of men," you said, "slowing things down. Know what I mean?"

The Mountie's cheeks were so pink that they appeared to have been rouged indiscriminately, like the cheeks of vain old women. He rooted around in his pants pocket, finally locating the keys to the rented car. "Well," he said, "it's been a pleasure meeting all of you, but I guess I'd better get going if I'm going to catch that afternoon flight to Goose."

Mama turned from the counter where she'd been valiantly trying to assemble, out of rags and tatters of dough, something akin to a pastry shell. "Are you sure I can't persuade you to stay?" She held up an apple, in a sad imitation of flirtatious behavior. "I've never known a man who could resist a nice piece of apple pie."

"Aren't you forgetting about Dad?" you asked.

"It's a tempting invitation, Mrs. Mowbrey," the Mountie said, "but I'm going to have to say no." He stood up, dangling the keys—I could tell he was trying to get your attention. "There's a low-pressure system moving in. Your sister, here, can tell you what that means." Awkwardly he began moving his feet, but he went nowhere, like a band member getting ready to march. "I know what you're going through. I remember what it was like after my wife's father died. A family needs time alone. Of course, they were very close. Very close."

"It's not an easy time for any of us," Mama said solemnly. "He was a good man."

"Oh, come *on*," you moaned.

Mama went over and took the Mountie's hand. "I just want to thank you," she said, "for all you've done. If it hadn't been for you, I wouldn't have my little girl back, safe and sound."

"Just doing my job."

Somehow, inch by inch, he had made his way to the door. I summoned up my courage, opening my mouth to see whether the sentence I'd been mulling around would, at last, emerge. "Do you think," I said, "if you see Jobie, you could tell him Kathleen sends her love?"

"Aha," you said, "Jobie. I was right."

The Mountie gave the thumbs-up sign, smirking in your direction. "Far be it from me," he said, "to stand in the way of romance." But I guessed, even as he said it, that he was lying. I knew that he never talked to Jobie, except to warn him about the consequences of trapping out of season.

I can't actually remember the moment when the door closed behind him. What I can remember is how the bright winter sun turned the car into a thing hard to watch: formless and plutonic, it vanished down the driveway and, with it, the last difficult evidence of Labrador. We all watched it go. I could tell that all of us—even you, Willie—were nervous, wondering what would happen next.

"So," you said, "who's this Jobie?"

"Someone," I said. I could hear the dripping of ice from the eaves, that sweet music by which winter tempts us into thinking spring is coming, when it is months away. "I'm going out," I said, pulling on my parka.

"Kitty has a boyfriend," you said to Mama. "How about that? Now's the time for some of that motherly advice. You know, the kind you gave me. Just because it didn't work on me is no reason to stop trying."

"Willie, please."

My hands, in red mittens, looked just like two hearts. "I don't know when I'll be back," I said, glancing around the room. "Has anyone seen my binoculars?"

"Why don't you ask Mrs. McGuire? Maybe she's dipped them in blood, or thrown them down the well." You grinned and swallowed the last of your milk. "Around this place, anything's possible."

"Be careful, sweetheart," Mama said, and I heard you laugh.

"Well, except for that," you muttered.

I walked with a great sense of purpose—at least insofar as my legs were concerned—towards the lake. Out of the snow, on either side of the road, dead asters proffered their slender bracts of fluff. This was the precise stretch of road where, a long time ago, you'd told me the story of Christopher Columbus. "This road looks flat," you'd said, "but it isn't." I remembered how you'd described Columbus, a handsome man holding up an egg, confronting the court of Queen Isabella. "A lot of them laughed," you'd said, "but not the Queen. Which is a lucky thing for us."

It occurred to me now that maybe the people who'd

laughed had been grown-up people with children—people who wanted nothing more than to protect their children from finding themselves, one day, poised in boats on the edge of the world, where everything stopped to be replaced with air.

The trees loomed up on either side as the road began to descend slightly, a neck dipping down to drink. In Labrador, I thought, I was the one who loomed above the trees: the birch trees there were no taller than my fingers, and their leaves were the size and shape of my baby fingernails. Here the trunks of the trees gave off heat, so that where each one of them disappeared into the snow there was a circular declivity, a place a person could reach into to draw out a handful of damp needles. I saw that a deer had been walking around, leaving the prints of its hooves, shaped like your lip prints on tissue. For a deer, I guessed, there was no obsession greater than hunger. I didn't think that they desired us—even when their eyes widened as if in recognition—to find their bodies beautiful. I walked lightly, on the tips of my toes. The sun was getting smaller and the day more cold, releasing spirits out of bottles; winds swarmed through the high-up branches of the trees, disturbing the regular pattern of shadows across the road. I could hear the soft tearing loose and dull fall of deadwood, deep in the forest, followed by random crepitations, and then, just for a second, apprehensive silence.

The forest opened its mouth, Willie. It opened its mouth and I walked in among the columns of the trees, the dark grooves in their bark extruding ice and the sorry, predictive smell of pencil shavings. Huge and motionless, they consigned all hints of agitation to their twirling green heads, as I made my slow way through the knee-high snow. Ahead of me I could see the lake, scarves of snow lifting and lowering across its frozen surface, revealing patches of black.

Now I was walking down the glassy tunnel of shrubbery that led from the forest to the dock. Pebbles were visible here, and smooth small rocks, the ones on which, in the summertime, you could stub your toes. But this was January: faint shells of ice encased them, and they crackled under my feet. The closer I got to the lake, the grayer the world became: a single, round cloud had flown over the sun. I could see, when I finally came out into the open, that there were more clouds to the west—larger, darker— and I thought, It's going to snow.

I sat down on the dock, reached into the pocket of my parka, and pulled out the Mars bar I'd been saving for this precise moment. The chocolate smelled wonderful. In fact, it smelled so wonderful that the taste was a disappointment, infected, as it was, with the flavor of paper and cardboard. I was sick and tired of being disappointed, Willie. I heaved the thing away from me and then watched as the first flakes of snow began to cover it up. When I couldn't see it anymore I felt better.

Far out, probably at the lake's center, where the raft would be once the summer people arrived, I thought I could make out a more concentrated and substantial form than that assumed by the falling snow. A man? From time to time the wind quieted, and I could see that it was, indeed, the figure of a man, seated on a drum-shaped object. I pulled up the hood of my parka and began to walk out onto the ice towards him, listening all the while for the sound of cracking below me—the sound that, by the time you could hear it, would no longer be a warning but the danger itself, spreading out under your feet. I walked faster and faster because, even before I could see the face, the great blue eyes and the slightly parted lips, I knew who it was. I passed seven tip-ups, their red flags dipped, meaning the fish had not yet taken the bait. I was running. I was running and, as I did, the flakes of snow got larger and larger, each flake original and distinct, testifying to the existence of a mind haunted by dreams of geometric precision.

Rogni was sitting on an upturned five-gallon bucket, jigging for perch. Around his feet there must have been forty or fifty of the things, their little golden bodies frozen solid, like the spilled currency of giants. Several of them, I noticed, had had the eyeballs plucked from their sockets, but this didn't upset me. I knew, from the boys in my class who went ice fishing, that the best bait for perch was the eyes of perch. "Tasty," Bobby Hallenbach had said, pretending to pop one in his mouth, whereupon the sissies among us had squealed.

"Kathleen," Rogni said. "At last." A line disappeared from his hand down a hole in the ice.

"What do you mean, 'at last'? You make it sound like all you've been doing is waiting around for me. Just waiting until I showed up. I don't understand. Maybe I'm awfully dumb, but I thought you were supposed to stay away from Willie. Wasn't that what you said?"

"You're right, Kathleen." He looked weary and, from time to time, it was almost as if I could see through his face, back to the shore where the cedars and willows gathered, where the dock stuck out like a tongue. "You're shivering," he said, and then he lifted a heavy black blanket from the ice and handed it to me. "Wrap yourself up in this."

"Hey," I said, "where did you get this?" It was the antique carriage robe that I remembered seeing in the barn, hanging over the wall of the box stall where your pony used to live. "I don't believe it," I said. "Why do you keep taking our things? If you're an angel, why do you need to take our things? I really don't understand."

I could see, rising to the surface of his body, a luminousness, the whole image sharpening into the points of a constellation I didn't know: northern, unmapped, an X. "I'm sorry, Kathleen," he said. "No matter how hard I might try, I could never *make* a blanket. Or a ring. Or a creature of flesh and blood. At least, not out of thin air. What I can do is arrange things into stories. And that's all."

"You can make a baby," I said. "Don't think I don't know about that."

Rogni bent his face close to mine and I could see the unmarked contours of his skin; a wave of heat broke from him then, scorching the tips of my eyelashes, even though they were protected by my glasses. "Remember," he said, "this is *your* image I've been created in. Prissiness doesn't become you, Kathleen. Believe me, I understand—better than I'd like to—what an unreliable thing a human body is. If it's taken me this long to get the story right, then it's *your* fault as well."

"No! You have help," I said.

"God has nothing to do with this," Rogni said. "I thought you knew that."

"I don't know anything," I said.

Which wasn't the truth. The truth was, I knew everything. I knew everything, Willie.

From the cusped blades of Rogni's shoulders feathers shot forth—the network of veins extending outward, beating against the cold walls of air. And then, at the very end of the row of tip-ups, a flag leaped, and from somewhere within the wide frozen world I thought I heard a scream.

"There was once," Rogni said, "a childless couple, well advanced in years, living together in a cottage on the edge of a great woods. This was in the second half of the twentieth century, when the men who ruled the world had lost sight of the dangerous connection between power and artifice. So, even though the woods in which this couple lived were no longer prowled by saber-toothed tigers, their lives were constantly in peril.

"Were they aware of this fact? They owned neither a radio nor a television set; they were sufficient unto themselves in the manner of the once-well-to-do, hiding all evidence of their decline from everyone but each other, where it took a form resembling their original passion: oblique and carnal. The old man, for example, bathed rarely; his wife let her gray hair grow long, and wore it unbound. Thus, even after they'd acquired the habit of sleeping in separate beds, strands of the woman's hair would detach from her scalp to drift across the man's face; the air she breathed would be thick with the smell of his body. Eros, once admitted through your door, will never leave. It is up to you whether you will make of this a good or a bad thing. It is up to you whether you choose to use Eros as a weapon.

"Of course, even the deadliest weapon gets dulled with repeated use: although the old man had inherited a fine and speculative mind, as the years went by, he spent more and more time bent over a Ouija board, watching as the planchette spelled out messages like LIFE IS BUT A DREAM. His constant companion was a yellow-crested cockatiel, which rode everywhere on his shoulder until, one bright morning in the wintertime, the old woman woke to find her husband stretched out glassy-eyed across the floor beside his bed. She yelled at him to get up, but she might as well have held her breath. The old man had had a stroke and, from that moment on, the cockatiel chose for its perch the back of his wheelchair, as if wary of contact with human infirmity.

" 'Wgghh, wgghh, WGGHH!' the old man would shout, to let his wife know that, even though he could no longer speak, he still had needs and desires.

"For her part—despite her occasional irritation at being summoned into the dark room where her husband sat, with his disturbingly sweet smell like milkweed—the old woman was happy. At last she could work on her needlepoint tapestry without the old man hanging over her shoulder, remarking on her choice of color or her sense of design. She had been stitching this tapestry for years, constantly revising the landscape, so that the saplings which had originally formed the lower border were now mature trees; through their branches you could just make out the surface of a river, likewise transformed over time from a restless flickering of silvers into a broad band, its depths hinted at in hues of umber and sable. Animals appeared on the far bank—otters and deer and fisher-cats—the old woman consigned their bones to the underbrush when they died. Their lives were so short! What did they know of old age's relentless self-absorption?

"In fact, only one creature in the tapestry had managed to resist the routine claims of mortality. This was a large fish, swimming closer and closer to the right-hand edge of the fabric, as if, at any moment, it might break loose and continue swimming through thin air. The old woman had loved this fish ever since it first leaped up out of the water, its emerald eye taking her in. She'd been a young woman then; when her husband turned to her in bed, she'd meet his ardor with a gaze like that of the fish. She had never wanted children. She was, in her own way, content.

"There was only one problem. Once it was certain that the couple was asleep, the cockatiel would sneak into the parlor, sidling up to the tapestry and snipping, with its hooked beak, the threads that were the body of the fish. It left the rest of the tapestry alone. At first, the old woman had wondered what was behind this destruction, but eventually, not too long after the old man's stroke, she caught the cockatiel in the act. Although she ordered it to stop, the bird ignored her, plucking out bits of wool and dropping them onto the floor.

"In the morning she confronted the old man with her discovery, at which the cockatiel widened its eyes in a parody of fear. 'Tattletale tit,' it said, 'your tongue shall be slit, and every little bird shall have a little bit.'

"Despite her hatred of the cockatiel, the old woman began to suspect that the fish's longevity was a product of the bird's tampering. Every day, as she re-created its sleek body, she tried to test this suspicion, devising complicated knots at the back of the tapestry, weaving in stronger threads. But no matter what she did, in the morning she would find a blank place where the fish had been.

"Late one evening, as she sat reworking the sky to include the Pleiades, there came a knock on the door. The old woman opened it to find, standing in front of her, two young girls. 'Good evening, granny,' said the shorter of the two. She was very pretty indeed, like a little elf. The taller one towered above her, and was wearing hip waders.

"The old woman invited them in. For a moment she forgot how strange she must look; for a moment she imagined herself to be enchanting, her long hair the color of ebony, her skin as clear and smooth as glass. These were the first children, in all the years she had lived there, to come inside her cottage. What were they doing in the woods? Had their parents abandoned them?

"The two girls walked cautiously across the threshold and peered into the darkness of the living room. Could they see the old man where he sat hunched over in his corner? Certainly they could hear him grumbling, softly at first, and then louder and louder. When the old woman offered them tea, they politely refused. It was so late, the taller girl explained. Her name was Lou, and her sister's name was Lina. They were lost, and wondered if the old woman could tell them how to get back to Owl's Head.

"Whereupon the cockatiel roused itself, flying up out of the shadows to land, all at once, on the coat tree. 'I am like a pelican of the wilderness,' it croaked, 'I am like an owl of the desert.'

"Had the girls actually jumped? The old woman laughed. If the bird was her affliction, at least it provided, as well, a source of amusement. She shook her fist at it, and then, quick as a wink, stuck out her index finger and jabbed it in the chest. 'An eye for an eye,' the bird commented, returning to its perch on the old man's chair.

"Lou clapped her hands. Such an unusual creature! But Lina, it must be admitted, was growing a little impatient. She pointed to the windows, black squares filled in with stars, and the old woman finally grew serious. Owl's Head, she informed Lina, was ten miles away, through the woods, on the other side of the mountain. The girls would never be able to find it at this hour. Every year children wandered into the woods, and no matter how long the parents searched, those children were lost forever. When the old woman took Lina's hand, she found that the skin was surprisingly cool. There was a bed in the attic, the old woman suggested. She could make it up, and then the girls would be able to get a fresh start in the morning. Lou and Lina glanced at each other in alarm, but the old woman was adamant.

"And so it happened that, despite their sense of foreboding, the sisters ended up on a lumpy mattress in a tiny room shaped like a slice of cake. Lina, who usually had trouble sleeping, fell asleep at once, whereas poor Lou remained awake for hours. To begin with, there was the sound of snoring: the low, rumbling snore of the old man; the squealing snore of his wife. And then, when she had finally become accustomed to this noise, and was starting to doze off, another noise took its place. A heated discussion was going on downstairs. Lou thought she recognized the voice of the cockatiel; the other voice was unfamiliar, deeper and slightly muffled.

" 'In the beginning, Sister,' said the bird, 'light was everywhere.'

" 'Ah, but you have never lived under the water, Sister,' replied the unfamiliar voice. 'There we swim among the souls of the drowned, and we teach our young to honor what is fleeting.'

" 'In the beginning,' repeated the bird, 'light was everywhere. And it did not have to bend around men.'

" 'Even the littlest ones among us come to understand, in time, how beautiful we are,' said the unfamiliar voice. 'You can take me apart as often as you like, but you will not change that fact.'

" 'You are a fool,' shouted the bird. 'And what about me? Look at my tongue: just like a tiny bud, is it not? You must believe my heart is no different. Incipience is a terrible burden, Sister.'

"The other voice grew fainter now, so that Lou could barely make out what it was saying. Something about the smell of river water? Something about a promise? The voice was sad, and the girl felt tears forming in her eyes.

"Eventually she fell asleep. When she awakened, she didn't know where she was. Indeed, the room in which she found herself was so small and lightless that, for a moment, she thought that she was dead and lying in her coffin. But there was someone else lying there beside her. Lina! And there was the old woman's head, sticking up through a trap-door in the floor!

"As Lou watched, the old woman's lips opened and closed, explaining that breakfast was almost ready. Her tone was pleasant enough, but there was something in her expression—a sly look—which made Lou wary. The moment the head vanished, Lou shook her sister awake. There was no question about it: the sooner they could get out of that place, the better. She didn't need to explain; Lina was in complete agreement. Still, it's unclear why Lou chose to keep secret what she'd overheard the night before.

"They found the couple sitting in the kitchen, the old woman pouring coffee into her husband's cup. An ordinary and cheerful kitchen, but Lou felt as if something was wrong. She couldn't quite put her finger on it: there was the sun, shining in through the window, lighting up pots and pans, plates and forks, Lina's thin white face, the old woman's pursed lips, the old man's bad eye, round like a blob of mercury. And then Lou realized what it was—the old man's cockatiel was gone.

"When she asked what had become of it, the old woman snapped her fingers. The cockatiel had flown away—just like that!—during the night. She didn't seem particularly affected by this event; if the old man was upset, it was impossible to tell. But, as the old woman pointed out, the food was getting cold. She urged the girls to sit down at the table, where they noticed, for the first time, a large fish, cut into four portions, on a serving platter. Such treats rarely came their way, the old woman told them. A gift? Lina wondered, but the old woman shook her head. She had caught the fish herself, that very morning.

"Of course, this was a lie. In fact, the old woman had taken the fish from Lou's wicker creel, which she had found on the front stoop in the middle of the night, when she opened the door to let out the cockatiel. She had stood there listening to the sound of its wings—the subtle sound of an expert magician shuffling a deck of cards—growing fainter and fainter, until she could hear nothing.

"Now, with great ceremony, the old woman set a portion of fish onto each of their plates. 'Eat it while it's hot,' she ordered. And then, just as Lina was hungrily reaching for her fork, the old woman grabbed her hand. 'There's one thing you ought to know,' she said, 'before you begin. There was a regent of Byzantium, the Empress Irene, whose reign was marked by discord. Still, upon her death she was canonized, because the faithful could remember only her devotion to graven images, to artifice.'

"Lou shivered. If she recognized the fish, she didn't say a word. You see, even though she was, at heart, an adventurous girl, she was also, by now, very frightened. She thought she could remember the last thing she'd overheard the unfamiliar voice saying the night before. 'My poor sister,' the voice had said, 'you have confused incipience with amorality, and I weep for you.'

"Lou opened her mouth to call out, but it was too late. As the old woman leaned forward, smiling, Lina took into her mouth a morsel of fish—that morsel in which was hidden the tiniest of bones—and, when she swallowed, that bone lodged itself unerringly against her windpipe, choking her to death.

"Some miles away, high up in an old poplar tree, perched

the cockatiel. It perched rigidly, the sun glinting off its yellow head; as the years went by, it began to gather dust until, in time, it toppled over and fell into a million pieces in the grass.

"'Awk, awk,' it said, 'gone but not forgotten.'"

It had stopped snowing, and a red light pressed out from behind the devious, twisting screen of branches at the lake's edge. I could feel nighttime's approach; already the hills to the west cast down across us their shadowy nets, preparing to trap the unwary—preparing to entrance a solitary child such as myself with promises of expansive silence, of deep purpose. The perch were covered up now, lying under a thin white sheet; the moon, likewise, was faintly visible under its sheet of clouds.

"I want to go home," I said.

"Bear with me, Kathleen," Rogni said. "I'm almost finished."

"But I'm scared," I said.

He motioned for me to stay where I was, and then he walked—an ordinary human figure again, in a dark coat dusted with snow—to the end of the row of tip-ups, where he drew from out of the hole in the ice a large, greenish-white fish, its sides and V-shaped tail dotted with red spots. "At least it's beautiful," he said, carrying it back to show it to me. He laid it down gently among the perch, and removed the hook from its mouth. "This is for you," he said.

"What do you mean?" I asked, horrified.

"A present. From me to you. Lake trout. The sweetest meat you can imagine."

He put the fish into my arms—it was already frozen, the lens of its eye opaque, withholding information.

"No!" I said. "How can you expect me to take this thing home?"

"A story is a story, Kathleen," Rogni said. "Trust me."

"*Trust* you? What are you, crazy?"

Under my feet I felt faint movement, as if the whole frozen disk that covered the lake had detached itself at the perimeter.

"I don't have time to argue with you, Kathleen," he said. "Take the fish. Does your mother know how to cook trout? High heat? Rapidly? An open pan?"

He was growing larger now and, as he did so, the many shapes of him struggled violently with one another for ascendancy. The monstrous—fiery cogs turning within a mantle sprouting eyes, erectile tissue, darting tongues—twitched, in an instant, into the beatific. I heard a crooning voice, saw the cream-colored arms of a woman lifting the lid of a blue box, out of which streamed stars, their bright faces regarding me hopefully. Hopefully, Willie, so that I drew closer, only to be repulsed by the overwhelming, mineral stink of metamorphosis. I thought I saw, for just a second, a white bear reared up on its hind legs, and then that shape was gone, and a hundred others swarmed in to take its place. Wherever Rogni's voice came from was rising up higher and higher into the darkening sky: it was becoming faded, disconsolate, like a memory of music: "A little salt? Pepper? Sweet butter?"

I cradled the fish in my arms and started to walk towards the shore. Abruptly the ice lurched under my feet, and then began its slow, horizontal rotation. It was as if I were trying to walk across the surface of a moving merry-go-round, but a merry-go-round empty of wide-nostriled horses and lacquered benches; of other children and the blurring, peripheral faces of happy mothers; of the chance to pluck, from thin air, a prize. I don't think, in all my life, I have ever felt so lonely. I was even tempted just to stand still, to allow myself to be launched, finally, fish in arms, into space. But, as you know, I didn't—by concentrating and picking up speed of my own to compensate, I managed to keep my balance. The closer I got to shore, the faster the ice moved, until, at the very last moment, I had to jump across a yard-wide gap filled with black waves, from off a wildly spinning plate.

When I landed, the wind got knocked out of me, so that by the time I looked back to where I'd been, all I could see was a thin thing coiling upwards through the sky, high above the gold and molten lake water. The fish, I was surprised to discover, was still locked in place within my arms. It was cold, chilling me even through the thickness of my parka; like any dead fish the smell it gave off aroused circumspection rather than appetite.

As I walked home I tried to figure out what to do. The clouds had dispersed into particles and vanished so that the moon was wholly visible, a full moon in a darkening sky. Such a difficult world, Willie, where the snow-covered road on which I walked was like your arm, reeling me in; where the fish that I carried was like a receptacle hammered out of metal—a valuable receptacle with a secret hidden inside. Just like you.

I can't remember at what point exactly I reached my decision. I think it might not have been until I turned in to the driveway and saw, as if for the very first time in my life, the windows of our house shining at me through the heavy arms of the pines. Was the choice between sustenance and retribution? I didn't think so, because the body of the fish itself was growing heavier and heavier, as if it carried a moral weight—the terrible gravitational field of doubt, out of which a single tiny feather tried to escape. The house increased in size. Believe me, what I chose was in the name of all things that were not Kathleen, that had their sources outside myself and that were, consequently, unfamiliar. What I chose was in the name of *you*, Willie. The house was now enormous, and I walked into it breathing hard, feeling my heart's consistent prodding of blood outwards, even to the tips of my fingers; feeling drop down around my feet the invisible garments of that faith in which I'd been clothed ever since the first time I'd heard Rogni's voice: they made puddles on the floor, the most ordinary puddles imaginable, reflecting nothing.

Everyone was in the kitchen: Mama at the stove, where steam rose out of many small pots; you sitting at the table playing solitaire, fending off the hissed advice of Mrs. McGuire, who sat opposite you, all dressed up and ready to go in her black coat and hat; Daddy at the counter, a newspaper flung into the air in front of him between his two fists.

"Kathleen," he said. "The prodigal returns." And then he whistled, admiringly, between his teeth. "Where did you get *that*?" he asked.

"What?" You set a seven of diamonds on top of an eight of clubs and got up, craning your long white neck to see. "I didn't know you knew how to fish," you said.

"I don't," I said. "A man gave it to me. An ice fisherman." I put the fish down on the table, its dorsal fin barely touching two exposed aces, and we all stared at it. The color had drained away during my walk; it was no longer beautiful, but it was certainly very large.

Mama ran her hand through her hair and looked at me, exasperated. "It'll never fit in the refrigerator," she said. "Maybe you could put it on the porch."

"What're you talking about, Constance?" Daddy asked. "We're going to eat it, right, Kitty?"

I stood looking at you. You were no longer interested in the subject of the fish: the expression on your face was strained and thoughtful, and you walked gracelessly to the sink, where you leaned forward to peer through the window, as if you were expecting someone.

"I can't imagine what's keeping Patrick," Mrs. McGuire said. "I told him four o'clock, did I not, Kathleen, and here it is five-thirty and still no sign of the boy. His sainted father, dead these twenty years, was no better—a month late, he was, for his own birth, so that his poor mama had swelled up to the size of a sea cow, and there was not a shoe this side of Sligo she could get her feet into."

I could see your back stiffen, the knobs of your knuckles whitening as you clamped down on the black rim of the sink. "Do you think," you said, "you could spare us the tales of childbirth?"

Mrs. McGuire ducked the pointy blade of her chin down into the place where the folds and pleats of her neck disappeared into the collar of her coat—it was an unconvincing display of servility. "Forgive me," she said. "If my tongue offend thee, pluck it out."

"Willie hasn't been herself lately," Mama said. "You'll have to excuse her."

"Ah," said Mrs. McGuire, "of course. It is hardly a week since the poor old man passed away, God rest his soul."

Little by little the fish was beginning to thaw out on the table, its contours softening in a pool of clear juices. I went over to the sink to get the sponge, and as I came up beside you, you put your arm around me and pulled me close. "Hey," you whispered, "I'm glad you're here."

"I'm glad I'm here, too," I said.

"If I can just make it through tomorrow," you said, nestling your small head down onto my big shoulder, pressing it in. "If I can just make it through tomorrow, everything'll be okay."

"What's happening tomorrow?" I asked. But I didn't have to hear your answer to know: tomorrow the little feather would be plucked out of your body; tomorrow you would be Willie-without-a-feather, and I would be

Kathleen-without-an-angel; tomorrow a whole glittering thread would be yanked loose from the fabric of our lives, and the residual pattern would either unravel into a kinked and colorful heap or assert itself, finally: two sisters seated together on a porch, smiling.

"So," Daddy said, "how about it? I can't remember the last time we ate fish for supper."

"Do fish sticks count?" you asked, nudging me.

Mama sighed. "What about the roast?" she asked.

"We can have that, too," Daddy said, pouring himself a tumbler full of Scotch. "We can eat our brains out."

"But I don't know how to *cook* it," Mama said.

Rustlings and squealings both external and internal accompanied Mrs. McGuire's decision to rise from her chair. Purposefully she drew pin after pin out of her hat, setting them down on the table in a pearl-headed cluster, like roe. "It has been many years, Mrs. Mowbrey, since I have seen a fish of such size and weight," she said, removing her hat and coat. "My dear husband, Angus McGuire, was a fisherman—for years he used to carry the head bone of a flounder in his vest pocket, and I have always thought that the consumption took ahold of him the day he lost that bone to Connor O'Toole in a card game. It was a fearsome thing to see, a big giant of a man like Angus with the flesh just melting off of him! Why, in the end he was no bigger than Willie here, and his hair the same shade of red."

As we watched, Mrs. McGuire lifted the fish and carried it over to the sink, where she ran it briefly under the tap. "I hope, Kathleen, that you did not step over the line?" Bending delicately at the waist, like a young girl, Mrs. McGuire located the biggest of the cast-iron frying pans in its drawer under the stove, and ran her finger along its surface. "It's been some time since you have used this pan, has it not, Mrs. Mowbrey? We shall just have to hope that the fish doesn't stick. It is the worst kind of luck," she told me, "to step over a fishing line."

"In that case," you said, "maybe we should have the thing stuffed and hang it on the wall."

Mrs. McGuire ignored you. It was as if, while you sat heavily in your chair, watching, she had assumed those properties by which we all recognized you as a dancer. Each of her movements was calculated and economical: at the flick of her many-boned and brittle wrist, the flame leaped up under the pan; her elbows stuck straight out from her sides as she dredged the fish in flour, and then her whole torso twitched from side to side as she energetically twisted the pepper mill; when the butter bubbled up she raised the fish and smiled. I realized I had never seen her smile before.

Dumbly—hypnotized, really—we all sat motionless as the fish hit the pan, sizzling, sending forth a cloud of fishy-smelling smoke. It was six o'clock: I could hear the Westminster chimes in the living room. We all sat motionless around the kitchen table as onto each of our sky-blue plates Mrs. McGuire slid a portion of lake trout: dark on the outside, white within. It smelled delicious.

From where I sat I could see your nostrils expanding and contracting; I could see you prodding at the fish with your fork, and then lifting the fork to your mouth.

A story is a *story*, I said to myself.

You chewed and swallowed. Then you looked at me and your face was lit up with inexplicable happiness. "It's so sweet," you said. "I never expected it would be this sweet."

In *this* world, Willie. That is how a miracle happens in *this* world. And then the door blew open, all by itself, on its hinges, and in poured the miraculous air that we've been breathing ever since.

ABOUT THE AUTHOR

Kathryn Davis's fiction and poetry have been published in *Esquire, The Atlantic,* and *Antaeus,* among other magazines, and have earned her Fellowships in Literature from the National Endowment for the Arts. She teaches fiction writing and literature at Goddard College, and lives in Vermont with her husband and daughter. *Labrador* was awarded the 1989 Janet Heidinger Kafka Prize for Fiction by an American Woman.